None but the Dead and Dying

None but the Dead and Dying

By

Ellen Behrens

BASKERVILLE
PUBLISHERS, INC.

Copyright © 1996 by Ellen Behrens

This book is a work of fiction. Names, characters, places and incidents are either the product of the author's imagination or are used fictitiously. Any resemblance to actual events or locales of persons, living or dead, is entirely coincidental.

BASKERVILLE Publishers, Inc.
7616 LBJ Freeway, Suite 220,
Dallas, TX 75251-1008

All rights reserved,
including the right to reproduce this book or portions thereof
in any form whatsoever.

Library of Congress Cataloging-in Publication Data

Behrens, Ellen, 1957–
   None but the dead and dying / by Ellen Behrens.
      p.   cm.
   ISBN 1-880909-41-3
   I. Title.
PS3552.E4147N66 1996
813'.54--dc20   95-47880
                                                                  CIP

Manufactured in the United States of America
First Printing, 1996

*To Mom and Dad who always knew
I would eventually do this,
and to my family and friends.*

1

It is the time of night when more people of the town pretend to sleep than sleep. Lights downstairs are off but glow from upstairs and back windows. Shades are drawn, kisses stolen on porches or in front seats of cars. The last of the day's newspapers are shuffled together, tucked in the trash. The faint smell of someone's barbecue hangs in the air. Down alleys and long driveways and in corners behind factories where it is so dark even the seeing are made blind, a few have given in to their restlessness and they linger, lighting cigarettes for each other, waiting to be old enough for the bars along Main Street. In a few minutes they'll meander in that direction, bored tonight by thoughts of starting dumpster fires, stealing car stereos, tossing park property into Waterworks Pond. They think about heading out of town, to someplace no one knows them, to other bars or other parks, but they have no car, the town closing in on them this way, holding them close like the heavy arms of a mother who won't let go.

Like those in their beds, they hear the music of the saxophone. Theodore Thompson plays in the attic of his mother's house, quietly, he thinks, so as not to disturb the neighbors.

The saxophone wails through the rafters, into the vacuous night. It is the cry of an animal trapped. It holds the neighbors to its rhythms and they blink. They turn even further into the softness of pillows and lovers but cannot block out the sound of Theodore's horn.

Tonight Theodore plays blues. No one who hears him knows the music is not his; they believe the music is his gift to the town, and for this reason no one thanks him. They're afraid if he finds out he can be heard he might stop. His music has been with them for so long they cannot imagine it ending. Yet Theodore grows old.

Almost no one can remember now what drove Theodore into the attic with his saxophone. Many do recall the boy with the horn, the boy in the high school band, the crepe paper ribbons, ruby red punch, the jitterbug—a full scholarship and on to college he went, a suitcase and his saxophone. He kissed his girl goodbye as if going to war, was so convincing Contessa Butler thought she would never see him again. Six months later, his instrument still wrapped carefully in its case, he came home. By then she'd married someone else.

Some say it's for love that Theodore plays. They say the mournful overtures to the night are to her, the lost one. Others know better.

One who hears, who knows, is Mamie Van Allen. Mamie is eighty. She sits on her porch at midnight to hear Theodore play. She used to chaperone the high school dances, used to watch the young girls swoon for Theodore. She wrote him a letter of recommendation to get him into college. She sent him money without telling anyone—not even Theodore, who was grateful, who said his thank-you's through the personal column in the paper alongside others' gratitude for flowers, cards, gifts, during losses of loved ones, hospital stays, births of babies.

Tonight she sits in the mid-June heat, listening, sipping her scotch. She listens to the cicadas humming in off-rhythms to the wail of the horn a street away, smiles when they hit rhythm for a bar or two, sometimes even for a whole tune.

She imagines they are both younger and he is playing for her. Soon she will finish her drink. Perhaps she'll go in to bed. Maybe she'll languish in the white wicker chair, and fall asleep here to awaken in the early sun. She has no one waiting for her inside; she has no reason not to stay and drink and pretend.

The music will outlive Mamie and she knows this. Thoughts of death come to her now and then and while she doesn't welcome them, she doesn't chase them off. Like the children who cut through her yard, who let the air out of her car tires a few years ago when she was still driving, she understands the why.

Her only concern about her death has to do with the details of it. People will come to see her off, she's sure of that. But to whom will she leave the house? Her things in it? So far she has left the will unmade and Matthew Miller, her lawyer and judge, calls every now and then to remind her it's a detail she must attend to, an end she must tie up. He's been calling more and more often and she wonders if he knows something that is eluding her.

She doesn't want to think about the will, doesn't want to imagine her things being auctioned on the front lawn. She's not sure you *can't* take it with you, so she's decided to be buried with something. Again, the indecision: what, though? Like the will, she decides to decide another night.

Maybe when Theodore plays jazz again, she thinks. That's when I'll decide. When he plays jazz I'll know it's time.

Contessa Welch pulls the peach-flowered curtain aside in her bedroom window across the street from Mamie Van

Allen's house and peers at the blur in front of Mamie's front picture window. She's been counting and knows this is the thirty-second time this year that Mamie has done this. On seventeen nights she fell asleep there; of those nights, nine were rainy and damp. "Old Mamie is sitting on the damned porch again," she says.

"So? You pay more attention to the old lady than you do me," Jack Welch says from the bed. The blue-green flickering of the TV flashes in the room like electronic lightning. "Jesus but Leno's no Carson. Same damn punch lines every night. Whyn't you come to bed with me? Why do I got to beg for you to be with me?"

She strains to hear past the closed window now that the air conditioning has shut off. "Teddy Thompson's not sounding too especially good tonight," she says.

Jack rolls toward the edge of the bed. "I'm going to turn the light on."

"Leave it, just leave it," she says. "What do you need it on for, anyway?" To annoy her, she knows. To lure her from the window and into bed. She drops the curtain into place, wonders if this will be night eighteen on the porch for Mamie.

She thinks Jack suffers from jealousy. They all graduated together—Jack, Teddy, her, Doris, Freda, Sammy, others. They don't see each other any more, something that's not strange to Contessa despite the smallness of the town, despite them all being in the phone book, despite seeing each other now and then on the street or in the grocery.

Back then, the pairings had been different: Jack and Freda, Theodore and Contessa, Sammy and Doris. Last year when Sammy died of prostate cancer, he widowed Freda. Doris moved East and moved back a few years ago, divorced, the mother of a college-aged son. Contessa dreads seeing her, dreads the conversation: "My Franklin has already been offered well-paying positions with Rockwell and ITT—and he still has another year to go!"

Once it had been Contessa he played for. Now she crawls into bed next to Jack while Theodore makes love to his saxophone.

Reverend Clayton Bleu ponders the keys of his typewriter. He's thinking of monks. Vows of silence. Hand-scripted everything, hand-copied everything. It is so easy these days, the reverend thinks, but why is it so hard for me?

His wife is asleep in the next room. She snores but Reverend Bleu isn't sure whether it's a genuine snore or not. He once tried taping her but of course the tape ran out after an hour and during that hour she hadn't uttered a sound. This pleased her but frustrated him. Then he began to see a pattern: she'd snore especially loudly after a fight, driving him from their bed; not snore at all after lovemaking. Tonight her snores are, he is sure, protestations against his late hour in the study.

Though he's been aware of Theodore Thompson's saxophone for the past thirty minutes or so, the music isn't what's keeping the ideas from coming.

He wanders to the window, pushes the heavy curtains aside. The street light near the house is fanning amber across parts of the yard and street. The light keeps him from seeing the sky. In their last house, in the Upper Peninsula of Michigan, he could see the stars. Nights like this he could step onto the back porch, light a cigarette, puff smoke and watch it fade, let the thoughts come. It's as if, without the stars, he can't think.

He'd like to do a talk—he never calls them sermons—too preachy-sounding, and who is he to preach?—on solitude. He'd like to use Theodore Thompson and his midnight concerts as an example. One man and the beauty of his solitude. He's thought of this many times, but he knows he'll never trespass on Theodore's life like that. He does decide he should visit the man and his aged, crippled mother. He's decided this before. Nothing, though, ever seems like enough.

In his office in town, Ben Stevens paces. He has things to think about, important things about the town, but Theodore Thompson's stupid horn keeps blaring, screeching around the corners of the neighborhood like some car with a teenager behind the wheel, the noise never fading into the distance, just coming around and around. Ben pulls the office window closed, locking it as if the sound will creep in otherwise, a thief out to steal his thoughts, his peace of mind.

The room will grow stuffy, sealed like this against the summer heat, and Margaret, who cleans the city building, who vacuums at dawn and empties ashtrays before most people are awake, will scold him if she finds out, so he makes a note to himself: OPEN WINDOW BEFORE LEAVING. He lays the note atop a pile of papers he came up here to review tonight, and taps it down with his fist as if securing them there forever. Nothing, he knows, lasts that long, though a lot of people think so. His own career at Feldspar Chassis—the parts manufacturer up on the lake—lasted not even twenty-five years, from the day of his high school graduation in 1968 two years ago, a far cry from the thirty years he'd wanted to put in with the company. He'd pictured it all the very day he first walked into Feldspar next to his father—the retirement dinner and pension that would come with enough good health left to take Mariann to Hawaii and anywhere else she wanted to go.

He never believed—none of them had, especially not folks like his dad who'd been around so long he remembered before unions and contract negotiations—it could be so easy, being "let go"—words picked to try to make them think of a sort of freedom from punching in and out, of vacations when the company set them, whether they were when you wanted them or not. "Let go" meant let go from pension plans and retirement benefits. No number of years mattered. The lay-offs cut deep and to the quick and for weeks they called each other as if to reassure themselves that being at home restless and bored and useless and worried was what they were supposed to be doing.

Even tonight, two years later, Ben can conjure again the look of that meeting: two or three hundred line workers after a long eight hour shift wiping grime from their foreheads and pulling plugs from their ears, all of them shrugging to each other, "What's this about?" because, though of course there had been warnings in reduced production and fewer squabbles with management over the latest contract, nothing had been enough. It wasn't going to happen, not *really*, and so even while the plant manager, in rolled up sleeves and loosened tie told them, "Not enough orders... foreign competition eroding our base..." and other things, Ben and his father and the others stood listening only for the rest of the speech, the part some of them had heard before that went, "We expect orders to increase again when GM/Ford/Chrysler steps up production on their new line and so expect to call you back in for your regular shifts around then." That part never came. Someone finally called out the question: "When will we be called back?" but the PM had only shrugged his shoulders, his hands empty and dangling at his sides.

That night at dinner he told Mariann. She didn't cry or rant or excuse herself to be alone but had only looked at him and said, "Good God, and there's no getting a job here in town, either," because the pressing plant on Route 20 was laying off, too.

Mariann started part-time at the drug store and Ben started selling Amway and ran for town council. He understood, he told the voters, his neighbors, about factories and manufacturing and the need to keep businesses in town. And so he won a seat on council and then was appointed mayor.

Now how to keep those factories and businesses in town is the question. What's happening at the pressing plant—a personnel cut to nearly a tenth of its full force of nearly two thousand—looks too familiar to him.

Ben stops in front of the sole window in the office and stares out. This is a historical building, they've told him, brick and stone with high arching windows that stick sometimes when they're closed too long, and this is why, his city manager told him, they haven't built a new municipal center despite plans drawn up every ten years or so. Ben told him he thinks they should look into renovations at the very least.

He steps back to his desk, finds a Herald Square yellow pencil. On a piece of city stationery he writes "Improvements" at the top, then "#1: Air conditioning in the city building. Reasons against: $. Reasons for: necessary to maintain constant temperature for computer equipment; probably safer in the event of fire (all those files in the attic could catch)."

He sits in his chair, an aging, high-back leather one that swivels but squeaks when urged closer to his desk. "#2," he writes, "New chair for mayor's office," then scratches it out, and, upset that he can't think of anything more elaborate for his improvement plan, wads up the paper and tosses it away. He leans back again in his chair, trying to ignore the shriek it gives him, then, with an image of Margaret at a table piecing together his paper puzzle clear in his mind, he leans to pull the wastebasket to him. He reaches in, collects the wad of paper, and shreds it first into narrow strips and then halves, then into quarters, letting the bits fall into the otherwise empty basket like a miniature tickertape parade.

In the quiet, the saxophone from two blocks away edges in to him. Ben strains to focus. "Business," he says aloud. "Businesses diversify when they need growth." He writes on a new sheet on the pad: "#1: Save the plant."

The saxophone slips up and down its notes. It's sad tonight. It is always sad.

Next Ben writes, "#2: Find a way to bring new $ in." He leans back in his chair, ignoring its cry, and closes his eyes, trying only to see the music behind them.

Crescent St. Clair sits on the floor of the belfry in the spire of the Catholic Church. This is the best place, she's decided, to hear old Thompson play his horn. She's tried lots of spots but always comes back here. Maybe finding the key to get up here has something to do with it. On a walk this past winter she found the key, dropped, she guessed, by one of the nuns. She saw it as further proof that sexual frustration can make you careless, distort your thinking, make you drop things. Up here she can close her eyes and imagine things she can't anywhere else.

Tonight she imagines a nun gone crazy with celibacy tearing the wood from the shuttered windows, shrieking insanely, laughing into the night, her black robes catching loose nails, tearing the cloth, the holy white of the wimple darkening with dirt and sinful thoughts. The nun thrusts her face into the harsh wet wind of a summer thunderstorm, the kind that flashes lightning like old movies and thunders through your chest, the kind of storm they haven't seen yet this season. Her sisters clamber up the same steps and ladders Crescent has already mounted to get here, clutching at the sides of the ladders to steady themselves, their feet unsure with the long skirts. She imagines the sisters taking hold of the mad one, calming her need to jump, quieting her before the folks in the nearby houses overhear.

Crescent leans into the night this way, seeing these things, listening first to the songs of the birds fade, to the whisper of leaves telling her the parts of her stories she has been missing. She hears the occasional cringe of screen doors being opened as the townspeople step onto porches, turn off air conditioners and open windows to withered breezes and the beginning strains of Theodore Thompson's saxophone.

The music is clear from here, the clearest. As it rises through the town it is transformed, expanding with the horizon. When she listens to Theodore play, she wishes for something of her own to love like that. Maybe an art. A talent. At seventeen she's already decided that men are too precarious to invest love in.

Theodore has played a long time tonight. This worries Crescent, who knows her father is right now beginning to wonder where she is, is beginning to pace and mumble, rehearsing his anger. The music is worth his anger. She closes her eyes, thinking that at least she has a real dad, someone honest in his anger, his frustrations, his demands, a man with grease in his life and fingernails from the plant, a man not like Hope Bleu's father who always seems someplace else, even when he preaches on Sunday morning. Maybe especially then.

Crescent wants to fall asleep here, beneath the huge bell that hangs over her like an interrogation lamp, bearing down on her conscience. She wants to ignore the heavy dust she can't see but can feel between her palms and the coarse, wooden floor. Amid the pigeons, settled and quiet for the night, she stretches her lean body across the blanket she's smuggled up here, and she lays her head on her arm, calming herself to sleep with Theodore Thompson's sax.

She would camp out here some night if she were sure the

bell wouldn't deafen her in doing its duty. If it weren't for the Catholics needing to be summoned by tolling bell to early mass, she would stay some night. But the Catholics show no sign of altering their schedule for mass, so she crawls up here, sinks into the weathered walls and Theodore's music, and thinks—sometimes profound things—until the music fades.

When she gets home she'll let her father accuse her of ducking out with Denny McMasters. Somehow trying to explain where she's really been is more complicated, and to her father, she's sure, more perverted.

Tonight, when Theodore takes his bow in his public attic and delivers the night back to silence, Crescent will loiter here in the belfry, conjuring reasons why Theodore spends his nights alone.

Where the streets of the town end, fields of corn, soybean and wheat stretch toward the horizon. So closely together do the town and country fit that someone walking down a brick or asphalt street, or even one of the newer concrete cul de sacs, could suddenly find the street a dead-end, the earth suddenly unpaved and, in the late fall, folded over into dark soil, while in the spring and summer the fields were a lush green or, in drought years like this one, standing in a pale hint of their true colors, whispering secrets only the surest of farmers could understand.

Up another road a few miles north of town, Landers Stone stands in a dark patch of lawn, the only patch surviving the scorching drought that has hit so hard this summer. Often, alone out here, late like this, Landers slips down to the grass, feels its coolness between his fingers, then wrestles his heavy work boots from tired feet, pulling once-white socks from his thick ankles and wriggling his toes into the ground. He knows that sometimes his wife sees him do this. The first time he discovered her gaze on him he was embarrassed. That was nearly twenty-five years ago and she has never said a word, has understood that there are no words for it, nothing he can say about it anyway, and now it is something they hold between them, unspoken and precious.

Tonight, though, Landers is too troubled to tug off socks and boots. It isn't that the grass turned brown months ago, would be sharp against his flesh. No, the very earth he has labored with these years is suddenly turning on him, and it isn't the drought. The drought, that's the kind of thing he's gotten used to as a farmer. Years of see-sawing weather that brings either too much rain or too little, years of see-sawing grain prices and bill paying, though the bank accounts never improve, only worsen. No, today, it's something different. A different way for the earth to work against him.

Rico Zamora had led the team of migrants to the digging, swore to Landers later that he'd done exactly as told, and Landers believed him. A hundred and fifty feet from the house, measured, angled, the first swipe from the backhoe and then the shovels came up with the first evidence: fragments, split and shattered white. Bones. The workers refused to dig further until Landers came to see for himself, and that had taken awhile. Landers had gone to town, his day to see about the loan at the bank, to share coffee with a few others who'd come into town, too. The farm hands, no longer patient, called him, finally, at the Country Inn, and Landers left his second cup of coffee still steaming at the brim on the counter.

The hole wasn't that big at first, but he could see right away what they were so concerned about. There was no doubt that they'd come across something. He knew he had to call the sheriff. Maybe there was foul play. Maybe something else, though he wasn't sure what.

Rico and the others stood in the hot sun, the breeze kicking fine dirt into their eyes, so they pulled red and blue bandanas across their faces like old-time outlaws, their dark eyes squinting into the sun, against the dust. A few of the men, Juan and Jesus, Rico's cousins, crossed themselves as Landers made his way to the edge of the hole. He asked them to dig a little more but to only uncover, to be careful not to disturb what might be there, but they looked at him with eyes that came the closest they ever had to disrespect. Landers told them to forget it, then. "See where we're at with the beans—we going to need to spray the end of the week?" he asked them, but they lingered at the lip of the hole and Landers, who couldn't blame them for simple curiosity, said nothing more.

Sheriff Guerra asked a lot of questions when he got there, taking no notes, his face hard to read with the sunglasses reflecting like mirrors the blowing dust and sullen faces that looked into them. "Who all you got working here, Landers?" he asked, and Landers gave him the names, as many as he could recall, then said, "But only a few were working on the backhoe and on this waterline."

"Don't matter. Could be we got a real problem here."

When the sheriff moved, the leather of his holster and belt rubbed one another and conjured in Landers an uneasy feeling. The way the man paused in his steps to cradle his hand over the butt of his gun was aggravating, too. It seemed a gesture of habit, the hand closing over the weapon like a fist over a gearshift in a car, even when the driver has no intention of moving from second to third gear, but prepared, no matter what, to do it just in case.

Strangers on his land—the land he has come to think of as his, anyway—strangers are learning its curves and secrets better than he to judge by the way the sheriff's men and the odd crew from two counties over with their all-white coveralls and get-up like astronauts sift through his back property like it was the moon. They made him want to turn to them all and say, "I'm glad we found this, but it is ours, after all, or nobody's, but in any case it's not yours and you need to just get off this property." But how could he say that to Guerra who was, after all, only trying to do his job? To Guerra, who has always been friendly, if not, exactly, a friend?

He learned long ago about law around here, about doing business, about keeping on the good sides of people.

"Don't you let nobody in this place," Guerra had said. "And let me speak to your workers."

The migrant workers gathered, shirts hanging open, straw hats hiding faces in the orange sun. "About the commotion up by the house, with the water line digging," Guerra said. "It's a sheriff's department investigation going on—not priority, just something we're looking into." A few voices mumbled along with him, translating into Spanish. Guerra dug the toe of his boot into the sandy dirt and sighed as though this was something he didn't think was really necessary to say aloud but felt compelled to anyway. "Since it *is* an investigation, I'm advising you not to say anything about what you've seen or experienced around here, okay?" He waited a few minutes for the translations to finish. "Understand?" He waited this time until everyone nodded.

The day is gone now, though it lingers in a long pink and lavender sunset and in Lander's mind. Why had the sheriff thought it would help to warn the workers not to talk? Surely he knows that they will, but innocently, to wives and girlfriends and other family members, will maybe speak too loudly to each other in the bar tonight and in this way the chain will begin, link by link, made of words and images and gossip and rumor.

Before leaving, the sheriff and his deputy took samples, ordered an all-night watch over the site, and, though Landers cannot see the good of it—surely the worst that could have happened out here has already happened—he posted a man.

None But The Dead And Dying

The man he's designated as watchman lives down the township road because the migrant workers already on the property—to the man—refused the job, even for double pay. When Landers asked Rico, his crew leader, why no one wanted to stand watch, Rico shrugged, uttered some Spanish as if hoping to find the English he needed hidden in it somehow, then said only, "Something. Is something here. Can't you feel it?"

Landers had shook his head, but now he wonders if he can feel it, after all.

He looks across the rolling flat of his land toward town where the sky glows a pastel orange, the color the lampposts there, reproductions, give off in the night. He knows of the night concerts in town, of the sound of the saxophone, has even, reluctantly, driven Bessie in to hear it. Tonight a drive into town, music echoing through the streets hushed to hear, would be a nice escape from this land that seems to want to take him in, swallow him whole, but tonight he'll stay and wait, staring across the fields toward the dawn until he gives up the wait, the night too long, stretched out like thin tempers and the worst growing seasons. Finally he will collapse into bed.

From his place here on the lawn he can make out in the shadows Diamond Richard's silhouette at the digging site as Diamond walks the perimeter of the hole, a hunting rifle shouldered. Those two years in the Marine Corps, Landers can see, are finally coming to some good out here. "Yessir, Mr. Stone, I'll stand watch tonight," he said this afternoon, grinning. "Any night you need it." He rubbed a stubble that was on his chin then but gone tonight when he showed up at the door. "Reporting for duty, sir," he'd said.

There is something, Landers thinks, and he knows it is something he could see and understand if only he looked a little more closely, if only he weren't quite this tired and harvest still so far away.

Later he will awaken in bed, his wife's back to him, her toes pressed into his calves as if they marked the starting line to a race. He will awaken, aware again of something crucial he's forgotten until that moment: that the land isn't his, but George Freeman's, and only under his guardianship. He will wonder then what old George will say, and will guess that he will say nothing, of course, but will only look at him with his frightened eyes, his retarded face twisted to make his words understandable. His attorney, though, will have to know. And Landers won't be able to sleep then, all the things he knows he'll have to say to Mason Pope circling and circling in his head like so many buzzards waiting to alight.

2

Trees and the three-story brick, stone and cement buildings of the downtown keep the earliest sun from shining on the two-block strip of Main Street, but it creeps through the leafy maples, buckeyes and pines that shelter Mamie Van Allen's front porch.

She blinks, lifts her arms slowly from the arm rests. They are dimpled with the pattern of wicker and age. She unbends her legs, straightens the knee joints, points her feet toward the porch steps. It takes a little longer each time to separate herself from her chair.

Last night, sipping from her glass, the music in her ears, she couldn't think of a reason to abandon this spot, to give in to the night, to turn inward to her own bed. In the dark hours it seems, often, to make more sense to sleep out here, where the rustle of squirrels, the call of blue jays and coo of the mourning doves awaken her. It sometimes makes more sense to her to be out here should she not awaken, out here where her neighbors and friends could find her instead of waiting to notice that she isn't out, that maybe something is wrong.

This morning, stiff and sore, her body cries a thousand reasons why she shouldn't be so afraid to be alone in there. She fits her hand around her glass, its melted ice and flat liquor floating a cricket on the surface. In a moment, when she stands, she'll pour the liquid into the bushes at the side of the porch. Right now she concentrates on one part of her body at a time. She limbers her toes, reaches to untie her shoes to free her feet, but a pain shoots through her lower back and she clutches at it, rubbing at the spot as if to blot that part of her entirely away, until a familiar ring comes down the street—the child-sounding dinging of a bell and the screechy wheels of Gasman George's rusty green bicycle.

Up Maple Street he comes, his body weaving side to side, balancing with some miracle. His pedalling of the bicycle's fat wheels is smooth, though his head jerks, a quick left then left again, right, and right again. He could be nervous in the street or pursued by private tormentors. He looks ahead, then back, then back again, his expression still startled, his mouth still round, his eyes still wide and searching. His face is a silent scream for help. He rides the town, pedalling and looking, sometimes carrying small brown bags from the grocery in the wire basket latched to his handlebars. His once red baseball cap has faded to orange, the brown dirt of his pants hiding denim underneath. Cracked shoes hold the pedals, control the speed, rough-knuckled hands grip the handlebars, steer the bicycle along the curb.

Mamie Van Allen knows his ride down the street will frighten young children back into their own yards, pull them onto porches until he is safely past. Older kids will jeer at him and he'll look, and look again, that startled, puzzled face of his fading with his distance down the street or around a corner. Adults he passes no longer see him; he's not a curiosity to them anymore, but shuffled into the realm of the invisible where anyone whose function in the town's mechanism isn't defined is abandoned.

Mamie waves to him, knowing he'll glance at her, then away again. "Hello, George," she calls. "How are you? Nice day for a ride."

None But The Dead And Dying

He drops his empty, frightened look on her, rides on.

George is no curiosity to Mamie. She remembers him as a child, Southern born and removed to this Ohio town with his odd voice, backwoods clothes, and no daddy. He smoked and swore before he hit ten years old and took any dare for a dollar the other boys could think up. He swung from tree to tree on ropes looped between them in the woods behind Waterworks Pond. He scaled utility poles on the spikes that used to jut from them for the linesmen to use. At the tops he would take dares on which wires were live and would touch any one he was challenged to. When his older sister would come to fetch him, she likely found him at the top of a pole or tree or balanced on teetering planks at construction sites or along steel braces in electrical towers. She lashed out at the neighborhood kids who'd egged her brother on: "Can't you understand he don't know no better? Whyn't you just quit and leave him be?" But they would laugh and George himself would say, "Ah, Sissy, it's okay. We're just funnin'."

When he was ten his mother placed herself in her car in the garage and, with doors closed, started the engine, let it run and run. Three days after her funeral, George imitated his mother's move. He sat and waited and breathed deep the nothing he was supposed to breathe and couldn't die. When he told the boys they said he lied, but he stood strong and when they dared him to do it again, this time with them watching a dollar apiece, he agreed. He sat in the car, in the closed garage, motor humming beneath him, for two hours. Nervous, the boys choked their way into the building and pulled the car door open. There sat George, smiling, listening to the radio. Gasman, they called him. But he didn't care that he'd finally been accepted into their ranks. He stopped taking dares, quit school, and hasn't spoken since.

Forty years later he rides from Birdseye Street where he lives to the grocery near the new Protestant Church or downtown to the pharmacy where he picks up prescriptions for his sister. Once upon a time she watched over him; since their mother's death he has watched over her.

That Gasman George doesn't acknowledge her greeting doesn't surprise Mamie. She greets him every time she sees him, is given back that same blank look every time. She imagines what it must be like at his house: George, trapped in his own silence and terror, sitting across the table from his sister who, Mamie has heard, babbles and laughs and makes no sense.

Maybe it's that he can't remember, Mamie thinks, watching the bicycle creak by, the man on it twisting back and back and back again to watch her.

But losing your memory when you get old, she thinks, is a kindness. It keeps us from remembering all the things we could once do but cannot any longer. Growing old gracefully is knowing how to pretend to forget.

A curtain in the window across the street flutters but Mamie ignores it, knows it is Contessa Welch watching her again. She ignores it to concentrate again on unfolding herself from the chair.

The Reverend Clayton Bleu watches his daughter Hope from across the kitchen table. Where oh where, he wonders, did the days of cold cereal with an extra teaspoon of sugar go?

Hope hunches toward her bagel and cream cheese, her blue-green eyes studying the book propped open by her elbows. Her blonde hair spills around her, untended like the yard of the empty house down the street. The other day, when he asked her if she combed it she said, "Oh, Dad." There was commentary in those two single syllables, but the message he was supposed to get passed him by. Later Sandra told him it's the style, the way everyone was wearing hair. "Everyone under eighteen," she said, when he started to challenge her. Why hasn't he noticed that?

With the same silent quickness of the coming of an Ohio spring his daughter's life has become foreign to him, the language something he thought he knew, but like the scriptures he spends so much time pouring over, a language of its own as well. At twelve she shared his love of the Mud Hens and nights at the dining room table playing gin rummy or Go Fish or double-handed solitaire. Now she inhabits her own world, a fortress. He imagines that the door to her world is oak and looks like the arched, wrought-iron-hinged door of a castle. He decides to knock on it.

"So," he says, clearing his throat, pushing aside a plate now littered with the crusts of toast and yellowy egg syrup. "What are your plans for today, Hope?" he asks.

She shrugs, doesn't look up, and he feels the rush of air as that heavy oak door slams in his face.

"Going to stay in and read?" He tilts his head to try to see the spine of the book, but though she's made no attempt to hide it from him, he cannot make out the title. It's a hardcover, something that doesn't have the gory picture of human grotesques so popular with horror stories or the ripped bodices of romance covers. This book is a flat, faded red, and somehow, because it isn't something he expects, it is harder for him to ignore.

"Probably not," she says.

"Going out, then?" He tells himself it's just like talking to the people in the County Home Health Center when he visits there. He tells himself it's a matter of patience.

"I guess that's the choice."

"Going to bring your friends around sometime?" he asks, and the look she gives him is the same one he's seen her direct at injury-accidents they sometimes pass on the highway. "What's the problem with that?"

Her eyes now beg the ceiling for help. "What is this, anyway? Why all the questions all of the sudden?" Her left index finger pushes the book closed and the reverend drops his eyes to the cover. A library book, no jacket. The book is out of sight before he can translate the faint embossing of the title into right-side-up sense.

Her fist hits her hip, a gesture her mother has. He wonders if she is learning to fake snoring, too, so she can avoid things. That should be a habit only for later on, he thinks. Later on when she's old enough and married enough to be in bed with someone. Not now. Not at fifteen—or is she fourteen? "I know what you're thinking, Dad," she says.

"You do?" He collects his used napkin from the table in front of him and crumples it up again.

"I know you're starting to wonder if I'm creeping around with boys, thinking of giving away that 'precious gift reserved for a husband.' Well, I'm not, so is that it or do you want to beat around the bush some more, maybe hoping to scare something else up?"

"Uh...no...." He drops the napkin, again, onto the table, then picks it up to place it on the plate. He wonders where Sandra is.

"Good," Hope says, and is gone. He pictures again that big castle door and decides to walk away from it, decides he really doesn't want to know what she does inside there.

The bulb dangling overhead is a spotlight. The concrete basement walls that echo the twanging guitar and thudding bass drum are billion-watt amplifiers. The cassette deck recording the notes with relative accuracy is a multi-million dollar studio. Denny McMasters, Cal Garnett, and Walt "The Wiz" Franklin aren't a gang of farmland instrument-bangers. They are the Stones, Starship, Def Leppard. Crescent St. Clair, perched in the corner of the cellar room on a teetering bar stool can see it all, has always seen it this way.

Crescent's history with Denny is long. At five they raced their tricycles from Denny's sidewalk to Mr. Lemon's asphalt driveway where they waited for him to walk home from his presidency at the bank, where they waited for the good-natured whacks on the behind he gave them with his rolled-up Toledo *Blade*.

At eight Denny introduced Crescent to picking tar from between the bricks on Cherry Street. Their fingers sticky, they'd roll the tar, hot from summer sun, into balls, compare the sizes, and determine the winner at dinnertime. When they were fourteen, Crescent returned the favor and introduced Denny to sex. Despite taking their experiments out into the world, they still believe a bond was made in this very basement, three years ago.

Denny has already written songs about her and they call her here, despite her need to flee. Crescent and Denny believe they will probably someday marry; nearly everyone they know believes this as well.

Soon the music will wear itself out but for now the music is changing. The room looks like a basement even longer this time, the other images flashing like the quick-cuts of the music videos Crescent and Denny study when they're in the mood to dream of their own. But not tonight, and not for awhile, and Crescent wonders if it will ever come so strongly again.

The sun burns into the flesh of the land, burns it leathery hard and creases age into it. Landers Stone feels the heat against the back of his neck and thinks about turning his Cleveland Indians hat around, but it seems silly and young and far too reckless for the seriousness going on around him. That he can't wear his cap the way he wants is evidence, too, that Landers has had to give over something of his management of this land, this patch of property, to the professionals in white safety suits. Something about maybe the "remains" being able to infect otherwise healthy men, a power from the grave Landers has never thought possible before.

The white space-suited looking people are back; yesterday two of them, today a half-dozen, and Landers has no way of knowing how many men, how many women, though he considers them all men, it not seeming right that women be involved in inspecting sites like this one. They cut cleanly through the earth with shovels—flat across the surface, one level at a time, and then, discovering something, they take photos and make notes. Landers guesses that most of the notes have to do with which pictures are which. He thinks the photos will probably look much alike after development: brown dirt and white slivers, bones, who knows what else might show up. It feels less and less like land he holds any responsibility for.

Sheriff Guerra stands to Landers' side, one hand resting on the butt of his gun, the other thumb tucked through a belt loop. Every now and then he pushes his sunglasses up his nose with a middle finger, but he has stood solid on this rise, watching the work before him with so little movement that Landers wonders about his training. Do they practice this? Do they plan ahead in case, like an animal trapped in its own habitat, they must stand rigid long enough to save their lives?

"What are you thinking about all this, Sheriff?" Landers asks, not so much because he thinks he'll get an answer that satisfies, but because he'd rather a few words, a grunt even, instead of the straight-backed silence. Landers told his wife at lunch, after three hours of watching the sheriff watch the men dig, "I'm 'bout to feel pretty near guilty myself, and I don't know a thing about it." Today he believes all the stories he's heard on television about people unjustly accused, about confessions coerced.

"I'm thinking it's pretty damn strange," Guerra says, turning to face Landers. "You say you just started digging here yesterday?"

"For the most part. I mean, we planned all this out but yesterday was the first we cut into the ground in a serious way. Just stuff the utilities folks did before to let me know whether it was worth digging along here. But the backhoe was yesterday, the first cut; till then nothing was touched hardly." Beads of sweat dribble down his brow, neck. The sun feels like an interrogation lamp. Even the word "hardly" suddenly seems damning, and Landers wonders if he should take it back, say something else, but to cover what?

The sheriff shifts his weight from one foot to the other and then balances his weight again between them, his feet spread about shoulder width. "That's what I thought. What was here before you started digging?"

Grass, Landers thinks, what else? "This's always been part of the lawn, you know, the yard goes way back and so that's one reason we figured we could do this, kids all grown and grandkids not here enough. Just been yard, that's all. Grass."

"Nothing atop?"

Landers shakes his head. "Lawn that got mowed more times'n me or my boy want to remember." He tries to grin but the sheriff is distracted by the shout of one of the diggers.

They step closer to the hole that grows wider though not much more shallow. A few of the workers scramble closer. One is pointing, crying out. Another skull.

A careful examination takes place, flakes drop into plastic Baggies, another dozen pages fill, pens run dry and are replaced.

A station wagon pulls from the township road into the

driveway, winds up the path to the ridge and three men and a woman climb out. Landers sees that the lettering on the side of the car says "Midwestern State University."

Portly but not very old, a man who's maybe in his early thirties with a scrabbly beard the same red of his hair and face and neck, comes toward them, sticking out his hand. He says, "Midwestern State University, Department of Natural and Physical Sciences, we can maybe tell you a little something about what you've got here."

Landers shifts his weight, taking the man's hand to shake it. "Morning," he says. "Landers Stone." Then he twists his hat around backwards after all.

"Michael Olson," the red-haired man says. "Professor of Archeology at Midwestern. This is quite a find, sir. I'm glad you gave us a call."

"I didn't," Landers says, and he has no idea who did, but word always travels quickly around here. He supposes maybe the sheriff's office called. Or maybe one of the migrants at a bar in town shot his mouth off. No matter what, it seems odd to call a college.

"Well, whoever," the man Olson says. "Anyway, we'd sure like to take a look." He is leaning forward as though the only thing keeping him in this spot are his shoes—if he moves them even a little, maybe he won't be able to control them, like a child warned not to go someplace who wants more than anything to sneak away there.

Landers holds out his arm to show where they've been digging and right away the university people call the white coverall people back—"You there! Stop! Wait just a second, okay?" All run toward the site as if they've been caged and just now are set loose. They collect the Baggies, as many as the sheriff will allow before he tells them to back off. One of the men, moustached and maybe no older than Landers' granddaughter, in college herself, hangs onto the sheriff with his eyes, follows him the way obedient pets keep to their owners' heels.

Into the hole they drop themselves, Olson, the man and the woman, these blue-jeaned university people and right away they begin picking through the unearthed fragments, their fingers delicate, pinkies pointing as though sipping from a demitasse. They lean in to look more closely, their voices hushed and murmuring. Every now and then a cry or silence amid the conversation, while Landers, the white coverall people and the migrants who've come to stare again ring the pit, watching, listening.

Olson emerges at last, the dirt dusting the cuffs of his jeans and white tennis shoes. He walks to Guerra and Landers, leads them by the elbow away from the site, away from the others. He motions the moustached man back to the hole where he, too, starts sifting the earth, combing it with fingers, whisking it with a fine bristled brush as though painting the ground.

"First," Olson says, "they thought you might have uncovered a mass or serial killing from perhaps the twenties, something connected with bootlegging along the turnpike run, but of course, given the artifacts with them, that can't be it." He holds up something that looks to Landers like a plain old chipped-up rock. "What you have here, sir, is an Indian burial ground. We'll have to do some checking, some analysis, but from what I can see this is an unusual site." The man's words come more quickly, the polished professional edge of them falling off his words. "This is a very rare find, Mr. Stone. Very rare."

"Christ," Landers says.

"You must be aware that this makes the site very valuable to our research," Olson says. He turns the sliver over in his fingers, rubbing dirt from it, studying it as he speaks. "So little is known about the trading patterns of the indigenous peoples of this territory that what we find out here is essential to the development of that body of information.

The burials here alone are a find, but add the rest of the artifacts and you've got quite a lot here that we can use."

He stops toying with the relic and looks Landers in the eye. "I'd like to bring in more people," he says. "We should excavate this site thoroughly but quickly. Certainly you understand the trouble bad weather can bring. I don't suppose you have any problem with us moving forward? Of course we wouldn't disrupt your farming."

Landers squints from the man's face to the pit where the sun streams in his direction, then back to Olson. "Did I hear a question in that mess someplace?" he asks.

Olson laughs. "Yes sir, you did. We believe it's imperative—very important—that we move quickly to get this site excavated, but we'll need more people. Your assistants here are fine individuals but this is not their forte—their specialty—no offense, of course, and besides, we don't wish to take your workers from their usual jobs. The specialists are forensics experts, I'm sure, but again, what are needed are experienced excavators."

Landers looks at Olson, studying his blue jeans that are worn but from sitting behind desks and not from the labor of a farm. He studies the smooth hands, hands free from heavy lifting, the furious tugging at the reins of a horse not yet tamed. He studies how the sun is also studying him, bearing into him, initiating him. Landers grins. "What's all this going to run me?"

"Run you?" Olson shakes his head.

"Cost me. What you planning to charge me to do this excavation?" Landers tucks his thumbs into the loops of his jeans, lifts his chin to stare down his face at the man.

"Oh, not a thing. The university funds the research. Government grant money. Volunteers. Wouldn't cost you a thing except for the inconvenience of having a few strangers around your property for awhile. And, actually, we'll do all we can to minimize our presence."

None But The Dead And Dying

The sky darkens and thunder rolls miles away to the west. Could move in, could fade away. Landers knows this, but watches the concern that slides across Olson's face. Landers says, "Then what do I get for it?"

Olson shifts his weight from one dusty tennis shoe to the other. "I'm sorry, sir, I don't quite understand what you mean."

Landers leans close. "What you going to give me for letting you do this? Don't everything cost somebody something? And if I'm not the one giving, then you must be."

"Well sir," Olson says in a way that makes Landers think he's trying to find an answer to the question, "Well sir, we'll be providing you with valuable insight into your land, into the history of it."

Landers gazes past the man, into the greying sky. He is taking care not to show a response to the words, though in his mind he asks the red-haired Olson what more he needs to know: already he's studied it, knows its curves and dips where water collects rainy years, where the sun beats the green out of it dry years, where the moles like it and where the crows roost.

But the man goes on, "By offering us this opportunity you'll be lending rare information to a limited body of research involving tribes we no doubt know little if anything about."

Landers leans against the Midwestern University station wagon, his palm pressing into the heat he's forgotten about and now must ignore. Sheriff Guerra has turned his attention back to the site, directing those who are now shedding their white astronaut-type coveralls. They brush hands through hair dampened with sweat and matted flat under the awkward headgear. They seem to be readying to leave, gathering up equipment, speaking briefly to the university woman before heading toward their own cars.

Lordy, Landers thinks. Lordy, lordy, where'd they all come

from? He wonders if the migrants are checking the beans for weeds, if Rico has got them in the right sector. He needs to check but this man Olson keeps talking. And the rain is maybe coming. It would be so good for the crops to have rain.

Olson is saying, "Surely you must agree that this excavation must go on, that we must learn all we can about this. We'll certainly compensate if we can."

Landers watches the van with the forensics people back down the long driveway. "How many people you talking?" he asks. The university woman is again in the hole where he sees her head bob up once, gesturing to the man standing beside him. They are finding things, many things, and they are excited. They are like bugs, Landers thinks, busy and quick to move, quick to multiply.

"Not many, Mr. Stone. I promise you we'll keep this under control for you. You'll barely know we're here," Olson says.

And Landers nods. It is not so much an agreement as a signal he understands, but Olson grins widely, shakes his hand. "Good," he says, opening a black leather book by unzipping it, a book Landers hasn't noticed in his hand until now. For a second he thinks it is a Bible, the kind his sister started carrying when she was saved years ago, but the man flips it open and draws a pen from a corner of it to write in it. It is an appointment book, but this makes Landers no less uneasy about it or about him.

The rental on the backhoe, Landers thinks. What will I do about that? "What about my water line?" Landers asks, and Olson looks up, puzzled. "What are you going to do about my water line? I can't very well finish it now that you want to do this excavating. Am I right?"

Olson clutches the black leather book with both hands at its top and presses it into his stomach. "How can I help that?" he asks, and from the way the question sounds,

Landers thinks the man Olson really doesn't think there is a way.

"I'm going to need to start all over with it, I guess, don't you think?" Landers gestures, starts walking along the strip of upended grass and dirt where it leads from the house to the barn where he's planned to splice a T into it to carry another line out. He points. "Easiest thing would be to use where this pit is, where this excavation you want to do is at," Landers says. He shrugs. "But of course, with that needing to be used your way, I got to find another way about this water line. Going to cost me extra, with the time I'll need to backhoe another direction or go around it. Haven't thought that through, of course. But something will have to be different, if you want to go ahead the way you talk." He looks at Olson.

The man holds the book in one hand now, at his side. He is measuring Landers somehow, not paying a bit of attention to the useless ditch and the idle backhoe. He begins to nod, bites on his lower lip, something Landers hasn't yet seen him do. "Okay, Mr. Stone," he says. "I'll see what I can do about that."

Landers turns his Indians cap around on his head, adjusts it to pull the bill even over his eyes. He turns and, head down, walks blindly toward the pit. He knows the ground this well that he can walk yards and yards without looking up, judging position by the changes in the way the grass grows, by the weeds, the bushes in his peripheral vision. This is property he has farmed and tended for years and years and he means to show these university people just that.

At the lip of the pit he holds his hand up, high, a stop sign. "Please don't bother yourselves any further," he says and the moustached man and the woman and the third man look up at him where he stands a little above them and the relics in their hands drip dirt and sand.

"Mr. Stone," Olson says, coming up behind him, "I need to make a phone call. I can't okay such an expense on my own."

So Landers leads the man back to the house, grateful that Bessie is in town grocery shopping so he can at least delay introductions and explanations, though they seem to get more complicated as the days shift.

At his side, younger but struggling to keep Landers' pace, Olson is going on about the dig, and Landers forces himself to listen: "...hunting ground, settled by only a few groups we know of—they'd settle a bit, then move on every dozen or so years. But there's something weird, just plain weird about this one."

"What do you mean?" Landers asks. They walk up the back steps where the cement crumbles, Landers can see, a little more today. He holds the screen door for Olson, who pauses on the back step.

"Breech burials, I call them," he says. "The burials found so far are all distinguished by their face down, north-south orientation. We've found a few this way at other locations, but this seems different."

Not sure what the man Olson means, Landers shrugs. It is like another language, another place, suddenly, and Rico's words, before anyone else even had a whisper of this, seem to be more and more right. He points to the telephone on the wall near the sink. The tap is dripping and he presses the faucet handle tight. In a few minutes it will stop but will be hard to wrestle on again. It seems that there is no in between.

"Thank you," Olson says, picking up the phone to dial. Turning to Landers, he grins. "I'll use my calling card, don't you worry," he says, and Landers nods, backing out of the house, but on the back step again, isn't sure where to turn.

None But The Dead And Dying

Word is spreading, from the counter conversation at the Country Inn to the gas pumps at the M&M Mobil station on Route 20, word about Theodore Thompson's ailing mother dying in the night.

Contessa Welch has heard the news and has already placed a casserole in the oven. She leans now over the stainless steel, double-sided sink and presses her hands into the foaming water, her eyes following first a squirrel, its tail twitching its balancing act on the branches, then the butterflies and sparrows, blue jays and cardinals. She can't see the mourning doves where they walk the streets out front, pecking blindly at anything that might be food, but she can hear their coo-cooing and she thinks how appropriate it is, though they do this every morning and it is Contessa who's never noticed until today.

She hasn't seen Mrs. Thompson since Theodore stopped wheeling her to church years ago. Contessa thinks it must be a relief to him. She knows he will be disoriented, not with the loss but with the gain. The freedom his mother has finally bestowed upon him will overwhelm him. Frighten him. Contessa understands this.

When her telephone rings she thinks it will be another friend who will stumble to impart news they're not sure she's heard, their babbling an effort to understand her reaction to it. Their memories reach as long in this town as the streets that stretch through the heart of things, streets that stretch into state highways and lead to places far away. Because of these memories the callers have questions, questions Contessa has answers to, answers she won't divulge. Answers that are nobody's concern.

She is thinking all of these things when she picks up the receiver, careful to make her voice somber in her hello. It is Jack, though, calling from the plant, an unusual thing, despite all their years of marriage. "I don't want you mewling over that man," he says right away. "Christ, everybody's been waiting for this, anyway."

He's smelled my casserole, she thinks, all the way across town, all the way through those metal walls and concrete reinforcements. She says, "I am going over to offer my proper condolences, if that's what you're so concerned about. I've put a casserole in the oven and when it comes out, I'll walk it over to him. I wouldn't think you'd have difficulty with that." But then I've seen you piss right into the wind, she thinks. "Try to have some compassion."

"Compassion? Crap. The man is probably glad. I just don't want you making some stupid fool of yourself."

Or of you. What could be more foolish than jealousy? "The timer is going off," she says. "I'll tell him you send your condolences, too."

She hangs up the phone. Through the sheers in her front window she sees Mamie Van Allen back on the porch, unusual in this heat. Maybe she's hoping for more excitement. Maybe she's willing her own death, hoping to be one of the three. Maybe she's trying to stay the executioner.

The timer buzzes.

So the word spreads. Mostly people are wondering if Cecelia Thompson might have died before, during, or after Theodore's music, the fact of her going easier to know than the when. So many years sick after the stroke, so many years of Theodore's tender care. There are hung heads on Theodore's behalf and then the speculation turns, as conversations do, like sharp-turning cars on two wheels: they begin to wonder if this means Theodore will play tonight. Surely, they say, we can't expect him to go on, not tonight, not after this, it must be such a shock to him.

And so the hot summer day stretches long, and even the children play more quietly, their ears turning, every now and then, to the sky, their eyes scanning the breaks between houses to peer toward the Thompson house, its Victorian spire hidden in the trees. They know they won't hear anything, not now, not yet, but they listen anyway, their breath catching at far-away sounds, at the hint of something heavy in the air.

In the rolling thunder of the afternoon a stranger tucks his thumb into the pocket of his jeans. It might be nice, he thinks, to settle for a little while.

He stands at the corner of Hamer Street and the highway, stands at the corner that started the town over a hundred and fifty years ago, and watches kids get ice cream cones at a local stand. He sees their eager hands, the quick tongues that lap melting chocolate and strawberry, but sees, too, that there is something silent beneath them, something in them that is waiting, and he wonders what it could be.

On down the highway he hikes, his pack light on his back, the sun fierce against it. He will take room seven at the Buckeye Inn and will walk the streets of the town, taking in broad white porches in front of pale yellow and green houses. He will feel invited to stay.

3

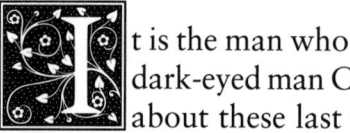t is the man who is new in town, the dark-haired, dark-eyed man Crescent has been hearing so much about these last few days that has caused her to slip on this black dress with the purple and pink flowers and walk to the funeral, then find a ride out here to the gravesite. She scans the crowd as she had at the church where she sat in the rear pew to watch the mourners file in, and though she has seen many people she doesn't know today, no one fits the description. Some of the talk around town was that he was somehow related—a cousin of some sort; perhaps, the whispered stories went, even illegitimate. But if he's not here, not here for any of it, then who is he?

Her eyes scan the bowed heads and catch Theodore Thompson. He ducks into the prayer as if he hasn't been aware of it until she spots him. She stares at the pink of his forehead and the albino white of his hair. She has heard the stories of this man, too: the musical genius gone crazy at college or lured home by the very woman they bury now, a woman trying to substitute the son for the husband whose sudden death left her so lonely so many years ago.

Crescent sees that Theodore Thompson does not cry here for his mother. She sees that his mouth moves to his own prayer, lips not matching those of the minister's. She feels a nudge from Hope Bleu.

"Pray," Hope says, but Crescent can only stare at the man, can feel the dark clouds hovering, but knows that the night is still far away.

A large green tarp sags on its poles around the pit because no one worked with it long enough to pull it taut and Landers stares at the sad circus it makes of his backyard. He wonders how they expect it to hold if the clouds moving in let loose. Maybe they've learned to gamble the sky like we do, he thinks, and today their odds-on favorite is No Rain—that the drought will continue, the earth, brown and scratchy and brittle, will make them all more frustrated than ever by this humidity that hangs in the air but won't drop into the soil. On this fourth day rain has threatened the clouds hold together like fat ladies auditioning, curved and teasing, skirting away to let their yeses fall someplace else.

To the northern part of his yard he can see that Rico is on the backhoe, making the new line, the money for the machine rental and lost wages and any extra piping promised by the university people. It only took that one phone call, so simple to arrange, and afterwards Olson and him both so much easier with each other. It was Bessie he hadn't imagined would be against it: "This is our property to manage, Landers, and I know you know that," she said when he finally needed to tell her, her rising so early in the morning telling him something was on her mind. "I just don't like that maybe this means we're on their side or something," she said, too, something he didn't understand at all and she couldn't explain, though she tried: "Maybe we'll owe them or something, is what I mean." But he said, "No, no Bessie, it can't be that way because this is so they can excavate. This is their way of paying us." She was dumping coffee gone cold, getting ready to make a fresh pot, maybe the third before noon. "That's exactly what I'm talking about," she said, throwing the old grinds away and measuring for twelve cups.

Now comes Mason Pope's voice from the driveway behind Landers, saying, "Well, just as they say it is," and Landers turns to shake the man's hand, a soft hand from a cushioned life, but Landers smiles because he must.

They walk up the new path to the edge of the site and Mason takes it in—the breeze flapping the tarp just enough to kick sand in everyone's eyes. The men and woman from the university and their two assistants apiece barely blink, too afraid such a blink could make it all flash away. They work quickly, carefully, each with their own job, stepping carefully over strings blocking the pit into orderly squares, a grid laid over the earth to organize it somehow. They trowel and brush and inspect and measure and seem to pour water over everything they find.

One takes compass readings, takes them over and over to make sure they're right. "At what angle Figure 7?" the woman asks, and the assistant reads from a pad, "North-northeast to south-southwest, head location southwest, measured orientation at 121°." She asks, "Make a note of the solstice angles, will you, Marty?" and he nods, jotting something down.

Someone bends over a sketch pad, neck to hot sun, hands working to draw the site. Another photographs, writing furiously in a notebook after every shot, sometimes using his own compass to calculate location, angle. Others brush and number and sticker each item, so many, like the object in Olson's hand the first day, still looking like clumps of dirt or homely rocks to Landers.

He scuffs dirt into the carved earth, just a little, as if by accident, and watches it tumble the five or six feet to the bottom of this hole, stretched now past any reasonable width for a water line. The hole has almost become another layer of property—on the upper, the house, barn, fields and the steady motion of that world needs to grow food, while on the lower, skulls and bones and broken pottery and objects foreign to these times. No one yet can tell Landers to his satisfaction when it was created, who by or who for, other than a few words like "indigenous" and "transient" and "unidentified," which seems to him no more than they knew the first day. None of the words is enough for him. Across the fields he can make out Rico's crew in bright scarves and wide straw hats bent over the hoes, chopping the weeds in the beans, saving the cost of another herbicide spray that probably wouldn't work in the dry heat anyway. At least the farm seems to keep going, somehow.

Mason Pope steps out from under the tarp, looks at the sky where the fat ladies crowd the line overhead. "Stopped by George's and tried to talk to him about all this," he says, and Landers nods. Mason says, "Of course he didn't know at all what I was trying to tell him."

That makes it your call, Mason, Landers thinks. He nods again.

"Seems to me, if it's not hurting anybody, why stop it?" Mason says. "And they are making up for the trouble with the water line?"

"Right," Landers says, and this time Mason nods. He smiles, showing white teeth, grasps Landers' hand to shake it with fingers bearing a giant college class ring with some colored stone in it Landers hasn't been able to identify. He stands waiting to wave at the lawyer down the driveway, but Mason is hesitating at the edge of the dig, then motions Olson to step aside. They talk and gesture, but are enough away from Landers that he cannot overhear. He cannot imagine what it might be about, so he turns toward the soy bean field. It's not his business, not really, after all.

Mamie Van Allen still sits on her porch where she took her supper a few hours ago. It has been quiet, the town hushed out of respect for Cecelia Thompson, perhaps. Contessa Welch, on her way to the church this morning, stopped up, concerned about Mamie's sitting in the sticky heat. Mamie asked her what the difference was between sweltering inside or out. Contessa had no answer for her, though she frowned, and tiptoed in her high heels back down the sidewalk toward her car where it awaited her across the street, engine and air conditioning running.

Mamie called after her, asked her to give Theodore Thompson her condolences, and Contessa waved and nodded, an agreement to do the proper thing. Mamie has wanted to call, even managed to sit by the telephone, find the number in the thin directory and dial it, but hung up each of the four times she dialed.

I've made my share of such calls, she decided, and I shouldn't be expected to make any more.

She's settled herself here, in this perfect spot on the porch where the trees shield the sun and make breezes when nothing should. When she sees the man coming up the street from Mulberry she recognizes his unfamiliarity. Foreign, too, to this town is his defined, straightforward walk that is not rushed. There's a self-assuredness about him she can spot from six houses away. His dark good looks are not those of anyone she knows in town, and she knows nearly everyone.

As he nears she sees he's probably near thirty. He's lean and firm but looks like he could hold his own in any barroom bet gone bad. He's sauntering up the walk to the edge of her property. He's returning her gaze.

"Evening," he says, his voice surprisingly soft, a voice not fitting the hard features of someone who's probably seen what she can only imagine.

"Good evening," she says, noticing for the first time the

uncertain beginnings of dusk. The grey of dawn has lingered so long, welded the day into a steel band of thunderclouds, strong in its surrender to sunset. "Nice night for a walk."

He smiles and again, the contrast. His smile is broad, easy in coming. "Long as it doesn't rain."

Mamie notices two things: the man doesn't say "don't" and his features are broad, eyes black. He reminds her of photographs she used to study of American Indians. She wants to speak again, to invite him up the steps, sit with her, listen to the night with her, but he moves on and she realizes it's probably best; he could be anyone. He could be dangerous. She folds her hands into her lap and wishes for the energy to get up from her chair to mix her drink, to have invited him to sit with her anyway.

Years ago, at the Christian Academy, Clayton Bleu was told by a pastor of a country church in southern Indiana that churches are still social places. "Don't let this preaching stuff fool you," the man told him. "People just come to church for companionship. To catch up on all the goings on. Study it yourself sometime. Without fail more people show up for baptisms, weddings, Christmas, Easter and funerals. I call them the Big Five. You got one of the Big Five planned and you'll see those attendance numbers go up." Clayton can't recall the man's name or even the church he had at the time, the church the man was later dismissed from for some reason. Clayton wonders vaguely if the stogie he gestured with finally got in people's way. Or maybe he finally ran into a congregation that didn't care about the money. Clayton remembers little about the man other than his words: "Put out the message that you're going to be talking about Moses or Job or John the Baptist and only the stalwart will show. Even then they'll be fidgety, looking at their watches every few minutes. Cut those Sunday services short, at least the sermon part. Add an extra hymn or have the pre-schoolers sing or the youth group put on a skit. That'll hold everybody as good as anything can."

Clayton shook his head. "People go to church to learn something, to be taught about the Word of God."

The man shook his head. "Sorry, boy. They don't even half the time read the Good Book. Sure they like having it explained to them, but only in little bits and pieces and in a way that makes them feel better for not reading it, so you got to make the thing sound deep and complicated and personal, too. 'God is talking to you—yes you!' That sort of thing. And always remember to set up more chairs than you do for a regular service for any of the Big Five." He watched while Clayton nodded his head, caught the look of suspicion in his eyes, then said, "Believe it or not, this is the best advice you'll get the whole time you're here at the Academy."

And the man was right.

Clayton Bleu sits now in one of the pews of the sanctuary, thinking about what he managed to find to say in here today about Cecelia Thompson. He had all the right elements. People seemed pleased with the service. He is always tired after any of the Big Five, and he always wonders if it's been worth it.

He leans back in the pew. Of the four congregations he's led, this has the nicest church. Simple lines, modern design. The altar up three wide, low steps, offering the minister easy eye contact with the members in attendance. The long altar table resembles a conference table blanketed in white linen, a thick brass cross and huge Bible propped open and flanked by long tapered white candles in brass sticks. Plain bleached wood pews angle behind and along the sides of the altar, rising a step at a time in three rows for the choir. Then, straight back, a huge plate glass window with a view to an outdoor grove where an eighteen-foot cross stands, spotlighted for evening services, washed in sunlight for Sunday morning services, purified in snow in the winter. In any season the cross enunciates its promise.

It is to gaze at the cross through the always-gleaming window that Clayton Bleu comes here. It is to elicit wisdom from his surroundings that he haunts the sanctuary. Tonight he contemplates Theodore Thompson. Cecelia Thompson. And himself, and why he never visited her.

On the drive from the church to the cemetery Hope said, in passing, that Miss Van Allen hadn't come out because of the weather.

"Miss Van Allen? Where did you hear that?" he asked.

"I talked to her."

He tried to picture his daughter having a full conversation with anyone and can't. "Where? When?" he asked, before he could dam them up behind common sense. She gave him the scowl he expected.

"Gosh, Dad, don't you talk to anybody?" She rattled her hair, done up with barrettes dangling beads and feathers and odd little objects that made him think of things you send underwater to lure fish. "She was on her porch and I sat with her for awhile."

He tried to picture Mamie Van Allen and his daughter chatting it up on that big porch. He saw nothing where the image should have been. "So what did you talk about?"

She turned to watch the houses pass. He knew their conversation was over. She shrugged. She said, "Nothing," but he knew that whatever it was, it meant something to Hope.

He watches, in the sanctuary, the cross fade to black in front of him. No services tonight, because no light illuminates it. Some of the parishioners object to this, want the cross lit in any darkness. The debate has raged the entire time Clayton Bleu has been minister here, has been raging since the erection of the church in the late sixties, and rages still. One faction says not lighting the cross is like laying the American flag out in the parking lot and driving Harley Davidson motorcycles over it. The other faction claims the boost in the electric bill will destroy the financial solidarity of the church.

So far the economists are winning, Clayton thinks, then decides that tomorrow he will go see Mamie Van Allen if only to feel closer to Hope.

He is drinking slowly, this beer warming already in his palm and he concentrates on setting the bottle down between swallows. There is no hurry, he tells himself. There is no place I must be. There is nothing I must have a clear head for.

He has walked the streets of the town today, has taken in the wooden and brick homes, the grass in front of them green from sprinklers or brown from drought. He ignored the questions of children playing: "What's your name? Why are you walking? Where are you going?" because he is used to that.

It is a friendly town, he has seen evidence of this, but it is also closed. As he sits he is aware that he is being inspected, observed, judged. He drinks slowly, setting his bottle on the bar between swallows. He turns down an offer of a cigarette from a man in a John Deere hat and denim jacket. "Wasn't we in school together?" the man asks, but it could be a test, the qualifier. If he didn't attend with someone the man knows, he is a stranger, an outsider. He could be asked to leave.

He shakes his head.

"Not very talkative are you?" the man says, watching him.

"Just enjoying my beer."

The man nods his head, showing for the first time his

drunkenness, then turns to the bartender. "Hank, you heard any more about Stone's place?"

The bartender replaces the man's empty Budweiser bottle with a full one, dropping the empty with a clatter behind the counter. He shakes his head. "Weird stuff going on out there, for sure."

Another man joins them, this one bareheaded and balding, a dark brown beard making his head look like it could be on upside down. "Burial grounds is what it is."

John Deere slams his bottle on the bar. "No shitting."

Brown Beard shakes his head. "No, man, I'm telling ya. First they thought it was some hideout for serial killer bodies or something—" He waits to continue while those listening nearby chuckle and laugh. "Really. Angie's sister's husband, he does work that's someways connected and that's what she says to Angie today. But now they don't think so."

"So there's more than one body?"

Brown Beard nods. "Lost count at about four. Maybe half a dozen, maybe more."

"So what is it, then?" the bartender asks.

Brown Beard leans close, bringing his listeners into a tight circle. "Something valuable, though, valuable enough for a night watch."

"Who they got to watch? Pinkerton's security or something?" a man a few stools down says.

"Diamond Richards," Brown Beard says, and the men laugh.

"So much for valuable," the John Deere man says.

The stranger unfolds himself from the bar stool, drops flattened bills onto the bar, waves his thanks to the bartender before heading out the door. He is remembering seeing a phone booth with a telephone book still hanging from the metal attachment, is trying to remember which street it was, along which sidewalk, thinking to look up an address, when he sees a young woman on the curb across the street.

4

rescent St. Clair has been waiting for the stranger, the soles of her feet burning against the asphalt of Main Street where she sits on the curb across from the Bahama Lounge. Her eyes haven't left the corner of the bar in fifteen minutes. From this spot she can see both the front and side doors. She's never been inside the Bahama Lounge, but she has imagined the inside so clearly that it has become real to her: the walls painted with tropical scenes of palm trees and long-tailed, bright red, blue, and yellow-feathered birds perched in the branches or suspended in flight between them. Behind the bar the bottles sit brown and amber and shimmering in front of a mirror decorated like an ocean beach. Paper oriental lanterns hang from the ceiling, casting dim light around the room. The tables and chairs, a few booths and a bar are the light colors of rattan, bamboo and bentwood. Cash Simmons attends the bar clad in Hawaiian shirts and white pants while girls from out of town wait tables in halter tops or strapless bikini tops and tight white shorts. This is their year-round uniform, with little skipper or sailor hats crooked on their heads. The men at the bar flirt with them and Crescent imagines the girls at the Bahama Lounge make lots of money in tips.

None But The Dead And Dying

Sometimes she likes to imagine the fight last summer that she heard tore up the place. Gregg Walker had thought his wife Loretta danced a little too close to Hoboy Brown so he slapped her and Hoboy delivered a quick right in Loretta's defense. By the time they cleared the place out two hours later, thirty-seven Bahama Lounge regulars had become a part of it and twelve people, including two deputies from the sheriff's department, were injured. People streamed out of both doors that night.

Crescent hopes that if there's excitement tonight that it's not a fight that might hurt the new man before she finds out more about him. She hasn't been told that this is where he is, hasn't seen him go in, but she has matched her image of the man with the image of the Lounge and has decided that this is where he is.

Crescent can hear the click of the traffic light in the middle of the intersection of Main and Maple, just a half a block away, when it changes from red to green to yellow and back to red to cast a ghoulish patina across the pavement and storefront windows. Crescent sits and stares and watches nothing happen. She hears footsteps along the sidewalk, coming closer to her from Maple Street. She suddenly wonders what time it is, how much time has passed since she first sat down. She glances to her left and sees the figure of a man approaching. Alone and a little stooped he is, and she tries to capture the walk that nearly crosses the border into a shuffle, tries to attach that walk to her memory of someone. She glances away.

The music from the jukebox inside the Lounge has stopped and only the lit Matilda Bay neon in the window tells her the place is still open. Pressing the tiny button on the side of her digital watch, she sees that it's nearly midnight. She realizes they've stopped for Theodore's music.

The steps come closer, then stop. She's glad the music has finished; they'll hear her scream if it comes to that. She remembers something somebody once told her about bears and backing down and she takes a deep breath and stands, turning to face the man.

It is Theodore Thompson and he is glancing toward the Bahama Lounge, his white hair soft like a ring around his head, like it has snowed but only on him, only on his head. "Fight tonight?" he asks.

Crescent shakes her head, swallows a few times to wet her dry throat.

"It's so quiet," he says. "All over town." He seems puzzled by this. "People on their porches, so late at night."

Crescent sees it, the question, unspoken. "Hot inside," she says.

He looks into her eyes, and she sees a kindness in his, though she is expecting something else, something haunted or lost. "It's as if—as if they're waiting?" A question, but not exactly the one she feared.

"For the night," she says, not knowing if it is enough, too much, the right or wrong thing. So much balances on these words.

She thinks it is a small smile that softens his face, but he says only goodnight before turning in the direction of his home.

When the man emerges from the Bahama Lounge he sees the young woman, all legs she looks like from this angle, while she watches an older man walk away from her. A familiarity mixed with their distance intrigues the man. It is a combination he has seen in people ever since he got here.

She is looking at him now, not moving from her spot near the curb and he knows that, despite his wish otherwise, she is not a small town hooker. He stands a moment, wanting a cigarette. "Hello," he says, drawing the curbs closer together, narrowing the street between them.

She says, "Hi. Nice night for a walk."

It almost isn't, the hot air so sticky, clinging to shorts, jeans, shirts, using sweat as glue. "It is," he says, knowing it is the thing to say, even though it would be better if it would just rain.

"You visiting friends here?" she asks, twisting her body from one leg's weight to the other.

He crosses the street near this heart of town. Along Main Street, no space for the skinniest shadows between them, stand two- and three-story brick buildings, old solid structures with new businesses on lower floors: Video Visions, Shape 'N' Shear, a hardware store, the Country Inn, insurance and law offices.

"Well?" she says.

He has learned to never say he's just passing through. "Just moved here," he says. For all he knows, it might be the truth that he speaks. He is always discovering his own truth.

"Oh! Well, I'm Crescent St. Clair, but everybody just calls me Cress." She thrusts her hot pink painted nails toward him in a handshake. "Welcome."

"Thank you," he says, taking her hand politely, quickly, surprised at her gesture. This one is so young, he thinks, she could be trouble. "Nice town."

"You think so?" She shrugs, sets the pace in their stride down the street.

"You don't?"

"Well, I mean, it's so boring! I can't wait to get out of here, find some real life. Why would you want to move *here*? Where are you from, anyway?"

"I don't think it's so boring, Cress."

"You've *got* to be kidding. Hang around long enough and just watching the traffic lights change will give you a thrill."

He catches his laughter in his throat; the sound of it has always halted the laughter of others, has always made them turn to look at him oddly. He wishes again for a cigarette. "It did suddenly get quiet around here," he says.

She looks at him as if she has a secret she wants to share, glancing around the deserted street. "We're waiting to hear Theodore."

He has been matching her stride, footfall by footfall, down Main. They turn now down Amanda Street where grass grows again between the street and sidewalk and the maples tip their leafy hands overhead. Long sidewalks trip away from their cement path to meet wooden porch steps.

"Theodore?" He's glad she doesn't seem to mind his accompanying her. She has many secrets she might yet share with him. Maybe she knows about this digging, these happenings at the Stone farm.

"He plays at midnight," she says. "He hasn't missed a night yet and even though he's late tonight—probably because of his mother dying; did you know about that?—I'm sure he's still going to play." Her ambling chatter matches her pace.

The man notices that she's avoiding the cracks as she walks. "Step on a crack..." he remembers.

"The best place to hear him," she is saying, "is from the church tower."

He sees the shadowy spire reach into the night a few houses away and another street or two over. "You go up there often to hear him?" he asks.

But she has stopped, nearly in mid-stride, her brows furrowed. Even the pink of her nails, he thinks, have paled. He follows her gaze, sees nothing. "What?"

"He can't stop, just because she died," she says.

Later he will remember her words and be amazed at how important the music of the man in the attic must be to her. For now he can only watch her struggle with the possibility, and feel relief when the soft, almost timid strains of saxophone emerge from the folds of the town and crawl from infant whimpering to screaming terror.

He wants to walk further alongside the long-legged teenager, wants to imagine the brush of her hair against his shoulder, his chest, but he can only stand and shake his head when she asks if he wants to hear the music from the bell tower. He watches her walk away, the strains of music floating all over the night.

Ben Stevens steers the new Buick into the winding driveway, thinking that he would rather have found a back way in, but country lanes and farming paths have never been familiar to him, their patterns around fields a puzzling grid, labyrinths only rural folks can find their way through. He feels exposed this way, his headlights breaking the darkness like a shattering gunshot on a quiet street.

He reminds himself that it doesn't matter if Landers Stone sees him, comes out to greet him. He's permitted to make such visits, and, after all the talk around town today, it's probably expected that the mayor make some sort of special visit. It's explaining the midnight hour that would be difficult.

Over the rise he begins to make out the shape of the ridge, and judges where the edge is, braking easily before it, aiming his headlights into the space ahead. It isn't as dark as he guessed it would be, enough light leaking from the house and floodlight to illuminate the area. He kills the engine and climbs out of the car, strides to the edge of the pit. Suddenly it is dark. A tarpaulin that has been suspended overhead and the depth of the dig hold the light back, so that the site is a dark spot in the middle of lit night. He crouches, resting his weight on the backs of his heels, and peers into that blackness. He can make out a soft white, here and there, as his eyes adjust, and he guesses these must be the bones he has heard about.

"Get away!"

The mayor turns to see an angular man pointing a gun at him. "Who are you?" Stevens asks, putting his hands up and rising slowly, the gesture something that comes back to him from childhood good guy-bad guy games.

"Who the hell are *you*, that's the question," the man says, waving the gun, stopping Stevens from taking a step toward him.

"Be careful with that, will you? I'm just trying to figure out who you are. I'm the mayor. Ben Stevens."

The figure lowers the gun, rushes to him. "Gosh, Mayor, I'm awful sorry. It's just that you wasn't ID'ing and I didn't know."

"No harm done, but you really ought to be more careful." He steps again toward the site. "Got a flashlight?"

"I'll get you one," the man says, and hops away, a few skips to start himself into a run.

Stevens wants to drop himself into the hole, sift through a little dirt himself, handle the bones, get the feel of the site, of the process that has been going on down here, but he is held back by the feeling that there is an authority to this that he doesn't possess, that this is someone else's domain and he is, at best, an observer.

The man is back with the flashlight and Stevens shines it into the pit, sees that he was right about the dim white being bones. He can see, with the aid of the light, that other items have been unearthed: pottery and chips of things that might be arrowheads. "Quite a discovery, eh?" Stevens says, more to himself than to the other man.

"Well, those college people are awfully interested, that's for sure. I think more's coming in the morning, too." The man is lighting a cigarette, his rifle propped casually against his leg, butt to the ground, and Stevens thinks that this is probably the way many people are shot to death accidentally.

He stares into the pit, his eyes adjusting further to the darkness. There are so many things in the earth, he thinks, that we just don't know about until they suddenly show themselves. The pyramids in Egypt. King Tut. Didn't that even become an international exhibit that toured the country? This is small, compared to that, but still...still it is something for this area. Something special.

"Ben, what brings you out this way this late?"

He turns to see Landers Stone coming up the rise to the dig. Stevens holds out his hand for the man to shake. "Just got to thinking about this, Bud, and didn't have much time till now to get out to see it."

"Light ain't much good this time of the night," Landers says, and Stevens knows it's his way of saying the welcome he's being given is a reluctant one. "Ought to come back around eleven tomorrow morning when the whole entire gang of them'll be here."

"Who's that?"

"Well, let's see." Landers holds up a hand of fingers for counting. "Must be about a dozen of those university people at least, and they keep saying more'll be here tomorrow and danged if they don't just keep coming. Of course there was some sort of police before that and they still come around some, mostly just checking things out. Curious, I guess."

"Been quite a circus, sounds like," Stevens says. A breeze kicks in from the west and a shiver runs through him. All these outsiders coming in. Motel rooms. Restaurants.

Landers nods his head, scuffs his feet in the sandy dirt. "Times during the day I just want to drop it all, cover it all back up and get back to normal. But I guess the university people got a point about us not knowing much about this stuff."

"We don't know about it because we got other things to worry about," Stevens says. "You just hang in there, Bud. Things get back to normal and you'll miss all this attention." He raps his fist lightly against the other man's shoulder.

Landers laughs, nods his head at the ground. "You're probably right about that."

They stand in silence a few minutes, staring into the pit as if willing something within it to move, to shift in the dirt.

"Your man's doing maybe too good of a job," Stevens says, then, gesturing with his elbow toward the figure with the gun who's moved away to scout the other side of the digging, adds, "Thought I was maybe dead there for a minute. Or maimed, anyway."

Landers laughs. "Poor kid's just been dying to play army since he got out of Vietnam."

"Had to wait awhile," Stevens says, feeling suddenly old and young at the same time, realizing that Landers is speaking of Diamond Richards, who graduated only a couple of years before he did.

"Always did like guns and war," Landers says. "Maybe if we'd had more Diamonds over there we'd done better."

"Better yet if more Diamonds had been running things." He's heard Landers talk Vietnam before, talk politics in general, and it's something he avoids when he can. It's hard enough to keep things around here together; can't people understand how much easier it is to talk than to do? He slaps Landers on the shoulder. "Thanks for letting me take a look around," he says.

Landers shakes his hand again. "No problem. If you'd called, though, we could've had some hot coffee on for you."

Stevens grins. It's like there's no such thing as trespassing. "Thanks," he says again.

"Come around tomorrow and meet some of the new folks," Landers says, and the mayor nods.

Climbing back into his car, Stevens takes another look at the farm that has been transformed. The tarpaulin flutters a bit in the night breeze. He returns Landers Stone's wave and decides that he just ought to do that, come back, meet some of the new folks.

Contessa Butler Welch lingers on the porch. Her husband Jack has called her to join him at least twice but she's lost track, hasn't really been paying attention to him, her ears lifted to the night music drifting from a block away, the sweet strains of the saxophone. Angry and sorry. Those are the words Contessa would use tonight to describe the sounds Theodore makes. It is a private game she plays because she doesn't know the songs, thinks maybe they are made up as Theodore goes along, but she needs names for them, something to categorize the nights, a way of knowing Theodore, still, through his music. And tonight it all seems the right way to close off what the day delivered up to him.

She holds onto the night and the music and the porch railing. She waves, quickly, to Mamie Van Allen across the street on her own porch, but Mamie fails to return the greeting. Contessa decides that perhaps the music and the night have put her to sleep. She looks down the street, because there is a reason other than the music that has brought her out tonight.

It is the man who is new in town, the man she has heard so much about. She is hoping that he will follow her curious call, her silent need for something different, will follow it to her door. She has thought carefully about what she will say. She has heard he is friendly, will stop to chat, will return the greetings offered him, and so she knows that if he will just come near the rest will be easy.

The screen door screeches open behind her. "Come on,

babe, come to bed," Jack says, and she can tell by his voice that he is ready for her, ready to hold her until she can barely breathe, hold her to the sweaty scent of him, nuzzling her so close she feels nothing but his weight, hears nothing but the grinding need of him, his words harsh and dirty that were once sweet and pleading and just what she wanted to hear, back when he drank.

Some men, she's heard, get violent and angry when they drink. Jack always got amorous, gentle and sweet, but he drank too much, too often, missed too much work and finally had to stop drinking entirely. An alcoholic he calls himself, though Contessa disagrees, and often wishes for the drinking days. She tells herself on nights like this one that she would learn to deal with the frequent memory lapses, the forgotten holidays and dinner plans if only she could have that one part of him back. He hasn't had a drink since Deborah died; she's wanted nothing but drink since that day.

"Come on, babe, let's make our future rich," Jack whispers from the half-open door. It is what he used to say to her when they were young, barely married, ready for children and Contessa was trying to conceive.

She hasn't turned to look at him, doesn't turn now. "Go on in. I'll be up in a few minutes," she says, but she knows that she won't, that she'll stand here past the last notes, that when she finally does pull open that front door to go in she won't venture up the steps, will collapse on the sofa, knowing that his mood will have passed, that she will have to listen to his morning grumbling but that she will be able to shut that out, too.

"I'll be ready, honey," he says, then snickers to himself as if he has a plan, an inside joke, and closes the door behind him.

Contessa leans against the square white pillar that reaches to support the tiny porch roof. She looks again toward

Mulberry Street, squinting into the dim light cast by the street lamps, and again rehearses the words.

He sits in his car in the South Main Street School parking lot, thinking of his visit to Mamie Van Allen today. She's never been a churchgoer and by all rights Reverend Bleu should think of her as a sinner needing saving, but he's never been able to get around to that.

She was sleeping in one of those wide white wicker chairs on that cement and brick porch when he walked up, and he couldn't keep from staring at her. Maybe it was his staring that finally woke her. She came to gradually, deliberately, reluctantly, moving first her feet, disengaging them from each other. Then, as if most of her thought and all of her energy were on the effort, she released her hands and shifted the balance of her weight in the chair. He was intrigued, embarrassed, by her stirring, and he felt dirty for watching. He looked away, into the boughs of the willow in the Johanson's yard next door. Two little girls played beneath the dragging fronds, calling each other "honey," playing house.

"To what do I owe the pleasure of your company?" Mamie asked, her body still unbending, slowly, gracefully.

He heard the tone, the intended message, the scolding. He couldn't be sure whether it was for his visit after a long lapse or for his visit as a member of the clergy she has never had use for. "You've been on my mind," he said, and he heard the defensiveness in his own voice.

"Hope was here," she said. "She's very bright. I enjoyed her visit very much." A cross-hatch pattern of the wicker cut into the pink flesh of her arms where they rested for too long on the chair.

"She mentioned that to me," he said. He hadn't been

invited to sit so he leaned against one of the brick pillars supporting the heavy, winding porch that fronts the Van Allen house. "I was surprised at how many people came to show their condolences to Cecelia Thompson, especially in the heat. I can certainly understand you preferring not to go." These were the rehearsed words, words designed to excuse her, to give her an out for not being there. It didn't occur to him then that she didn't care either way, had no use for the social escapes he designed on her behalf.

She was focused on the girls under the weeping tree. "I'm not surprised," she said. "Cecelia Thompson had a good number of friends in this town, all of whom will miss her."

She has always been so proper, Miss Van Allen; despite the hostility that everyone knows existed between her and Cecelia Thompson she is still lady enough to have put him in his place this afternoon. The reverend felt the blush in his cheeks. "I regret that...I mean, I'm sorry if I sounded disrespectful...." And he was fourteen again. Despite growing up in a Nebraska town and not this one, he still heard in her words, felt in her presence, that sharp slap of a ruler against his palms.

"I understand, Reverend Bleu." She leaned back in her chair, fanned herself with a folded up portion of the *The Blade*, the town's own weekly not out for another few days.

The giggles of the girls next door tumbled over them. A neighborhood boy had entered their sanctuary and the girls seemed startled by this. He asked if he could play, too. "You can't play house," one girl said. "You have to play with dolls to play house."

Mamie Van Allen offered up something to him about Hope—she'd noticed her ears were pierced now, noticed how Hope had sat so straight in the chair. "Primly" had been Miss Van Allen's word. Bewildered, he had no response for her. He was trying to remember her at breakfast—today? yesterday?—trying to picture the earrings. How is he missing these things?

She looked at him as though offended by his unfamiliarity with his daughter. He changed the subject, asked about the burial site. He'd forgotten how she hates gossip, she'd told him so to his face once, implying that his tongue wagged looser than it should, though she never seemed eager to interrupt if she were only asked to listen.

Then he was glad he was standing because it made it so much easier to give her a little wave, an even smaller excuse, and quick-step off the porch.

A police car passes the lot where he now sits and he starts the car, tries to make it look like he's maybe just stalled or is turning around. He needs to go someplace but tonight the church and his house aren't good options, so Clayton Bleu isn't sure why, but he drives down Main Street, makes a left onto Route 20, and pulls his Chevette into the lot of the 24-hour Pizza House restaurant. He parks and heads into the square brick and green building, feeling exposed without Sandy or Hope alongside in such a place. He isn't really hungry. Maybe it's the station wagon in the lot that says Midwestern State University on the side.

They take up a couple of shoved-together tables in the middle of the room, and as the door closes behind Clayton they burst into a laughter that makes him want to check his hair, his face, his fly, but of course it isn't him, he knows this, they aren't even looking at him. They are away from home, from family, for a job digging in dirt but here they look like family—brothers and sisters, one older woman with wiry grey hair that escapes her scarf as though fleeing it. She reminds him of what Mamie might have looked like twenty-five or thirty years ago if she'd had a different life, a life of learning maybe instead of teaching.

Clayton takes a deep breath and ventures closer. When they look at him, their laughter done but smiles still shining, he stops. It has been a long time since he's needed to extend a welcome to complete strangers. "Hello," he says. "I'm Clayton Bleu." They nod, glance at each other; there are maybe a dozen of them around this table. "I'm minister of one of the churches here," he says, and then they offer him a seat, a slice of pizza.

"Sans meat," a woman younger than the first one he noticed, says. She is maybe thirty, as is the red-haired man next to her. The others, all men, look much younger, barely in their twenties. They are all comfortable—loose shirts, jeans, arms relaxed across the backs of chairs, legs crossed ankle-to-knee beside the table. They are easy in this way with each other, with him, and in this place that they've so quickly made their own.

"Sans—?" Clayton says.

"Vegetarian. Lots of mushrooms, olives and peppers," the woman says. "I'm Kathy."

"Nice to meet you," Clayton says.

"Michael Olson," the red-haired man next to him says, and they shake hands. More names follow, a Craig and a Jim and Clayton loses track after that. He accepts the chair someone has pushed at him, sits on the edge of it, pulled near the corner of the table, and accepts, too, a wedge of pizza that looks a bit foreign to him without the pepperoni and bacon and ground beef he usually orders.

"It's funny," the woman Kathy says. "We were just talking about what a friendly town this is." Some chuckling follows this, and plastic glasses are filled from the pitcher of water on the table.

"Well," Clayton says, picking at the pizza on the plate in front of him, his fingers not sure where to start, something he has scolded Hope for. "We're just glad to have you," he says, and it seems that, with these words, they are quiet again if only for a second, and Clayton wonders why he's said this, because they aren't really, are they?

"Thank you," Olson says. "We appreciate that, Reverend."

It occurs to him that the town, their ways, must seem quaint to them, trading kind lies with the local reverend over pizza. "We don't have many choices," he says, biting into a slice.

"Excuse me?"

"I'm sorry. Not many restaurant choices. McDonald's. Subway. Pizza places too many to count. Did you know there are the same number of pizza places as attorneys, the same number of bars as churches and beauty parlors in this town?" He swallows an offered glass of water.

"No kidding," they say.

"No kidding. There are as many motels as there are used car lots and one more funeral home than new car dealerships. When you combine all the restaurants, there are more of them than any other type of business."

A few of the young guys at the far end of the table toast this news with their drinks. "The women must look good going to the bars, then," someone says.

"I did a talk about this one Sunday," the reverend says, and they listen as if waiting for him to launch into the lesson but he doesn't, he just says, "It was all about how we show ourselves to others. I mean, coming in from out of town, you must have noticed a few things yourselves."

They nod and chuckle and look at each other but they say nothing except, "It really is friendly."

"Maybe you can make it to church this Sunday. We'd be happy to see you there." These are automatic words, words that shoot out of him as needed, but they never fail to embarrass him. He stands to leave.

"Off so soon?" Olson asks, and the reverend says he guesses so.

"Visit us at the site sometime. You'd be amazed," Olson says, and Clayton wishes he could say the same about their visit to church.

"I might just do that," he says, and thanks them for the pizza before slipping back into the night. It has been more difficult than he imagined to sit in this familiar place making conversation with unfamiliar people. How long has it been since he last met someone new? Since he last was reminded that his world has been collapsing to fit the size of this one town?

Tonight, outside the Pizza House, Theodore is still playing. The music slithers out to him these five or six streets away, wraps itself tight around him, and Clayton breathes it in. For this first time, he knows that if he could, he would breathe it all back out again, too.

5

ontessa Butler Welch is trying to concentrate on what Bonita Franklin has been saying, but it's church talk so she has no interest and this complicates things, because she must still appear interested, must still smile and say, "No, really?" every now and then.

"I can't believe," Bonita is saying, "that Sandra Bleu is surprised at all that I got off the prayer line. I mean, you know I'm long distance. Everybody knows Green Springs for whatever unearthly known reason is long distance from town. Add that to the fact that Josephine Andrews is just ahead of me on the line and she hates to call long distance from town, so she saves up the names so she can call me with them all at once. Add that to the fact that it might just be a month or more before she calls me." She pauses here to empty another cream into the coffee that's just been warmed up. She is also waiting for Contessa to prod her, so, despite an impatience with melodrama over trivia, Contessa obliges with, "No wonder."

Bonita shakes her head, continues. "So you can imagine how mortified I was when I got to regular prayer meeting last night and the ladies were going around the circle, asking for prayers for Mamie Van Allen and that entire McMasters family and the usuals, the Walkers and Browns, of course...."

Contessa nods through the woman's list until she can't bear it and says, "Yes, so?"

"Well, I didn't hear Cecelia Thompson's name so of course I said that we mustn't forget dear Mrs. Thompson and they looked at me as if I'd just raised the dead, which I guess I sort of did. Anyway, Sandra Bleu says, 'You must not have heard that poor Mrs. Thompson passed away last week.' And there I was, didn't even know about the funeral or any of it." She sipped her coffee.

Contessa frowns, makes sympathetic noises with her tongue.

Bonita takes this as a cue to go on. "That's bad enough, but it wasn't even the first time. Remember when Mr. Peters passed away—when was it—January? No, couldn't have been, the crops were still coming in, had to have been fall sometime, though it was a late season, what with all that rain...."

She goes on, sorting through a fragmented re-telling of a story she has already told more than once, losing Contessa at last. So Contessa sips her own coffee and wonders if she looks as bloated as she feels after her luncheon here.

Lula Burks comes around, offering them for the second time a piece of cherry fluff pie, and Contessa shakes her head again, but Bonita gives in, sending Lula back across the linoleum floor of the Country Inn to find a plate and fork.

Lula, Contessa imagines, will die in this little dinette, poised at a booth with her order pad in her hand and that intense interest and concentration on the customer's order etched on her face, sweet half-smile, half-furrowed brow and all. Contessa can see the funeral—Lula laid out in her powder blue uniform, her monogrammed Cross pen (a gift from her proud husband the Christmas of 1966—she tells everyone this if they should happen to remark on it) clipped neatly into her apron pocket next to a brand new, never to be used order pad.

Contessa is picturing this, stirring the sugar in her coffee again, when the new man walks in, the bell on the door jangling his entrance. She knows it is him, though she has never seen him, his dark eyes, his black hair pulled behind his head, the angles of his face and that feeling he sends through her. He pauses just inside the door to locate an empty booth or table, and Contessa stops stirring her coffee.

She both wants to catch the man's eye and wants to avoid his glance. It is the hint of something—a look of familiarity in the strangeness, or the mirage of memory—that teases her. She's heard the talk about him, and he fits it all.

He nears the table, heading for a booth at the back, and she presses her hand against her chest, presses against that flat skin at the base of her neck above the rise of her breasts. It's a place that hasn't felt hollow until now. She feels his eyes on her as he passes their booth; she crosses her right leg over her left, squeezes her thighs beneath the table. Her hand, she realizes, is trying to press her heart back into a regular rhythm. She scolds herself for being such a teenager but can't help wishing she'd dropped the yellow cotton sundress with the belted waist around her instead of this smockish green thing. After all, for her age, her figure still turns a head now and then.

Bonita is nudging her. "Did you see him? That's him, right?"

Contessa nods, reaches for her coffee but it has cooled, she knows it, and doesn't want it, so she lets it sit.

"Is he here with the stuff going on at Bessie Stone's?" Bonita asks.

Contessa shrugs. There is so little she has learned about him. A loner with a single at the Buckeye Inn out on Route 20. Spends nights at the Bahama Lounge. She wants to saunter up to him at his booth, extend a casual greeting, invite herself into conversation with him. She wishes she hadn't walked out of the Welcome Wagon meeting a few months ago over something that now seems so stupid as where the annual banquet should be held, but then, they never made much effort to introduce themselves to people living in motels.

"What do you know about him?" she asks, but on this subject Bonita has nothing to say.

Landers Stone drops the curtains closed, room by room, around the house. It's a shame because something they've always liked about the house is the view. To some people, Ohio countryside is dull, flat, looks the same for miles, but for Landers and Bessie the flatness means fullness—so much more sky, so much more ground. Winters they awaken some mornings in the midst of white—sky, ground, trees, buildings, cars, road, all white. When the snow stretches around them like that they don't think of themselves as blocked off from everything on the face of the earth, but as the dimple on that face, the gleeful sign that there's a smile somewhere.

Usually it's August before Landers begins to miss the snow, but the summer is moving too fast and too slow at the same time this year. Fourth of July is still a week away, but around here, every day, there's been that sort of excitement. It all interested him at first, the dig, the find, the meticulous way Olson and his people go about things, and then it got ordinary. Olson has so far kept his promise that the water line would get finished, that the farm wouldn't be disrupted. But there has been disruption from the outside.

Mason Pope, of course, and Ben Stevens have come out, and other friends from town, curious, just checking they say, and that's okay because this isn't too much different

None But The Dead And Dying

than a fire. Word spreads and people want to see, want to be able to say they've been by the place, want to offer help or just talk. But this is different from a fire, too, because it keeps on going, the on-site crew never finishing, back every day.

And just as the site becomes normal, something new. A phone call yesterday from the town's newspaper editor: "Say, Landers, I hear something really interesting's going on out there. Mind if I come take a look? Won't be but a few minutes, don't even really have to see you if you've got things to do. So many folks have questions, you know, and maybe something, not much but something, will keep some of the rumors from getting out of hand."

First thing this morning he was out but he had a camera Landers wasn't expecting. What was he going to do? A few pictures, a few words for the local paper, for the local readers, seemed okay.

He pulls another shade in an upstairs bedroom. This used to be Pam's room but it's been a sewing room now for nearly thirty years. Landers pauses, looks through a back window to the green tarp silent in the still air.

All that time, he thinks. All that time they were back there.

It takes him a second to imagine the lawn again the way it was. So much has rushed to happen in such a short period of time.

The telephone rings and he wants to ignore it but can't—it could be Rico on the cellular phone in the fields with an emergency or it could be Bessie over in Fremont at the Super K looking for an answering machine.

When he answers it a woman says, "Mr. Landers?"

"Landers Stone, yeah," he says, hoping it isn't yet another press person.

"I'm so sorry. Mr. Stone, this is Angel Baker from WCLE-TV in Cleveland and I would just like to ask you something about your find there. May I?"

"Just," "really." These media people make it seem so incidental. "A few words," "just take a minute," "only a few photos," "really won't be in your way at all."

"Of course," she is saying, "if this is a bad time, I would be happy to call at another time."

"No, no," he says, sitting down to take the questions that are all beginning to sound alike and to answer them with words that come back to him more and more easily.

Mamie Van Allen raises her scotch in a late-afternoon toast with the dark-haired, dark-eyed man in the chair matching hers. It seems early, in this prolonged sunlight, to begin drinking. Winters it's black outside by now, darkness a thorough cover for the clatter of ice in fat glasses, for the quick click of toasts. She looks at her watch, seeks reassurance in its dial, hands marking seconds and minutes even when she's not peeking. The man is watching her, she sees, when she looks up.

"You're the Mystery Man, you know," she says.

He smiles, drops his head to shake it at the grey cement slab of the porch floor. "I'm no mystery man, ma'am," he says.

"Please," she says, words fast on the heels of his, "call me Mamie. 'Ma'am' makes me feel old. Nothing worse than feeling old when you are old."

"Then you'll call me by my name and not 'son,'" he says.

They nod their agreement and smile and lift their glasses to seal it. His faded jeans are frayed to white at the knees but hint at lean legs, and his pale blue tee shirt is stretched across a muscled chest. When he lifts his glass his arms flex and tighten around his developed shoulders. She is glad that even if she must suffer old age she can still see, can still feel desire, can still imagine. She is glad for her scotch, tries not to wonder if he would have chosen to sit with her years ago when she had so much to offer. Or, she wonders, did I have less to offer, and that's why I spent those years alone?

He crosses running shoes so tattered they look as though they are bound together by the laces and necessity alone. "Eddy," he says. "Eddy Light Sky."

She nods as if approving the name.

He looked startled a little while ago when she invited him to sit, to share her drink. Now he seems glad, even relaxed, sort of studying her, maybe imagining her with ironed skin and bright eyes, younger hemlines revealing trim thighs, firm calves, tanned arms. His thoughts embarrass him, she can tell. He is violating her with his vision of her, and she knows it, can see all the way through to that. She is flattered by his attention, surprised to know it like she knows herself. It is very nearly a frightening thing.

On the porch across the street Contessa Welch waves and Mamie returns it. It's odd for Contessa to come out in the heat like this, with some hardcover book of all things, as if she were an intellectual of some sort, and in that dress with the halter sort of top that is much too young for her.

Mamie turns back to her visitor. She says, "I wish I'd been given a name like that. What does Mamie Van Allen mean, anyway? What does it say about me?"

He leans nearer. "It means you are one of a blood line called Van Allen. German, right?"

"That's all obvious, mundane stuff," she says. "But 'Mamie'? What kind of a name is that? Of course I'd rather it than 'Wilhelmina' or something."

He touches her hand. It is warm, soft. Her fingers clutch him. She can't remember when she last touched someone, when someone last touched her. "Mamie's a terrific name," he says. "It's alive and fun."

"Think I could change it? I don't mean legally, of course,

but you know, get a name like yours."

He sits, holding her hand this way, their fingers clasping over the table between them. "What name do you think fits you better?" he asks.

She twists her mouth, scowling. "I've never thought about it. Is it that simple?"

He lifts her ribbed, unevenly-colored hand to his lips and presses a kiss into it. "No one knows," he says, "how it might be for someone else. For some it takes vision quests and fasting. For you, maybe it will come to you so you won't have to go to it."

She squeezes his hand and smiles and wishes that tonight he would fall asleep next to her here, but of course he won't. He stands soon and kisses her hand once more before letting loose, then he is off again down the steps. He heads down the street in the direction away from Contessa's house and Mamie smiles about that in the orange sun that can't set for her too soon, tonight.

The early evening sun shines golden against the sides of houses and barns on this stretch of Sandusky County Road 33 and Mayor Ben Stevens flips the visor down on his Buick. Blazing brilliant and sharp, the sun finds him through the gap between visor and rearview mirror so Stevens must squint to see. He hopes no one he passes knows him—they might, after all, think he's looking at them, commenting without words over something equally unspoken. He is always careful not to offend or upset anyone. This is his role as mayor: to smile and shake hands and get the business of the town done while upsetting the fewest number of people.

He turns onto a township road with the single digit he can never remember, knowing the turn only because he knows all the farms out this way—the Colliers and Nessors and Winngates. Their barns and silos and aluminum-sided houses are the landmarks he navigates the country roads with.

Nearing the Stone farm things begin to look different to him and he sees right away what it is: the road is lined with vans and cars, the vans with satellite dishes and TV station names on their sides, WTOL and WTVG from Toledo, WXYZ from Detroit he recognizes, still others that mean nothing to him. He slows the Skylark to move between them but the Stones' driveway is jammed and he must drive on nearly a half-mile to find a spot along the road to park.

He hurries to the driveway in shoes not made for cracked township roads, the clacking of their soles against the pavement the only sound in a quiet that is made almost eerie by the signs of activity that lure him further inward. Black birds walk the front lawn, pecking at the ground, squawking at each other, and the yellow-flower-patterned sheets on Bessie Stone's clothesline flap. Voices begin to come to Stevens as he nears the head of the driveway, follows the path beaten into the grass leading to the site.

The green tarp is gone though the poles for it jut into the air, pointing to the sky at crooked angles like accusing fingers. Stevens' breath comes more quickly and beads of perspiration burst on his forehead. It is the heat and the walk but also much more. He pauses to wipe his face with a cotton handkerchief before going the final steps to the edge of the dig.

A blonde woman and a dark-haired man in shorts and tank shirts point cameras into the pit which is even wider now than it was last night. They shift their positions, their aim steady on the dozen or so workers in the pit, their cameras swallowing up images of dusty bowls, stones, bones. A couple of others, in shorts as well, their arms showing lines from having worn different lengths of sleeves in hot sun, direct the camera people. "Did you get that one where the skull has that dirt still in the eye sockets?" one of them asks. They are all young.

To one side, a red-haired, pudgy man with round-framed glasses speaks to another camera, speaks to a handsome, dimpled man Stevens recognizes as a Toledo TV reporter. Another reporter, a woman from a competing station, stands nearby, almost close enough to them that Stevens marvels she isn't in the shot. He has sometimes wondered, watching her on the evening news, if she is as pretty in person and he sees that she is but that the location shots and desk shots never show the wide hips and broad thighs he can see now.

Along the far ridge a dozen or so migrant workers stand watching, their arms crossed or clutching cigarettes. When a TV crewman approaches them, says something to them, they move away, only one or two making a comment back. Stevens sorts through the crowd for Landers Stone but doesn't see him, though Diamond Richards, rifle in hand, is smiling for photographers who click away with still-shot cameras, while someone else chats with him.

Stevens moves closer. It is important that the right things about the community get said. He recognizes a Fremont *News-Messenger* reporter and says hello.

This is all it seems to take. They all want the mayor's reaction.

Q: What do you think about a find like this outside your town?

Stevens: It's been very exciting.

Q: What role do you see the community playing in this?

Stevens: The community of course supports Mr. Stone and the efforts of the university team and we feel doing our part is making them feel welcome in a community that is unfamiliar to them.

Q: Well, Mayor Stevens, Mr. Olson says he and his crew have met with nothing but friendliness since arriving, so you must be pleased with the community's response.

Stevens: Oh, without question. We've always been a friendly place so when you combine that with the hospitality of our motels and restaurants and businesses, you've got something that's truly special.

Q: And, of course, this ancient Indian burial site certainly adds to that.

Stevens: Absolutely.

Q: One final question, Mayor Stevens. I'm sure many of our viewers would be interested in personally exploring the site, the location of which, for the time being, is held secret. Have you or are you planning to open the site up to visitors?

Stevens: This is something that will have to be decided. Mr. Olson and his people must be permitted to work and, while we always welcome visitors to the community, we wouldn't want the work out here to be disrupted.

Q: Then let me ask you this. What about children's groups? Don't you think Boy Scout and Girl Scout groups, for example, would find a visit to such a working archaeological dig valuable?

Stevens: Oh, I agree. I'm pretty fascinated myself. But we need to work it out.

Q: Thank you, Mr. Mayor. (to camera) That's our live report from here, Jerry and Diane. A terrific historical discovery down here, but so far off limits to history buffs.

The interviews done, Ben Stevens looks into the gathered crowd where the *News-Messenger* reporter chats with people from the Bellevue *Gazette* and the *Sandusky Register*. They give him thumbs-up signs and he wipes his brow with a flourish of his white handkerchief. The red-bearded, red-haired man walks to him. "Let's walk a bit," he says, extending his hand, introducing himself.

"Only for a bit," Stevens says, chuckling. "These shoes aren't made for much more than a bit around here." The man Olson is earnest, and Stevens tries to think of what he's said or done or not done to concern the man. He knows that whatever it is, he must correct it because they need this man here, now.

They walk the length of Stone's back yard, the mayor stepping carefully, watching the grass ahead of him. He's learned that country dogs run wild, so he walks with his head down, his eyes flitting from the ground to the man beside him.

Olson seems not to care. His hands are jammed as far as they'll go into the back pockets of his jeans—to his first knuckles—and he peers at Stevens through the round eyeglasses. "One of the reporters told me you're thinking of opening the site up to visitors, kids groups, maybe tourists," he says. He stops, facing Ben Stevens with his hands still behind him, his chest and belly heaved forward, Bessie Stone's fresh laundry on the line next to them.

Somewhere this man has a mother, a father, and they are proud of him, Stevens thinks, studying this man who doesn't nearly seem old enough, this man whose family must brag about the work he does to add to history and science. Stevens wonders for a minute what they must have thought when he told them he was going to keep digging in the dirt, even as an adult, and maybe get paid for it. "I said it was something to consider, yes," Stevens says. He tries the smile again.

"It's not."

Beside them the sheets whip the air with the breeze and it seems to Stevens that even from here he can smell how clean they are. The voices from the site don't carry this far, though the farm seems humming anyway, a backhoe not much further from where they stand, digging a trench in another direction from the burial site. The Mexican-American at its controls shouts his moves to someone on the ground, someone who looks to Stevens to be more a part of the university than the farm. They move slowly, and it occurs to Stevens that they are continuing the water line, carefully checking for signs of anything this way being unearthed.

They watch the backhoe a few minutes until Stevens looks at Olson again, smiling yet. Though Stevens wants to wrap his arms across his chest to do something with them, he understands about body language and holds them at his side.

"It's not something to consider," Olson says again, looking him in the eye. The sheets flip again, then hang still. "You have to understand, with all due respect, that having a lot of people around here is a very bad idea. The media and everything is plenty as it is."

"We could put up some rope fences around the pit, back a bit so they'd still be close enough to see but not close enough to interfere. We could take small groups, max them out at ten, hold any others down the driveway. We could control it." Stevens gives in to the urge, crosses his arms against his chest, holds himself in.

"You don't understand," Olson says. "I agree with the idea that people ought to be able to experience the excitement of a dig." He shakes his head, folds his own arms across his chest, then drops them. He looks out toward the fields where the migrants have returned now that supper is over and there are a few more good hours of sunshine. He turns to Stevens. "What's in that pit is valuable, you have to understand that."

"Sure it is," Stevens says. "Adds to what we know about history, all that."

"I mean the relics. Indian artifacts these days are a big trade. Even some of the smallest arrowheads not in the best of shape can be worth a buck apiece. A site like this one here is chockful of terrifically intact pieces."

Stevens whistles under his breath, turns without thinking to look again at the media crowd swarming the pit, the university crew ringing it, trying not to look protective, but marking its perimeter from the inside, keeping others out, watching the people who watch them. "I had no idea," he says.

"Unless you're into the trade or you're on this end of it, you don't. Most people don't realize it," Olson says. "But with word out now through the media, the treasure hunters are going to start tracking this place down, and they'll find it. You add a mess of tourists to the mix and you won't know who's who or what's what and your Diamond Richards watchman won't be near enough. Believe me, Mr. Mayor, that's a Pandora's box you don't even want to peek into."

He studies Olson, absorbing his words with the setting sun. There had to be a catch. Had to be, and this is it, he thinks.

The back screen door of the house slams and Stevens turns to see Bessie heading their way, heading for the sheets on the line. "Evening," she calls to them, waving, her white plastic basket swinging from her other hand. They return her wave.

"So are you removing this stuff, then?" Stevens asks. He's not even imagined the pit could be worth money other than through the revenue from the people it could bring in.

"Oh, it's not ours to remove. We only obtained permission—and just oral permission at that—to study, not to take. We would like a few pieces, and have gotten Mr. Stone's permission to remove a couple for testing purposes, but everything is being left pretty much as is for now. A museum on the site would be ideal, something we could probably raise money for, something that would allow people to see it, something that could be made safe from looting."

Stevens watches Bessie unpin the sheets from the line, gathering them in her arms from one end to the other, then folding them into the basket. She manages all this without ever touching them to the grass.

"A museum, huh?" he says, and Olson nods, and they

are walking again, heading back to the site. "Now that's worth some thought." Finally he sees Olson smile.

Crescent balances her weight over the center of the teeter-totter. One leg presses, then the other, and she rides high on one side, then the other. "He is so cute, too. Up close, he's even better. Hope, you've got to meet him. You've just got to."

"Denny's going to birth a brick if he finds out," Hope says, snapping off the end of a Milky Way bar, chewing quickly in a race against the sun and the melting of the chocolate.

"Not Denny and nobody else, either, owns me. If I want to hang out with this guy, then I will." Standing, she skitters in aerobic shoes down the wooden plank, skips over the handle and onto the ground.

Hope licks melted chocolate from her fingers. Her tongue digs into the crack of her life line. "So what's this guy's name, anyway?"

Crescent has been afraid she would ask. "I don't know—yet. But I will."

"So have you found out yet where he's staying? Maybe he's married or has a girlfriend or something. Maybe that's why he's here in the first place. You've got to find that stuff out, you know."

They wander to the slide, lean on its sides where it starts to curve in the middle. Crescent strides to the back of it, mounts the steps. She stands at the top.

"I don't *got* to do anything," she says. It's like a pronouncement from on high. "Besides, if you came into some town from far away to be with a boyfriend, would you spend all your spare time in a bar by yourself? Oh, wait, how would you know? So much experience with guys and all that." She sees no reaction on Hope's face to her comment, so she runs down the length of the slide.

"Let's go see if Miss Van Allen is on her porch today," Hope says, wadding the candy bar wrapper up, careful to keep it from smearing her fingers with any more chocolate than she's already had to lick off. She spots a dumpster at the corner of the school building.

"Why not?" Crescent stops her walk back up the slide to vault over the side. "I didn't know you and Miss Van Allen were such buddies."

"She's just a nice lady. I think she gets lonely. I mean, wouldn't you? That house and nobody but you in it and you sit on your porch just hoping somebody interesting might come by." She hooks the candy wrapper into the deep hollow of the dumpster as they pass it. "I can't imagine getting old and being alone. That must be just the worst."

"Well, honey, if you don't give it up to somebody someday, you'll be alone, too." Crescent tiptoes along the parking lot curb in front of the school. She looks at the way the bright school-bus yellow of the curb clashes with her fluorescent pink and blue shoes.

"Do you think that's why Miss Van Allen is all alone?"

"Why else?"

They kick a stone between them along the sidewalk. When it pops off the cement and lands in the grass, they adopt another until Crescent stops at the corner of White and Main Streets. "Do you think she'd tell us if we asked?"

Hope's expression reminds Crescent of the time they shared a sour pickle at the fair—her lips twisted in her first and last bite.

"What's the worst she could do to us?" Crescent asks, knocking a stone the size of a ball for jacks along in front of her. "Maybe throw us off her porch or call us names. Nothing too bad."

Hope isn't keeping up her end of the stone-kicking and

lets her turn pass. "You can't just ask somebody something like that."

"Why not? Like I said, what's she going to do to us?"

"It's not that. People need certain things to be theirs. Private. Like that guy you're talking about. Maybe he's here because of that Indian burial ground thing," Hope says.

Crescent stops. "What Indian burial ground?"

Hope has walked a few yards ahead but now stops as well, waits for Cress to catch up. "Out on the Stone's farm north of town. They go to my dad's church. They even had it on the news tonight."

"No."

"Yes. I'm telling you, Mr. Stone was digging a water line and found it. There's all kinds of stuff in it, pottery and arrowheads...."

"Bones, too, right?"

"Well, yeah, I guess. They did show one. It was just a skull they showed, with dirt still in it right where the eyes should have been and it really looked creepy."

They walk again, ignoring the boys who hoot at them from the open windows of cars. Every once in awhile one of their names gets called and they wave or neglect to, depending on the owner of the car.

"So maybe that *is* why he's in town," Crescent says. "We should go out there and see."

This time it's Hope who stops, throwing her hands up, pushing a hand to her hip and leaning her weight on one foot. Crescent knows the gesture, knows it means she is exasperated, one of those moves she has that makes her look too much like somebody's mother instead of a teenager. "What?" Cress says. "What did I say now?"

"What was I just saying about people's privacy? If he is out there, you shouldn't go out there bugging him."

Crescent kicks a loose pebble down the sidewalk. She kicks hard but the stone doesn't go very far. "That's not what I meant. I meant we should go to see this Indian burial ground to see *it*. Aren't you just the eensy-weensiest bit curious? Think of it, bones and skulls and stuff."

"No thanks."

A dog in a nearby yard yaps at them. Walking into the yard, upsetting it even more, Hope lets out a few barks of her own.

"Hope! What an embarrassment!" Crescent crosses the street to wait her out. When Hope doesn't want to do something, she has to get creative about convincing her. Hope is the most stubborn person she knows, the one person, despite being three years younger, who isn't and never has been intimidated by Crescent.

In the eighth grade Crescent noticed her, that new sixth grade kid on the playground after school who was being bullied by seventh graders who teased her about a warm jacket she wore on one of the earliest, sunniest days of spring. "It's not *that* warm out," she was saying, shooing her hand at their bare arms.

"Ah! Poor baby! She's cold! Needs her jacket! Brrr!" they teased.

And then she'd dropped her weight onto her left leg, her left hip jutting out to hold her left hand, and she said, "Showing me you're tough because you don't need a jacket *really* impresses me."

When she walked away from them, the biggest girl popped her from behind, scattering her books and papers all over the playground, throwing her off balance, though she was still standing. They snatched at her jacket. "Lay off, you'll rip it!" she yelled, so Crescent went to what she would always call Hope's rescue. With a couple of twists of fingers and wrists and yanked hair, they were gone.

"Whatdja do that for?" Hope demanded, scooping up books and papers.

Crescent knew that saying she was helping would have

been the wrong thing. "I just felt like it, I guess. I can't stand those crimps, anyway." She grabbed a few papers the wind threatened to steal away.

"Those what?"

"Crimps. Like they crimp my style," Crescent said, handing the papers over, looking around for more.

"You mean *cramp* your style."

Cress laughed, then, imitating Hope's hip and hand gesture, and said, "Yeah, right, like I'm going to call them cramps."

Even now there are other girls they call cramps and Crescent sometimes wonders what Ohio State will be like without her around.

Maybe something like this flashes through Hope's mind, too, there's no way Crescent can know, but Hope follows her across the street, says, "Okay listen. If you can get Denny to drive and you promise you won't ask Miss Van Allen about her you-know-what virginity, *then* I'll go."

"Have it your way," Crescent says, careful to make it sound as though she is giving in to Hope instead of getting her way, after all.

Hope nods, accepting the terms. So they walk again, dodging the little kids on bicycles who ride the sidewalks without looking up. Down along Main Street they walk, ignoring the boys in a pickup truck who holler at them when they pass on the street.

"Have you ever noticed," Hope says, "that none of these guys will borrow the family van?"

"How cramp it would be!" Crescent says and Hope punches her in the arm.

They turn up Buckeye Street, nearing Theodore Thompson's house, and they see something different about it, the stark wooden porch in front of the large Victorian house has a chair on it, a brand new outdoor chair, white plastic with a white plastic matching side table next to it. The girls look at each other. Theodore Thompson is sitting in the chair with the newspaper in his lap, but he seems not so much to be reading it as simply holding it. He is watching them come down the street.

Crescent waves. "Let's go up," she says, knowing Hope will follow.

When they skip up the steps to say hello, they notice a tall cola with lots of ice sweating next to him. A huge yellowjacket climbs around its rim, dipping down to take a sip now and then. A second white chair with a fat blue-striped cushion on it sits next to the table.

Cress parks herself on the porch railing and motions Hope to take the chair. She leans her back against one of the porch supports and raises her bare feet to the railing, balancing herself.

"Please don't fall," Theodore says, stretching a hand toward her, a gesture of warning and saving at the same time.

"Don't you worry, Mr. Thompson," she says, "I have lots of years of practice doing this." The yellowjacket careens toward her in the air and she bats at it.

"You're going to make it mad," Hope says, but Crescent ignores her. Hope raises her eyes to the porch ceiling, shakes her head at Theodore. "I'm Hope Bleu. And that's Crescent St. Clair."

Theodore stretches his legs. They are skinny and white in his outdated shorts. "You're the minister's daughter," he says, and Hope nods. "He did a nice service for my mother."

"Thank you."

"Can I get you girls something to drink?"

Hope shakes her head, says, "No thanks," and Crescent shoots her a dirty look. "I'd love one. Whatever you're having," she says.

He folds his paper and places it on the table. "I'll be back in a jiffy," he says, and vanishes into the house.

"Why'd you ask for the drink?" Hope says, leaning,

whispering, harsh.

"I didn't ask. He did," Cress says. "I'm thirsty. Can you believe his knees?"

"Oh, please." Hope drops her weight back into the chair and the plastic creaks a little. Kids playing across the street squeal and yell to one another. One of them hops into a Big Wheel and cranks its noisy plastic wheels down the sidewalk, the weight of it bumping loudly at each crack.

Crescent leans toward Hope, careful to keep her balance. "Maybe we should ask Mr. Thompson about his you-know-what virginity," she whispers back. Hope's face turns a mortified pale that Crescent loves to conjure. She gives Hope one of her you-just-wait-and-see looks, watching her face twist further with her horror.

Screen door slamming behind him, Theodore Thompson emerges with a tray holding two glasses of cola and a small plate of store-bought cookies. "We'll have to keep the bugs away," he says. "I brought you one anyway, because I'll bet you're thirstier than you say because you want to be polite."

Hope blushes but they all ignore it and settle in a semicircle to watch the street as it fades into the evening, the parade of women and strollers, kids on their way home from the pool, towels wet across their handlebars or around their shoulders.

"Do you girls go to the pool much?" he asks.

"Too many little kids there," Hope says.

Crescent points across the street. "Like those. We go to the reservoir. There's a better breeze and the water's not got all that chemical stuff in it."

"Oh," he says. "I see."

They sit, sipping their drinks. Crescent teases Hope, motioning to her in mime when Theodore is looking the other way, even starting to say something before Hope interrupts to say something about it being too bad about his mother.

When they fall silent again, Hope flashes silent warnings to Cress not to even think about that question.

"Maybe I should buy a new car," Theodore says after awhile. The girls, who can't remember him driving anything but an old red car collectors would kill for, look at each other, shrug their shoulders. They have no idea if he means it or if he plays with this idea every summer anyway.

Crescent decides to take him at his word or call his bluff. "Ooh," she says, "a new car! What kind?"

The yellow jacket has drifted back into their midst, teasing Crescent about tasting her drink and she flicks Pepsi at it, shooing it away.

"Well, that's really what I've been trying to figure out. You know, what I'd like," he says.

"Get a sports car, Mr. Thompson," Crescent says.

"Red," Hope says. "Or black. But the blues—Pontiac's, I think—are great, too. A deep blue, not exactly turquoise, turquoise can be so—tacky—but a deep blue-green is so rich looking."

"Oh, definitely," Cress says. "Blue-green. Maybe dusty grey, you know, charcoal." She flicks her hand at the yellowjacket again. "Whatever you do," she says, turning her smile to him, "don't get one of those powder blue cars that look like old ladies' bathrooms on wheels."

Theodore laughs, a titter with a blush. "Maybe blue-green, but I don't think a sports car."

"Why not? Live it up for once, Mr. Thompson," Crescent says. She strokes the water off the side of her glass, licks her fingers.

He shakes his head, crosses his legs at the knee, swinging one leg the way Crescent has seen women in movies do, dangling petite shoes from painted toes. "Can you see me in a sports car?" he asks. "A Corvette, say?"

"Of course!" Crescent leans across to touch the knee jutting below his Bermuda shorts, green plaid to contrast his yellow polo shirt. He stops swinging his leg. He is the pale complexion of winter, his white ankle socks tucked into sandals are only a little whiter than he is, his trips around the library behind the mower not often nor long enough to give him more than a pinkness that isn't even a sunburn but is the color of health, the color of him breathing. "You might want to lose those socks, though," she says. "Get some sun—"

"Cress!" Hope's voice is a hand up in warning. "Maybe Mr. Thompson would rather—"

"That's all right, Hope." He leans into his chair, stretches his feet out in front of him, tries to steady his gaze on Crescent. "I'm interested in what Cress has to suggest."

"Actually, not much. I mean, you're an okay guy the way you are, you know?" Crescent obliges.

"Well, thank you."

She takes her fingers from his knee, stretches her back straight against the porch support. He reaches for his drink and she sees that the yellowjacket has miscalculated just once, landing himself in the brown liquid. She wants to warn him but something in his glance tells her he sees it, so she is surprised when he sips at it anyway. He sets the glass back down, wipes his upper lip. "Are you okay?" she asks.

"Of course," he says, as though startled by the question. "You were saying?"

"Well," she says, "I was going to say that you probably could stand to get out some. Like, this is good, sitting here."

"You think so?"

"Sure. Lots of people don't even know you. I mean, you take care of the library and stuff, and people see you around, but you're still kind of a mystery," Crescent says. She draws her legs up under her on the porch railing, strokes her feet with her fingers, weaving them between her toes. Her anklet is a silhouette heart that catches the light of the street lamp which is brightening in the deepening night.

"Me, a mystery?" He laughs in a way that comes from

the surface of him.

"Well," she says, "you left town, came back. That's mysterious. Romantic, even."

He stands to dump the floating yellow jacket and the rest of his drink into the bushes. "Maybe to you it's romantic," he says. "Would you like another drink, ladies?"

"No, thanks," Cress says, "and you're trying to change the subject."

"Maybe he doesn't want to talk about it," Hope says. She sets her glass on the small plastic table that matches the white plastic chairs. It seems to bow a bit with this weight. It is more fragile than it looks.

Crescent eyes Theodore. She says, "Makes it even more mysterious. Shrouds it, you might say."

With this he goes someplace deeper than the laugh, leaves them for a few minutes, they can see him go, his gaze on the street but somewhere else, too. They wait for what he might say when he gets back.

The day stretches out in a blazing sunset they glimpse through the trees, in openings between houses and down streets. The sun, this time of the year, takes its time leaving, like the kids across the street who fuss and cry when their mother calls them in.

At last Theodore blinks, and says to Crescent, "Maybe someday I'll tell you. It's not so much a mystery, though. Really." He swishes the glass, forgetting it's empty.

6

t is rummage sale day at the church. Reverend Bleu stands near the back entrance, ready to greet those who think to come. He stares through the double glass doors into the parking lot.

Fifteen years after the move from the building at the corner of Elm and Birch streets this is still being called the new church. In the fifties the church had plans drawn up for a new building. Parking would be more plentiful than the hit-or-miss street parking that the first location offered. As it was, everybody had to park in the back, go in to services through the back door because the front door was convenient only to those coming into the church on foot, from the north. In the winter the front door was bypassed entirely when folks parked along Elm and in the tiny bank lot across the street. With the Baptist church behind, their lot was of course full at the same time. Every few Sundays voices were raised between members of opposing congregations over the few spaces along the curb before they were herded into the churches for sermons on neighborliness.

The proper women of the church, thinking ahead to the weddings of their daughters, pushed for a new design: a formal front, a wide-open portico under which cars could pause to set free their passengers without damage of wind or snow or sleet or hail or rain. The minister had visions of greeting the congregation before these doors as they left to waiting cars.

The building of the new church took years. Money, in this farm and factory community, was slow but steady in coming, the people of the church patient, citing God's Will as reason enough for delays. A decade later, the new sanctuary christened, the people were so accustomed by then to entering from the rear that the front doors, double wide with deeply carved doors and gleaming brass handles, went unused. Reverend Bleu's early months in the church here were spent shuffling from door to door, the elderly and infirm coming and going through the front, the younger, more able at the rear.

It is still, though, a back door church, for back door people.

Mundee Manway is the first to cross through the back entrance into the church for the rummage sale. Reverend Bleu has been expecting her. She is always first, convinced that should she wait the best buys will elude her, snatched up by quicker hands, earlier risers.

He smiles. "Miss Manway, how very nice to see you," he says.

She has dressed for this shopping day out. Rummage sales are Mundee Manway's malls. Her uneven shelf of white hair scrapes the shoulders of a yellow paisley dress. Across her middle she has hung a lavender cloth belt, and around her shoulders she has tied a green shawl splashed with red in a pattern that might be flowers. Her white ankle socks match her heeled sandals. She is perhaps seventy and walks everywhere she goes. The reverend marvels at her shoes. A straw hat and bag accessorize her outfit.

She pauses near him, but peers past him into the open room where the clothing bunches atop long tables, where handwritten signs on white typing paper taped to the edges of them say, "Women's Clothing, $1 each" or "Men's Clothing, $1 each," or "Children's Clothing, $2 a bag."

She teeters a bit on her heels and he catches her elbow. "Ah, Reverend, sir, how nice to see you," she says, and smiles a crooked, grimy grin. Three of her front teeth are gone. A dimple shows in her left cheek.

"You look so nice today, Miss Manway," he says.

His words are a match, lighting her face, and she leans nearer. Her tone is secretive, her breath DeWar's. "Thank you, Reverend. You know I only shop at your sales. This is where the best-dressed ladies in town bring their things, you know. I tried once at the Baptist's, but it weren't near as good as this one. Here, you know what you get is good."

"I'm glad you think so," he says. She tells him this every time as if it is a secret, but it is a secret she shares with everyone. "I hope it's a good shopping day for you, Miss Manway," the reverend says, and she grins again and pats his sleeve and waddles across the wide, linoleum-floored hallway to the multi-purpose room.

Reverend Bleu greets with a nod of his head a pair of women he doesn't know, wondering for a second if maybe they're Lutherans, then turns to make sure Mundee Manway has found a chair to rest in. After her long walk, she will need to catch her breath.

Squatting for blocks in deep red bricks and black windows high along the sides is the stamping plant. A strip of green grass holds in the teetering flagpole, the stars and stripes hanging limp along the silver pole this still morning. The cars aligned in the lots that circle the building steam in the early heat. Inside the plant the temperature will hit 120° before the shift ends.

Eddy Light Sky expected them to hand him a broom and

point him in some direction, vague instructions following his back. He always expects this; it has never happened until today. Usually they put him on some machine, taking the time to show him how it operates, what it does, where the switches are, what to do and not do, what to do if something goes wrong. "Take pieces of your body, one at a time," he's been told too many times to count. Jeep in Toledo, a steel plant in Gary, or any of the other dozen or so places he's paused to work, it doesn't matter, they're not much different from each other, the noise, the food from vending machines, the catwalks where men in ties keep an eye out, and the wallets super-glued to cement floors for a few hours of fun.

Today there are no jobs operating machinery and he knows right away it has something to do with the union. Floor sweeping is something so far down the hiring hierarchy that they can spare this strong-looking silent man this particular job. "Just act like you got your card," he was told when he signed personnel papers, and he nodded. Mouth shut, eyes and ears open, he'll survive, always has. Head low enough to keep from catching stray shrapnel from any direction.

Walking the plant now with spare light bulbs to replace a strip over Line 3 he blocks out the heavy breathing of the machines that seeps through his earplugs. He sees the looks he is getting: curiosity, anger, resentment. He ducks his head, keeps walking.

The humidity leaks around the town, into houses, onto flesh. It clings, shining its unwillingness to let go. Even in her skirt Contessa can feel dampness behind her knees, between her thighs, beneath her breasts, on her forehead. She steps into the house again, heads for the shower, undressing as she goes, dropping the garments into the laundry hamper inside the bathroom door.

Icy water pounds at her shoulders and she drops her hands along her body. What if... she wonders. What if he were here? What if he let himself in? Watched her undress?

She imagines those dark eyes falling across her, imagines stopping in the living room, the hallway, at the top of the stairs or here in the bathroom, stopping to let him see. To see him. She imagines his lips parting into a smile, into a kiss, into a touch of her, a hungry touch, a long lick along her, into her, and she moves to catch that rhythm, that image, with her fingers, and straddles the tub, the cold spray. Unhooks the nozzle to hold it closer, flicking the dial to pulse, relaxing into the porcelain beneath her, feeling it melt with her heat but seeing his face, feeling his mouth, hands, unable to imagine further, having no need to.

It is a pleasure she has only felt when alone.

The moment she steps from the shower the heat is upon her again, a virus of wetness, despite the air conditioner's hum. She dusts her face, arms, breasts, abdomen, legs, with the fat peach towel and then must start again with her face, the dampness back again that fast. From her closet she draws a beige linen dress and drops it over her naked body, startled at her ease with it.

When Jack comes in, she holds herself against him, feeling his rusty sweat drip into her, her near-naked body against him, remembering his hardness against her when they danced in school, when they danced to Theodore's saxophone. But all she feels is his belly between them, all she smells is the factory on him, the metal and grease and something he ate for lunch.

He hesitates, backs away. "Connie, honey, I need a shower, then—"

She releases him, wonders how, when he emerges from the shower still sticky, she will resist him, avoid the mood she's no longer in.

It was hard to start the car this morning, despite temperatures heading into the eighties, then it stalled at Woodland and Maple. Even so, Crescent considers it lucky to have its use after the scene with Denny's mom. I should have known, she thinks, I should have known.

Hungover, Crescent could tell, and drinking again already, his mother was. There in the kitchen, pressing cigarettes out in a Cedar Point ashtray, for maybe the first time she looked old enough to Crescent to be Denny's mother. In her mid-thirties and already a grandmother by Denny's fifteen year-old little sister, Delores McMasters' long, brown-rooted blonde hair fell limp and dirty against her shoulders. Tiny wrinkles outlined her fading blue eyes and her breasts sagged beneath a Budweiser tee shirt. Her stomach pulled the middle of the design off center. Everything about her looked off—her gaze, her walk, even her words.

In the end, Denny slipped the keys from the counter, palming them so smoothly Crescent didn't even know he had them until he climbed behind the wheel and tried to start the car.

Of course Delores heard them then, came running and screaming from the house, her burning cigarette forgotten in her two-fingered vise. Denny swore, kept trying to start the car. When it finally turned over, his mother was by now slapping at him through the open window. He chewed on the inside of his cheek, something he did without thinking until he bit too hard or too long and felt the pain of it.

"You're too drunk to use it anyway," he said.

Delores looked at him as though the words surprised her, the meaning coming to her slowly, then, "You shit! Gimme those keys! This is my car, goddammit!"

"Consider this a favor," he said, revving the motor to

scare her hands off the side of it before backing out of the driveway.

On down the street, he lit his own cigarette and puffed it quick before putting it out again in the ashtray, a courtesy to Hope who would smell it anyway, when they picked her up. "Fuck," he said. "She might just call the cops."

"Why?"

"Stolen car or some shit. Who knows? She's pissed, hard to tell." Without the cigarette he kept his fingers busy tapping on the steering wheel, against the window frame, anywhere.

"She'll go back to sleep and forget all about it," Crescent said, hoping she was right.

"You won't tell Hope?" he asked, and she heard the whole question. "Sure," she said.

So now the three of them ride down Limerick to South Main, make the left to head them toward town and beyond it.

Crescent pushes the buttons on the radio but the station doesn't change and Denny reaches over to twist the knob. "Forget it," she says. "The hunt isn't worth what we might find."

"What is it?" Hope asks from her spot near the door. They are crammed into the front seat bench of the old Plymouth.

"IOT," Crescent says, trying to hold Denny's hand, but he can't keep it still, has to move it, keep moving it, trying to forget and ignore. "You sure you know where this is, Hope?" she asks.

The wind coming through the windows blows Hope's blonde hair into Crescent's black hair into Denny's brown hair. "Five, I think," Hope says.

"I'll watch for it," Cress says, squinting ahead at the tiny green signs that mark the intersections.

"Then?" Denny asks.

"Then we look for the TV vans," Cress says. She presses herself into him; he rests an arm along the back of the seat. "She'll get over it," she says.

He looks at Crescent, frowns, checks to see if Hope has heard her. "There's no asking her for help with a new guitar, now," he says.

"When I get my school loan I'll send you enough to cover it," Cress says. She leans to kiss his cheek but he turns his face away.

"That's September," he says. "I don't know why I care anyway." He runs a hand through his brown hair. "I thought you were watching for the turn," he says, and she squints at him, squints out the front windshield.

The road curls under them, winding and curling, a patch of road that drifts closed in the winter when the wind blows snow and nothing stops it. Farms stretch wide as though the farmers, two hundred years ago, all hated each other, wanted to be as far apart as they could while still keeping a careful eye on each other. Not even fences—not wood nor silver chain link—interrupt the spaces between farms except where cattle, horses or goats might be tempted to wander into the road with them. Over undulating hills, under curvaceous clouds, meadows, fields and orchards border these skinny, cracked strips of country road.

Denny finds the turn onto this road, one-laned with ditches on either side. "What happens if somebody comes from the other direction?" he asks.

"Somebody'd have to give way. Back up. Find a driveway, I guess, why care?" Crescent says because she is mad now and he is making no sense to her.

Buzzards circle overhead in huge loops, their wings arrested and flat out. They are ugly, even from down near the ground, but they are also graceful and huge and Crescent and Hope watch them through the windows until the car passes under them.

"You were right," Hope says. Ahead of them a string of TV vans line the road. In one driveway a station wagon with writing on the side sits. The mailbox says "Stone."

"What if they don't let us in?" Hope asks.

Denny stops at the right side of the road, the same side as the farmhouse, leaving the car running. Across the road a small cemetery sits, chalk-white markers jutting at odd angles from the green grass. A larger stone, a monument of sorts, spires upward. "Pope," it reads. On a smaller, "Nessor," and on another, "Spivey." These are names Crescent knows from town. She guesses if she walked the cemetery she'd recognize nearly all of the names. Beyond the cemetery, over a patch of woods like so many that scatter the farmland, the pair of buzzards circle.

"What are we even here for?" Denny asks.

"Don't you even want to see it?" Crescent asks. "Aren't you even curious?"

He shifts the car into park, shuts down the engine and they get out. The sun hovers in a blue sky but the air is cooler, a breeze whispering to them. It is silent except for crickets. They walk toward the driveway, following a man in shorts who carries what looks like a long coil of black cable.

"Hey hey hey hey—where do you kids think you're going?" A man calls to them, they can hear his voice before they see him where he emerges over a rise about twenty feet ahead of them. He looks shot through with Vietnam flashbacks, his jeans worn all the way through one knee, his tee shirt dingy and hanging loose and shapeless down his chest. On his head the sort of cap Crescent has seen on the captains of US naval vessels, dark blue with gold braiding.

"I know that guy," Crescent says. She walks toward him, picking her way along the driveway between a station wagon and a pickup truck. The sand is hot on her bare feet and every now and then a sharp little sliver pokes at her soles.

She tries to ignore the rifle in the man's hands. He holds it loosely and she figures she will stop only if he raises it. She tries to place him. Her brother's age, graduating class. No, he's too old. Her mother and father. Yes, that's it. Vietnam like her dad and her uncle but didn't come back quite the same way, some say. And some say he was never quite right to begin with. She wonders who gave him the gun.

"I know you," she says to him. "You know my mom and dad. Dirk and Evelyn St. Clair. I'm Cress."

He is so rigid in his stance she isn't even sure he's heard her until he says, "Boy, you're getting big. Growing up, aren't you." He says this without even the twitch of a muscle, like he is at attention.

"Yes, well, we just wanted to see what everybody's been talking about," she says. "We won't be in anybody's way, we probably won't even be here only a few minutes."

"Promise?"

"On a bed of nails with a guillotine next to me and forty daggers pointed at each eye." She makes a signal to show she means it, something her father taught her when she was little, and she sees that he recognizes it. Behind her Hope and Denny are silent; overhead, across the road, the buzzards fly.

"Okay," he says. "But let me take you. You also got to promise me you won't tell nobody because what's here is stuff some people think is pretty worth it, I guess."

"Really?" She walks toward him, motioning behind her for the others to follow.

"That's what they tell me. So do you promise?" He is peering at her and she can see now that his hands on the rifle are sure and comfortable. Over the ridge behind him she can hear excited voices, someone calling a name that sounds like Mike to her.

"Promise," she says, "on a bed of nails and all that other stuff."

"The sign?"

She makes the motion with her hands, a swirling of her arms, a clasping and unclasping of her fingers, a final clench of them together. "Okay," he says, and he relaxes the gun and turns to lead the way.

They follow, Crescent closest but still behind. She twirls her finger near an ear, points to him, letting them know he's crazy.

They leave the path before the rise in the ground, circling near green corn that scrapes their calves, crops disturbed by the newly dug earth and the path they now follow. As they start up the rise from this other side, Diamond motions them to get down and they obey, crawling up the ridge, flattening themselves out along the ground.

Over the top they peek. Below them a pit of nearly twenty-five by fifteen feet lays open to them, a rough-edged hillside carved down about five feet or more in some places. And in the pit, dozens, maybe hundreds of things. The first that they notice are the bones—white and almost glowing in the June sun. Full skeletons shimmer and their reposes startle her. Crescent hasn't expected anything but is surprised to see they aren't laid out the way bodies are in caskets, straight and restful looking. These are crumpled, some of them wrapped into each other, maybe even atop one another. They are different sizes, a few are children. Almost all face north.

Strewn about them are things she cannot make out, guesses they are arrowheads or artifacts, she can't even imagine what they could be. Would this be like burying somebody today with a TV remote or a favorite wok?

In the pit, about a dozen workers, male and female, most young but a few older, talk and joke and keep their hands and bodies busy with the once-buried.

"Aha!" a guy calls out. He stretches up not far from where Crescent and the others hide. He holds a blade in the air, sweat on his body glistening, the sun catching a glint from the blade that isn't stone but bright and blunt. He lowers it to measure it quick with a tiny tape measure in his palm. "This one's bigger," he says. "Yo, Gary! Mine's bigger than yours is!"

A woman near another cluster of bones says, "You've been waiting for a chance to say that." She is dusting away at something with a small brush.

Crescent feels the sun on the back of her legs, arms. She wonders at the pit workers who seem not at all annoyed by it. They work steadily, spending much time on a particular object, brushing it, measuring it, drawing and photographing it, using compasses and other things she's never seen before. She wonders at their patience, too, the way they court an object so thoroughly before opening the door to see what the next might offer. Cress knows if she were in the pit she'd be shoveling dirt like a maniac, digging for as many things as she could find, rooting through the site like a kid on an Easter egg hunt where the first one done with the most eggs wins.

And so she is absorbed by the activity in the pit until the television crews that set up and break apart distract her, making reports or deciding not to, she can't be sure from here. That activity, though at the edge of the pit, is somehow separate, coming from another world from the workers in the pit who sweat in the bright day, their skin slick and clothes damp, absorbed in the little things around them, these things from the far away past.

They have been watching for some time when Crescent realizes that the Indian man she's expected to see here is nowhere around. The people in the pit, the TV people, everybody is sunburned or tanned. Everybody is white.

He asks not the first person he sees but a man who looks like he does maintenance or cleanup, a man who should know as well as anyone the way around the plant, but this man with long black hair braided down his back, a man Ben Stevens thinks might be Mexican-American, this man can't seem to help him, says only, "Sorry," and ducks away.

So Stevens wanders in a direction that is random, not believing he has forgotten this quickly the shattering noise and sharp light of a factory. He can't believe how much he wants out again.

He finds his meeting place after following three sets of directions that lead him through a maze of equipment and lines, dies suspended overhead. The heat closes around him so he feels he must walk harder just to make the same pace, a cloak, this heat, covering him in sweat that beads on him like tarnished metal studs.

Settling into a chair in a perch of an office that reveals most of the plant floor below, he tries to catch his breath in the air conditioning here. Someone hands him a can of cola and he pops it open, ignores the foaming over his fingers, gulps it.

"We'll just be another minute," the plant manager, Frank Jessup says, and Ben nods, still drinking.

He turns to watch the activity below, spots the man with the braid where he is pushing a dolly stacked with pop cases, heading to a cafeteria or break area, Ben guesses, to fill machines. Menial labor. Probably doesn't even have a high school diploma, many don't. All over the plant floor people repeat their job tasks. Ben rubs his arms, an old habit, the pain coming back to him now only when the weather gets mean, a scar that doesn't show from his time at a machine. Office workers whine about carpal tunnel syndrome but they don't even begin to know. He wonders for a second if fighting to keep the plant open is such a good idea after all.

"Mayor Stevens," a man says, reaching to shake hands. A handsome, graying gentleman in a fine suit, he smiles.

College, this one, Ben decides. He hated the college men

at Feldspar, a four-year business degree, sometimes more, and a bunch of classes in operations management, maybe a few months in a plant, but never long enough, any of it, to even begin to understand why the workers booby-trapped lunch boxes or rigged other pranks, why so many used drugs or drank. Here and there, shuffled from one station to another to "get the feel of things," was never enough to understand that for the regular person at that spot there was no next job waiting, that all the talk on the floor of "just hanging on to this until..." was bullshit, nobody was ever going anywhere. It was never enough to see people get hurt, even with OSHA, somebody you worked beside until something completely screwy happened and then lost fingers or limbs or worse. It was never enough to know what more cost-efficient labor in Mexico can do on a plant floor, to ever begin to fit the links together: steel from Pittsburgh or Gary to a plant like this one or one in Detroit.

"Neil Christianson," the man says. "I represent the owners."

Ben shakes the man's hand. "Thanks for meeting me on such short notice," he says, but he knows already that no matter how he pleads for the town, for the people who trust him to do this, they are going to do what they intend to, no matter what. They will follow their charts and graphs and computer printouts straight out of town.

"We need a contingency plan should you decide to close," he says, watching their faces, but they are blank, they are smiling, they are going to tell him nothing.

The town's side streets cross and re-cross like granny quilt designs, lawns and houses and cars in driveways and garages are all gray and deep blue and black, their lines and shapes blurred in the night. Cherry Street and Bertha Avenue and Duane run so far they run out of town like outlaws at dawn, spilling their followers into turning wheat or green corn. The houses are within twenty yards of each other in town, but out here, on the fringes, they stretch away from each other, reaching for shoulder room, space to yawn and stretch, distance enough to sleep with curtains wide to see stars and no neighbors.

The ground is soft enough but not damp, curved enough for comfort but no cramping. The spacing is good for houses and fields and private moments. Dirt trails for leading farmers to back acreage find other uses after sundown. The town has no "lover's lane" but has dozens, facing any direction, some inviting hasty, dry retreat while others stand always in enough mud to tempt excuses and require tractors to extract those foolish enough to drive them.

Tonight Denny McMasters has walked Hope Bleu down one of these lanes, held her hand, captured her kisses. Tonight Hope's bed is never turned down. Denny tells her she can't break a curfew that doesn't exist and his smile makes her smile, too. He tells her that even if he is a minister, her dad and mom probably are so distracted they won't notice when she comes in. She says he's probably right.

They hold each other in the dark and in the dark of the earth, imagining what wonder might be buried beneath them.

7

His dreams are of ancient people—the women stooping to grind grain amid his corn, the men roaming the woods at the back property. Hunters and gatherers who laugh sometimes but he doesn't know their language so he can only stand nearby, watching, useless. They ignore him in his bib overalls or blue jeans. Their children scurry from the fields when he steers the tractor or combine or corn picker along the rows, but they imitate the machines, raising their little arms to their sides to imagine themselves bigger, whooshing big noises from their mouths to make the sounds. They are teasing him but he cannot care about them because it is harvest and everything has ripened at the same time—the cycles strangely out of sync with the calendar yet in sync with each other—and he must harvest them all.

Early this morning, in his dawn dreams, they are celebrating or perhaps mourning, he cannot tell which. They chant and beat their drum. The voices of the men call out and he thinks they could be calling to him, but he cannot know for certain. He can only listen to the thunder of the drum and the lightning of the voices. They will never stop, he thinks. They will never stop.

The sun is at the very start of rising when Landers Stone

awakens to the sound of the drum and at first he thinks it is the dream, lingering, and then he hears the chant begin again, hears the voices through his open bedroom windows.

Out the side window that faces the driveway he sees that the sky is no longer black with the night but is coming lighter into day. Birds are full in their morning songs. The clock says five something. This is early even for Landers. He reaches for his jeans and shirt from yesterday, pulls them on near the window, listening to the rhythm of the drum, the chanting of words he doesn't know but sound like many hey-hey-ya's strung together.

He wishes for the farm's floodlight but it has been disconnected so the energy can go to lights farther back by the burial ground, something that can be triggered by Diamond if ever he needs it. Downstairs, he flicks the back porch light on, opens the back screen door.

Diamond is standing, legs apart, his rifle at ready but not aimed, in the middle of the driveway. Further up, toward the road, also in the center of the driveway, a group of people sit in a circle, the drum he has been hearing to one side of it. A few women sit nearby but mostly the song and drum are from the men, young and old both, black and silver hair streaming down backs or cut short near collars. A few are wrapped in blankets against the cool morning, some wear jackets, one of them a Detroit Lions windbreaker. Their pickup trucks and cars—four of them—line the road.

Great, Landers thinks. When just yesterday the media decided the story is dead—"so to speak," they said.

A well-built man who might be in his thirties or forties, his hair in two long braids down his shoulders, his deep skin and dark eyes telling Landers he could be Mexican but is probably Native American, walks toward him. Landers waves Diamond Richards back, Diamond with the eager defense, Diamond whom he never would have hired on as human watchdog if he'd had any notion things would go the way they have.

"Landers Stone," Landers says, extending his hand.

The man shakes it. His face shows a few lines where smiles have creased it. "I'm Daniel Yellow Wolf," he says. "I'm sure you know why we're here."

"I got a pretty good guess, I think," Landers says. He is thrown for a second by the man's English, after so many of his dreams now, nearly every night since the digging began, hearing the people in them speaking something so foreign to him. "Tell me what it is you want."

The man Daniel looks him in the eye, gestures behind Landers and past Diamond where he stands with his legs at shoulder-width, his rifle easy at the ready in his hands. "Our ancestors must be allowed to rest. The digging, the excavation, must stop." He represents, he tells Landers, The Native American Council of the Great Lakes, a group of unified tribes. "You've thought we were all dead, or maybe invisible," Yellow Wolf says. "But here we are."

The chanting and beating of the drum behind Yellow Wolf continue. The sun edges higher, dyeing the sky bluer little by little. It will be another clear, cloudless, hot day. Landers feels the heaviness in him from his lost sleep. "I'll talk to them about it," he says. "That's the best I can do."

"Who do you mean, 'them'? Isn't this your land?" He gestures, a wide sweep, he could mean everything the eye can see.

"It really isn't in my control," Landers says.

In an upstairs window of their bedroom, he sees Bessie standing, her summer robe clutched to her chest with both hands. Watching.

"You've given over the land to the university people?" Yellow Wolf asks.

The university people, Landers thinks, is just how I think of them. But the man asks questions as if it's a simple thing. He shakes his head. "It's complicated, Mr. Yellow Wolf. It will take awhile to explain. Would you like to come in for a cup of coffee? I really need a cup," Landers says.

In the kitchen, Bessie is already busy with the coffee maker, nods at the man when Landers introduces them, then excuses herself to change. The men settle at the kitchen table.

"This isn't exactly my farm, first of all," Landers says, offering Yellow Wolf a box of donuts.

He shakes his head, draws a pen and pad of paper from his back jeans pocket. "Not exactly?"

"I lease it."

"Who from?"

Landers leans back in his chair. It squeaks. The water in the sink drips and he tries to ignore it. "Listen," he says, "I'm really sorry. I want to help you out, but none of that's really going to make a difference. You're not from around here, you don't understand how it is."

Daniel Yellow Wolf studies him, shrugs. "It can't be much different here. Small towns, small farms, big plans and big politics," he says. He smiles the barest of smiles.

Bessie comes back in, her pale blue polyester pants and white shell top tugged around her body. She hands the men mugs of steaming coffee, sets a quart carton of milk and a bowl of sugar on the table but both men ignore them.

"Mr. Stone," Yellow Wolf says, "I was educated at the University of Michigan and Case Western, passed the state bar exam four years ago. Took me awhile to get through all that school, to realize I could do it, finish. Now I work for my people, speaking for those who can't and playing politics for those who won't. I understand more than you think."

"I appreciate that, Mr. Yellow Wolf," Landers says. "I sent my kids through college and know all about what it takes. What I'm trying to tell you is, I'm not the one making the decisions."

The man sips his coffee, nods. "I'm beginning to see that. All I want to know is, who is?" His fingers, wrapped around the mug from K-Mart, are decorated with turquoise and silver rings.

"George Freeman owns the farm, but he's not in charge of it." Landers pauses, watching the man write, thinking this will cause more questions, but Daniel Yellow Wolf waits him out. He reads people, Landers thinks, reads people the way I read the farm, to know the best days to sow, the best to harvest. He goes on, "George, well, he's not exactly right in his head, has trouble getting along except in the most basic ways, so we farm the property for him, make a little living, and George gets a little money to live by as well. Farm came to him from his folks, years ago. Mason Pope, attorney in town, he keeps track of George's legal affairs."

Yellow Wolf shifts in his chair. He's not a big man but he fills the room. It is his youth or confidence, but whatever it is, it's something Landers feels he must give space to.

"And it's Mr. Pope who's determined the site must be excavated?" Yellow Wolf asks.

"What other alternative is there?" Landers asks.

Yellow Wolf rises from the chair, pushes it against the table. He walks to the window in the dining area facing east and the sun covers him. "During the flooding of the river Mississippi a few years ago, when the water rose higher than people could remember it rising, the papers ran a photograph of a cemetery that washed away—coffins swept along the current. It disturbed a lot of people."

"I saw that," Bessie says. "It was awful." She wipes her hands in a dishtowel though they are not wet.

"Out there," he continues, "across the road, is another cemetery. What do you suppose would happen if you decided to start digging to see what you could find? Maybe there's jewelry buried there, maybe a couple of antiques. But the idea appalls you, doesn't it?"

He turns to face Landers who rises from the table as well, leaning against the kitchen counter next to Bessie. It is Bessie who nods her head.

"It disgusts you, doesn't it, to think that someone would do that." He watches her nod again, move closer to Landers. "Now, picture the next step: you've decided for some reason to remove the remains, to put a little sticker on each and every bone so you can reassemble them if you want to. But first there are tests—you'll chip and drill and analyze and who knows what all, maybe just to see if these people, good Christian folks, no doubt, died of something we're now calling AIDS, or maybe something else like Alzheimer's we want to know more about. Maybe along the way you start to feel a little funny about it all, because these bones once were people, standing, talking like we are, but then you think, 'But this is for the good of science. Someone will benefit,' and you go on with the drilling and chipping and sticking the numbers on."

He argues this way as if he is in a courtroom and they are judge and jury. He is near them again, calm still, his voice never raised. "Why should the disinterment of certain graves be considered immoral robbery while the same thing—only worse—when done to tribal burials is considered scientific advancement? A cause for celebration?" He looks into each of their faces, slowly. "The only thing that should be done is bury the site again," he says. "The only right thing to do is that. Nothing else is acceptable." He waits for them to take this in, then, his pad and paper in his hands again, says, "Now, how do I find Mason Pope?"

Bessie rummages through the drawer in her kitchen desk, pulls out the local telephone directory, the pages quivering in her hand. "Would you like his number, give him a call in a few hours?" she asks.

"Just the address, please," he says, and Bessie copies it down for him. She and Landers both know his office, easy to find in town, but this is what the man has asked for, and so she gives it to him.

"His office is right on Main Street," Landers says. "You can't miss it."

Yellow Wolf nods his thanks. "I know what I've said makes sense to you because you're good people," he says. "We aren't as far apart as you might think." To Bessie he says, "Nice to meet you Mrs. Stone. I appreciate the coffee." He closes the door without letting it slam behind him.

Landers pours himself a second cup and sinks into his chair again, the chants and drums going silent outside at least for a little while.

The hump of green grass and stones stretches for miles around the deep water of the reservoir, blue water reflecting blue sky. Small sailboats catch the quick breezes and float from one side to the other and back again or they follow the perimeter, tracing the paths made by the shouts of kids along the jagged shore. Families, clusters of young men and single old men, cast lines from rowboats, from motorboats, or from the edge of the water that slaps every now and then at the grassy, stony embankment.

"Just a puff," Crescent is saying, holding a lit cigarette in Hope's face. She holds her hand steady but it is an effort and this surprises her. Surprises her that she is today so impatient with Hope, that seeing her in Denny's car when he came by her house this morning has upset her so much. Why should she care? She has interests other than Denny McMasters, right?

She has been watching the way they keep track of each other, him in the water, nearly submerged, his hair matted to his head but still with an eye out for Hope.

"Just a little one," Crescent says. "You don't have to inhale. Just breathe a little in and hold it in your mouth. Then let it out. It isn't even really smoking, anyway. This is the way actors do it when they really don't smoke but have to look like it."

The paper burns back, the ash grows more fragile in its balance on the end, and Hope waves it away.

"Chicken to even try?" Crescent inhales, deep, stifles a cough from the burn that hits her chest, chokes the rumbling back and sips her Diet Pepsi as camouflage. Hope ignores her.

Denny drags himself out of the water as if pulling himself from the depths of the ocean after being lost at sea for days. He flops onto the edge of Crescent's towel, face down. He groans.

Crescent jostles him on the shoulder. "Wimp. You and Hope both. Why do I even bother to hang out with you guys? I should have stolen my own car and gone back to the burial site."

Denny raises his arm to give her the finger without even looking up. It is his way of scolding her for the unkindness she has waged at his mother through him, and she regrets her words. More and more she feels alone, not just here, but in general. She can't seem to think of the right things to say; nobody seems to understand her anymore. It's like being in a raft in the water, floating farther and farther away, calling for somebody to help but they don't hear, maybe they think it's a game and they might wave and call to her but they don't do anything to pull her back to shore.

Hope is face down on her own towel, her tan legs and arms damp with sweat and lotion. "Maybe you hang out with us," Hope says, "because we're the only ones who bother to hang out with you."

Denny laughs and Crescent punches him quick and clean on his upper arm. Her hand hits muscle, lean and hard from holding the guitar, balancing it and running rhythms and chords and things musical through it. She winces.

"Hard as a rock," Denny says. He rolls toward her, picks

the cigarette from between her fingers, takes a drag from it. "Bug up your ass sounds like it's giving you some real trouble. Sounds like maybe time for the exterminator or something," he says, watching Hope to see if she laughs.

"Fuck you, Denny." Crescent takes the cigarette back before he gets another whiff and she finishes it off, tapping it out against a flat rock the size of her hand, telling herself it was stale anyway, though she has no idea what a stale cigarette would taste like. She points at Hope. "She's the one who's bugged. Problems or something. All mopey and dopey and being a bore."

"You're just whining because I wouldn't smoke your stupid cigarette," Hope says. She leans to pick up her watch, decides it's time and turns over, squirts white lotion in three even lines down each leg—sides and back—and leans to smear it in.

"You tried to tempt young Hope into something?" Denny lights another. "Crescent, shame on you." When he exhales, he turns from Hope, blows away from her.

"Like I said, 'Fuck you, Denny.'"

"No, I'm serious." He's watching Hope stroke lotion into her arms. He takes the bottle from her, she turns her back to him, lifts her hair. "Wish I'd never started," he says.

"Really?" Hope clutches her hair with her right hand, balancing herself on the blanket with her left so her suit won't pucker where Denny might see beyond tan lines.

"Wrecks your voice, you know." His hands circle her back, trace her shoulder blades and the edge of her tank suit, smoothing until it fades into her skin the creamy liquid that smells like coconut cookies. One of his hands covers more of her shoulder than it would of Crescent's. His touch is unhurried and even.

"The great singer," Crescent says. She's drawn into watching them because of the way he touches her. Hard and passionate Crescent and Denny have always been, driven to each other with a rough energy that never leaves room for tenderness. Now she realizes she's never thought of Denny as gentle before. "When are you guys practicing again?" she asks, jabbing her finger into his back where it leaves a white mark that fades right away, a jab that she knows hurts him, but for this second she doesn't care.

He turns on her. "Cut it out, Cress." And then he is rubbing again, massaging into Hope what seems to Crescent to be more oil than a body can absorb.

"Sorry," she says. She picks up his abandoned cigarette, wishes it were pot. She reminds herself it won't be that long before she is packing the family car for Columbus.

She leans back, willing herself to relax but can't, images of Denny's non-guitar rhythm pounding through her won't work with Denny next to her, his hands on Hope. When she peeks at them she sees they've swapped roles, Denny's knees crossed in front of him, head declined like he was worshipping at her church, eyes closed, mouth "ohh-ing" while Hope presses cool lotion into him, pressing her fingers along his back in a way that makes Crescent, for a second, wonder about Hope and boys and this one in particular.

The occasionally cool, watery breeze that smooths across her she tries to imagine being from the night, from the window in the bell tower, and the quick waves slapping the stony embankment of the reservoir she imagines are the birds and night insects, and Hope's easy laugh and Denny's exaggerated stories are Theodore Thompson's saxophone.

In the Country Inn at lunch the word comes around in a way that Ben Stevens imagines is close to the way word used to travel in the Old West. They are eating and swapping the news of the day when someone comes in and says to someone else, a little too loudly, "There are Indians at the Stone farm." Conversations stop. A third someone says, "Say that again," and then conversations flutter to a new level. People like Ben Stevens flip bills next to uneaten specials and hurry off to the farm.

He hears the drum before the farm is near enough for parking and he sees that the news media are back in full force, even a few stations he hasn't seen out here before. He opens his glove compartment, extracts from it his spare tie.

His car parked, he hurries to the driveway where the press have assembled. He loops the tie around his neck as he goes. Voices chanting—"Hey-ya-hey-hey-hey-hey"—and the drum mix with the people directing the movement of cameras and equipment. More people from the town and neighboring farms are gathered. Migrants hang to one side, hands in pockets, looking on.

He can't tell quite yet if this new development is a good thing or not. He nudges his way to the front of the crowd. There is a circle marked off with string tied to sticks planted in the ground. Just beyond sits a drum and around it are a half-dozen or so men and women of different ages wearing jeans and shorts and tee shirts but also bandanas across foreheads or long hair sometimes in braids. Each of the drummers holds one stick, rapping in rhythm with the others. One or two men and a few women wear traditional regalia—leather skirts or leggings with fringe, bells and jangles, ribbons of all colors scattering in the air, trailing their quick-step circle dancing. A few men clutch feathers, another holds other items Ben can't make out. With each strike of the drum the dancers step, their rhythms building, the drums and bangles punching heavier, faster, until they ease back, a breeze of sound bursting across the open air, fading, gusting and dying.

A cameraman sets up nearby, aiming at the group surrounding the drum, but as he begins adjusting his lens, a man with two long braids and rings on his fingers steps in front of it, his hand up. "Please only film when you are told you may," he says, "out of respect." His voice is strong and even and permits no response except obedience.

"Excuse me, sir," Stevens says, and the man looks at him. He is not a big man, in his clean linen shirt and black jeans, but his eyes are steady and strong. Ben reaches his hand out to introduce himself. "I'm Ben Stevens. I'm mayor." He pauses, waiting for the man to introduce himself, but he stands also waiting. "Perhaps we could have a word together?"

The man glances at the camera, sees that it is on. However, it is not pointing at the chanters but at himself and the mayor. "Daniel Yellow Wolf," he says. He does not shake Ben's hand, a refusal Ben's not accustomed to. It leaves him off-balance.

"Might we just have a few words privately?" Ben asks. He is smoothing his tie, regretting now having put it on.

"I spoke to Mason Pope this morning, Mr. Stevens," Yellow Wolf says. "I'm sure there's nothing more you can offer, given your respective positions." He turns, walks toward a waiting reporter.

"I guess he told you, Ben," one of the Nessor brothers says, grinning.

"I guess so," Ben says, edging out of the circle, away from the crowd. He finds Landers fifty feet back near the site of the digging. He walks to him, looks with him into the pit that widens and deepens every day. More remains have been unearthed, more artifacts. The university people brush and measure and calculate.

"They want to stop this," Landers says. "Did he tell you that?"

"Wouldn't say squat to me," Ben says. Mike Olson and Kathy Shephardson, his partner, others whose names he's heard but can't recall, exchange waves with him. Olson climbs from the pit, shakes Ben's hand.

"So what's the story?" Olson asks, gesturing with his head to the driveway where the drumming and chanting persist.

"That's what I hoped to find out from you," Ben says. He pulls the tie from around his neck. If the news crews want comments from him, he'll slip it back on. "What did Mason tell him?"

Landers looks at him. "Told him to get his people and their butts off the property."

"So?" Ben says. "Why haven't they?"

"Well, that's what he told them to do but I guess he figured they would and that would be that because he went out of town."

Olson's face, Stevens notices, is red from these days in the sun, and it seems to him that it gets redder and redder but never tans—he wonders just how red it might get, how hot it must feel. He wonders if he presses his fingers to a cheek if he would feel its heat. "Can't they be told they're trespassing? That the owner doesn't want them here?"

Landers shifts his stance. He is a big man, keeping his height even as he ages, his towering bulk still over six feet but softened by his silver hair and the lines on his face—creases from years of sun and worry. "Tried that," he says. "Out of local police jurisdiction. Referred me to the county sheriff and Guerra said from what he knows about it the owner would have to make the complaint himself."

Stevens twists the tie in his hands, wraps his hands in the dark blue with red horseshoes that are so tiny they look like speckles. It is a winter tie, he realizes, and he wads it up and thrusts it into a pocket where it bulges, the tongue of it hanging out. "Well," he says, "I would imagine that getting warnings, which they're ignoring, then getting toted off to jail, local or county either one, is something they probably wouldn't mind because it's publicity for their side. Right now you can just see it as a way to keep the unwanteds out, the more folks around here, especially at night, the more secure we can keep things."

Olson crosses his arms against a sky-colored tee shirt with the words "Follow Your Bliss" on it in script. "On that we disagree. I'm not saying I distrust Yellow Wolf and his people, but the more people there are around the tougher it is to keep track of what's going on. I'll put my crew on shifts to help Diamond out."

Stevens looks out across the fields, green under startling blue sky. In two directions everything looks as it did a few weeks ago. Maybe the crops have matured some, but other than that the land stretches the same way, meets the horizon with the same landmarks posting the way. In the other two directions entirely new worlds have been discovered and settled. The activity of the pit, the migrants lingering near its edge, the media, the driveway newly jammed with cars and drum and Indians, the township road edged with more cars, pickups and vans with satellites. In the other direction, behind the house, the backhoe chips away slowly with a crew of three or four on the water line that started the whole thing and will probably be done and buried before the rest is.

"Do you think they'd be okay about the museum idea? If they knew one possibility is that nothing will leave here?" Ben asks Olson.

"Museum?" Landers says. "If you're going to talk to Yellow Wolf about a museum, you better have talked it over with Mason first."

Ben nods. "As soon as he gets back," he says. The chanting gets louder, the drum is hit harder. "Won't be soon enough," he adds. He turns toward the driveway to head for the road, trying to spy an escape route to his car that won't lead him past the media. Today, it's turned out, he has nothing to say.

Contessa Welch stands again to walk the length of the lavender and white living room. Her iced tea glass sits ignored on a coaster on the coffee table and the radio pipes easy listening music into the room but isn't loud enough to squelch the racket of the swallows and sparrows and mourning doves in the trees lining the street. She sat at her sewing machine earlier but lost patience when the thread broke twice in a few minutes. She sat to read but realized she was flipping pages at regular intervals without any idea of what she had read. When she turned the television on, game shows and talk shows and the earliest-aired soaps of the day flashed in bright colors and designer clothes and expensive people but none of it held her attention.

Now she paces, tries to remember what she usually does while Jack works at the plant, what she's done to fill her days. She tries to remember what they did this past weekend, Jack home but she can't remember how long he sat in front of the television, sports announcer voices whispering golf or yakking baseball. Once, passing through the room, she even thought she heard the voices murmuring in conspiracy, vulgarities from the dead they sounded like. She looked closer to see what he was watching but the colors ran together and the hushed voices blared into a commercial and she backed away.

She tries to remember what they used to do during the long bright evenings of summer but it is as if their pasts are gone today. There is something about fishing but she can't quite see—standing at water's edge or teetering in a shallow-bottomed boat, its motor cut. Without the complete image she doubts the truth of it.

The ice in the tea clinks a new settling, a rearrangement in the glass, a giving in to the warm air. It startles Contessa into quick breaths and she wonders why she's wandering through her house, she has so much to do, but she can't think of what it is.

At the phone, she dials her sister's number. Elizabeth answers on the sixth ring. "Connie—are you all right?"

They haven't even said hello and already Elizabeth has sensed her mood, something in her voice, her call that has come without reason. "Of course," Contessa says. "Why shouldn't I be?"

"Who knows? You just sound strange. I thought maybe you were nervous about the plant."

"What about it?"

"Don't you and Jack talk about anything? They're saying it might close."

"Close?" Contessa is trying to remember when Jack mentioned this—it's too important for him to keep to himself, though maybe he has wanted to protect her somehow. She says, "Maybe it's just talk."

"That's what everybody thought about the last strike they had, remember?"

Contessa is sorry she called. "Mostly I just called to say hello, see how you're doing," she says. "I really didn't have any news."

"Are you sure? I mean," Elizabeth says, "you're sure nothing's wrong? You sound sort of odd, like something's on your mind."

There is, Contessa thinks. I just don't know what it is. "Not a thing, really."

When she hangs up the phone she picks up the book and starts turning pages. She thinks of asking Jack again about the new man at the plant. All he would tell her last time was that he was put on some general custodial detail, that lots of the guys aren't happy about it, can think of plenty of guys who'd take that job in a second just to be back at work, and it isn't fair somebody can waltz in from the outside and swipe somebody else's job. She'd wanted to get him to invite the man to dinner some night, say something about how the man probably didn't know many people, but of course Jack seemed so angry that she didn't dare.

She turns another page of the book, seeing the words but not reading them, and melts into them, into the day.

Eddy doesn't see the accident but hears the cries of the men, the screeching of metal turned loose, set free to send the forty-ton die that stamps fenders crashing down, the smash of its arrival on the plant floor sending shudders through the building, through the men and women there. Even those who don't see it, like Eddy, feel it, feel the sinking in them.

People start yelling and buzzers sound that signal that the lines have been shut down but the machines keep moving for what seems too long. More people move, run, calling to each other, heading for the center of the thunder.

"I seen it," a burly man is saying, 'Mel' stitched in red in a white oval against his midnight blue uniform. "I seen it, that die just gave way, just fell and nothin' he could do, happened so fast."

"Tried to call out to him," another says, "tried to warn him. I forget sometimes folks can't hear nothing in here."

Foremen and supervisors in ties asking questions already and trying to get some control. The die, Eddy can see, has come down square, sparing nothing below. He eyes the ceiling, traces the track of the crane above, sorting through the suspended lights and girders and bracings, searching, like everyone around him, their heads up, searching for some sort of clue. Dangling, broken now, still swinging a little with the momentum, the chain is thick as his wrist but weaker than any man's will. They shake their heads, all of them, back and forth.

"Did the siren go?" somebody asks, and some say yes,

they heard it, the warning that a die was coming overhead, to clear just in case, why didn't he move? "Like he couldn't or something," the burly man Mel says. "Shoulda known, he shoulda known."

Eddy stands, watching calls for ambulances and inspectors and another crane to lift the die, watches until the call goes out that equipment in other areas is back on line, waits for the others to leave, for the paramedics to load the shattered remains of a man, waits for someone to tell him what to do next because he has never been in this position before.

When the ambulance is dispatched to the plant a few kids near the funeral home that also contains the EMS unit pedal their bikes hard to keep up a block or so, wondering where it's headed, who it's for. If it were a fire, the location of it would be scribbled on the chalkboard inside the firehouse so late-arriving volunteers would know where to go. But with ambulances it's hard to tell.

The siren shears through the early afternoon of the town and Theodore on his porch and Mamie on hers hear it. The Reverend Bleu slows his car against the right curb of Main Street to let the ambulance pass. Contessa Welch, turning pages in her book, hears the wail over the hum of her air conditioning and closes her book to wait for the phone to ring.

From her porch Mamie watches the cars, the people shuffling in and out of the Welch house. It has been a long afternoon, the air heavy with the cries of relatives and Contessa's odd laughter and of rain aching to come down but suspended yards above the treetops like low-flying balloons, ready to burst, clustered, strong enough to lift the town upwards, dangling it like a basket at the base of a hot air contraption.

Mamie has been watching the sky above and the house across the street. She sips her scotch, puzzling now over Crescent St. Clair's bouncy approach. When she bounds up the steps onto the porch, the window behind her rattles.

"Hi, Ms. Van Allen, how are you? Nice evening, huh?" She drags her tan arm across her forehead. "Shew! Sure is humid. Hot and yucky. Maybe it'll rain, what do you think?" She hitches her thumb in the direction of the Welch house. "Lots of cars across the street there."

Mamie shrugs her shoulders, wonders what Crescent wants. Hope never seems to have a reason to stop by; Crescent is another story, she's sure. "Jack Welch died at the plant this morning," Mamie says.

Crescent is slapped sober by the words. She leans against one of the porch pillars, hugging it, watching the people come and go across the street, some getting into cars while others lean into them, talking, shaking heads and nodding and wiping hands across faces. "I think my mom and dad knew him," she says at last.

No doubt, Mamie thinks. Jack Welch was older, maybe a generation or so, but Crescent's dad works at the plant. Nearly everybody knows each other here. "There's some Coca-Cola in the refrigerator if you'd like a glass," Mamie says. She doesn't drink it but has started to keep it on hand for Hope.

"Oh, thanks but no thanks. I just drank a bottle before I got here." Crescent drops into a chair. She seems done with the topic of Jack Welch. "Shew!" she says again.

"I haven't seen much of Hope in the last few days," Mamie says, watching Crescent's eyes dart down the street again. Who is it she's waiting to see here? Hope, maybe?

"Oh, you know. She's got lots going on, I guess. We been up to the reservoir to swim a few times. Plus she and Denny

McMasters are hanging out a lot, I guess," she says. Then she straightens, pressing her palms into the arms of the white wicker, crossing her legs. She strikes a pose.

Mamie stretches to follow Crescent's gaze, sees that Eddy is strolling toward them. Tonight he wears a hat she's never seen on him before, an old western cowboy hat that looks spent from long days and longer journeys. He strolls up the street toward them, giving the Welch house a quick glance or two. He exchanges a smile with Mamie and Cress.

"Evening," Mamie says, not wanting to divulge more than this, holding their familiarity close if that's what he wants.

But he surprises her. "Evening, Sweetheart," he says. He tips the black hat to her, the silver conch band around it jangling softly. "And evening to you, Cress." Coming up the porch steps, he removes his hat entirely, looking like a polite yet shy new sheriff in an old gold town where his skills and prowess with the gun will eventually be called upon to help save the widow whose ranch swindlers are after.

"Can I get you a drink, Eddy?" Mamie asks. Only Eddy could call her "sweetheart" and flatter rather than enrage her. He's shaking his head. Instead of sitting, he leans against the railing, his arms folded and eyes studying the Welch house where lights pop on while the evening light fades.

"It's just awful about Jack Welch, don't you think?" Crescent asks suddenly, and Mamie thinks, she is an actress, a bad one relying on eyelashes and scripts to get her through these tough scenes.

"I didn't really know him, Cress. But I'm sure it's hard."

"Oh, I'm sure, especially for poor Mrs. Welch," Crescent says. She turns to Mamie. "Perhaps I would like that drink now."

"Help yourself," Mamie says, gesturing toward the screen door. "You shouldn't have much trouble finding the kitchen."

"What can I get you, Eddy?" Crescent asks, using the eyelashes to help out the question.

"Nothing, thanks, but maybe Mamie'd like a refresher, while you're up."

Mamie tries to read him, but she can't tell whether a smile shudders beneath the surface or not. When the screen door clicks behind Crescent, she asks, "Are you okay, Eddy?" He nods. She thinks of what it must be like to have to go back to work there, after what's happened. "You sure?"

He nods again but she doesn't believe him. A nod is vague, could maybe be a legal lie. But words. Words are truth and this time he doesn't use them.

"I just wanted to make sure you're doing okay," he says. "Just wanted to pay a visit." He leans away from the post, turns his hat in his hands, plucking at loose threads around the headband. "I should get going," he says. He grins then and she is rewarded for her patience. "I'll come by another time."

He leans to kiss her before he kicks down the steps, waves his hat as if departing on horseback, and when Crescent emerges from the house, sees that he's gone, Mamie can't help grinning herself.

Crescent smacks a mosquito from her arm, rubs her other limbs as if her touch will keep all other insects away. She wonders again where he is, if his head start from Mamie Van Allen's has him inside already. She can only sit on the curb under one of this string of antique lamp reproductions, her feet in Main Street, keeping an eye out for the things that nibble in the night. She crouches at the side of the barber shop across the street from the Bahama Lounge, the bushes that trim the yellow brick building shielding her from the lit street.

None But The Dead And Dying

She wonders what time it is, wonders if she should give it up for the night, be content that she not only spoke to him but saw him already on Mamie's porch, her plan nearly perfect except for going into the house, letting him get away like that.

But now, coming around Buckeye to Main, she sees him. She cannot let him get into the Lounge tonight, that would be letting him escape twice; she would be hours waiting for him to come back out. The plant, she's heard, might be closed tomorrow for an investigation so he could be in the Lounge until it closes at two.

She brushes her arms and legs with her hands and stands, whisking her hair forward then back to add "instant body" the way her girlfriend Lorrie in cosmetology school has shown her. He is walking and seems not to see her, so she side-steps onto the sidewalk to amble toward him, pacing herself to meet him a few storefronts from the Bahama Lounge.

She gives him the sort of look she thinks he'd expect if she were surprised to see him. "Oh, hi!" she says.

He's caught off guard and nearly steps by her before he recognizes her. "Oh, hello Cress. I thought you were visiting Mamie." He looks at her from under the brim of the old hat.

"Well, I was, then I thought a walk would be nice, waiting for the music."

"Is it that time?" he asks.

She holds out her arm; next to hers, his skin is rich. "No watch," she says. She's glad she chose the white shorts, the midriff pink top. He glances at the vee of her neckline, he did that at Mamie's too, and she presses her chest firmly into her blouse, readjusts her stance to pose just so. "Damn," she says. "How will we know when it's time?"

"I guess we'll know when he starts," he says.

"What'll we do in the meantime?" She crosses her arms

against her chest, below her breasts, pulling her top a bit lower, catching his eye again.

He smiles. He has, she decides, a juicy smile. "Wait."

"In the bell tower?"

He nods and she takes his hand to lead him down sidewalks splotchy with yellow street light. A breeze chills her and she feels her nipples harden.

She unfolds a tattered blanket, throws it over dust and spiders' webs, then drops onto it, gesturing for him to join her. He smiles, lights a cigarette. He hasn't smoked in days, but bought a pack, today, after shift. She is too eager, her face telling him more than he wants to know, so he turns to lean against the wall near one of the four gaping squares in the spire. He's expected there would be a view from up here, even in darkness, but all he sees are roofs and treetops and here and there an asphalt street but only for a few blocks, then more trees and roofs, greens and browns and blacks and grays. Outside the bell tower it is quiet, the evening songs of the birds done, people in bed or waiting and listening, and Theodore, he imagines, is the only one who has something to do.

"Come sit by me," Crescent says.

He leans his long arms across the frame of the opening. "Tell me about Theodore."

"What?" She shifts, posing to show off her breasts again but this time he won't let himself fall for that.

"Tell me about Theodore, the saxophone man."

"Give me a cigarette."

He tosses her the pack, the lighter, leans again to the opening, to the breeze, listens to the shimmer of the leaves fanning themselves after a hot day.

"Light it for me?" she asks.

None But The Dead And Dying

She's changing her game plan—from innocent youth to savvy sophisticate. Next, he thinks, will be the bitch. None appeal to him.

When he stoops near her to light her cigarette, he knows she will hold the smoke in her mouth, exhale it, try to carry the illusion of smoking. He kneels and she touches her breast against his knee as she leans toward him. Her hands on his are warm. The cigarette glows orange and he backs off, away, retreating to the open air. At the window again he says, "So tell me."

"Nothing to tell. Lived here all his life. His mother was sick and she died just a few weeks ago—"

"I mean about his music. Tell me about that."

He can hear her exhale. "Why are you so interested?" she asks.

There are a lot of reasons, none he will tell her. He says, "Forget it," and, remembering the way they came up here, heads in that direction.

She scrambles after him, the blanket wrapping around her legs, tangling her up. "Hey, wait a second—"

He sees her confusion, the dying cigarette at the end of smooth fingers. She is mismatched, he thinks, like I am. "Look," he says, "you're cute and all that, but let's just listen to the night, okay?"

She pouts, but he won't indulge her. He walks again to the opening in the spire, taking another drag on his cigarette. The night silence is broken by a distant dog barking, by nearby crickets. She'll guess, he thinks, that I'm just shy or a gentleman and she'll bide her time. She'll think she's waiting me out.

He decides that for now it will do.

"Sure, okay," she says. "You know," she giggles, "I just realized I don't even know your last name."

"Light Sky," he says. "I'm Eddy Light Sky."

She wants to say something about it, he can tell, her lips

pursed that way, but before she can Theodore Thompson, a few blocks down the tree-covered streets and roofs, puts that name to music, starting easy tonight, but they know it won't last long, that he'll give in to it and chase after it in a fury.

Eddy leans further into the frame where the slats are missing, leans into the air to listen. A lot of notes come from the man's horn, but Eddy is remembering something an old musician friend once told him: "The dropped notes mean more than the played ones. In the dropped notes are symphonies, if you know how to listen." Tonight, maybe they will hear symphonies from the saxophone, if they listen well enough.

8

everend Bleu shifts the gray Chevette into park and turns the key to stop the motor. In the short drive from the church to the Welch's driveway he's already started to sweat and he mops his forehead with a hand towel he carries in the car with him. When he opens the door the heat surges, surrounds him like the enemy. His suit pants stick to the vinyl car seat and he brushes his hands across himself in quick motions, hoping he isn't sweating through his clothing. He hates summer. The uniform of the minister isn't made for summer, the starched collars and polyester pants, tight tie, hard shoes.

When he knocks on her door his hands are empty, though the clutch of his fat black leather-bound Bible would have calmed him, given his fingers something to hold, to press their nervous grip into. But approaching the opposition unarmed, he's always believed, is the fastest way to gain trust. Trust, he's been taught, is the main thing. "How can you expect them to hand you their souls if they don't trust you?" was even a question on an exam in theology school.

The wreath on Contessa's door is pale yellow and green with twisted, dried corn stalks as a center. Ribbons wrap silk flowers and buds against it, drop streamers from it. In a few months she will change it again, maybe to the rattan guitar with roses or the straw bonnet with pink and blue ribbons. It will be a sign of her coping, if she remembers to change it.

The heavy, glossy white door opens and Contessa looks surprised to see him. "How nice of you," she says, opening the outer screen door for him. She looks radiant and this, of course, baffles him. Where are the deep circles that show troubled sleep and too much crying?

She leads him into the house and he sees that she is alone, the house quiet with the absence of friends and family. She sits in the corner of the sofa nearest an upholstered chair in matching blue and white and lavender print. She motions for him to sit here, and he does.

"How are you, Mrs. Welch?" It is the obvious, he knows, but it is a start. His hands can't find anything to do; one of them tinkers with a small photo in a brass frame, a little girl, maybe the one he has heard about.

"Fine," she says. Her hair has been combed straight through without attention to curl or style, and her gaze wanders from him to the window behind him to the vase of white and pink carnations on an end table.

He tries to read her, to follow her lead. Everyone handles these things differently, he knows this. Some want to pray, some want to talk, others want to sit silently, perhaps holding his hand. Contessa Welch sends no signals. She fidgets for a few seconds, then is calm. She seems scattered, then focuses. It is hard for him to follow her. He crosses his left knee over his right, can't help jiggling his left foot, kicking air.

The pale pink skirt and white polo top accent her curves, cutting for her a figure younger than what he suspects are her years. "It is quite a shock," he says at last. "We were so sorry to hear."

She fumbles for a glass that sits nearby, its ice melted to a band of water atop the brown drink. She nearly knocks it over. This helplessness in her reminds him of Hope last summer when mononucleosis dropped her into a month of bed rest. She was delirious during the worst of it, watching him as she struggled, while he prayed at her bedside for a fast recovery. Through the same hot, sweaty eyes Contessa Welch looks at him now. "I'm sorry I'm not much company today," she says.

"I didn't expect you to be, Mrs. Welch," he says, his words lumbering after their meaning like yoked oxen reluctant in a muddy field. "I understand what strain you must be under." He stops his jiggling foot. "What can I do to help?"

She looks at him as if she hasn't comprehended the question, his implied offer. She blinks at him. There is this vacancy between them, and he knows he is the one who must fill it. It comes from her not going to church, he thinks. If she had been going, I would know her better, would know her not from what I hear about her, but from what I see when with her. And now she needs me to understand and I can't. He says, "It's in God's plan, Mrs. Welch."

"Please don't call me that. He's gone, after all," she says. She steadies her gaze on him, smiles at him. She uncrosses her legs and parts them, her skirt dropping low enough between them to shield him from a glimpse of thighs. "Call me Tess or something."

His eyes wrestle to hold hers; his mind's eye envisions the legs split further, the skirt pulled higher, hinting at deep, creviced hair. His own thoughts shock him, they come from someplace so far away from him. The air conditioning is on, flipping again to full tilt but droplets of his sweat form around his hairline, beneath his clothing.

"Would you like to pray, Tess? Pray for strength or understanding?" He grips her hand, forces it to join his, pulling her next to him to kneel on the carpet. "Dear Father," he begins, "we ask your strength be with Mrs. Welch—"

"Tess, I said. Call me Tess. Or Connie. Or Tessie—"

"Please," he echoes, cracking his eyelids to see her eyes on him, her body pressed toward him, her breasts rounding out the white polo shirt. She is smiling the empty smile he's seen Mundee Manway carry. "Please help us to do your work... to understand more clearly your ways... Let us know Your will so that we may follow it..."

"He's already dead," Contessa says. "He's already dead, what good is it? They wouldn't let me see him, they wouldn't let me see—" Her smile gone now, her hands fluttering in the air, touching her face.

"Mrs. Welch, Tess, you must understand—" He stops, realizing that what he wants to say he doesn't understand himself, can't say aloud, so awful to try to understand. "You couldn't. You just couldn't." He reaches for her hands, to still them, to silence the screams they let out that she cannot. He holds those hands quiet and smaller in his own. He tries to think only of these hands.

"But why not? Why did they hide him from me? I was here, waiting when they called and told me and I wanted to go to him, that's all I had been waiting for, to go to him, to see him one last time, but they said no. I had to stay and make cookies, but I wanted to go—"

"You couldn't, you have to under—"

"Nobody understands!" She lets go of him, stands to pace the room, her words like a cry or laughter. "I never saw my baby, either, except at first—I never saw her except—at first. It was hard. Sometimes I wonder if she's just hidden away someplace, and now maybe they've just hidden Jack away, too, because how can I know unless I see? Unless I can see for myself?" Her eyes shine but she doesn't cry.

He walks to her, pulls her to him to quiet her, pat her hair, her back, soothing her. He whispers to her what he doesn't want to say. "There isn't anything to see, Tess. The die was so heavy—"

She wails and he holds her tightly, guides them both to

their knees. "Would you like to pray about it?" he asks, though it isn't right, it's more of his training, more of a chant, but he has nothing else.

She reaches her hands to her eyes, wipes tears and mascara into her cheeks. When she smiles he tells himself it's shock, it's the strain. He's heard rumors of her fragile mental history, the trouble after her daughter, has even heard that when she got the news about Jack she heated her oven and baked cookies, just as she's said.

He struggles for the words that could help, wants to close his eyes but doesn't want to lose track of her, her smile wider now, her face brilliant, almost jubilant, and he thinks of the faces at revivals he used to go to in Nebraska when he was growing up, faces of the newly saved, the Born Again. He sees this smile that freezes him, it has taken him so off guard, sees her free hand leave her face, feels it stroking him where his wife refused for so many years he finally stopped asking, feels himself grow into her hand and he knows that he should make her stop but knows he cannot. He feels the strength of her fingers, the control in them her mind has lost.

Oh God, he thinks, and wants to pull away but doesn't in time and when he explodes across himself in the already damp clothes he feels good but awful at the same time. "Oh God," the words aloud this time, and his eyes are clenched shut, keeping her out but her hand is still on him, her other hand still covered by his, poised for prayer, and when he opens them her smile still shines and he thinks the craziness has gone out of them. He shivers.

She takes her hand back, closes it into the other, and says, "Oh yes, God, grant us your three wishes—one of them that Jack sleep well. Amen." She touches her cheek to his. "I'm so glad you visited, Reverend Bleu. I feel so much better now."

Contessa is the first to rise from her knees, and she guides him to his feet. "I really must lie down now. You'll show yourself out?"

Before he can answer she has turned, her skirts flouncing, and heads out of the room. He finds his way to a bathroom, an antique medicine cabinet over the porcelain sink, brass fixtures gleaming. He dabs at himself with a dampened washcloth, locates a hair dryer and plugs it in. It shakes in his hands and he leans against the walnut-stained door frame and closes his eyes to right the room again before he opens them. He wonders if he will ever stop shaking.

Somehow he finds his way out of the house, the driveway, the town, to the sloping edge of the reservoir. He grasps his knees in his arms, teeters back and forth on his heels and is amazed at the size of it, that boats are sailing and sputtering across its surface, that kids and dogs are swimming in it. The sun is hot on his head and neck and hands and he feels the sweat dribble down his back, chest, inner thighs but is reluctant to remove his jacket or tie or loosen his collar. To do any of these things would be to admit his need.

He needs to cool down, to forget, but touch is real, it makes even the imagined real. Touch is truth. And the truth, of course, can be terrifying.

A gull screams overhead and he's startled, picks up a stone and skips it over the surface of the water—two, three times, then it suddenly feels its weight or remembers it is a stone and slips under the water. The Reverend Clayton Bleu skips stones, thinking about bees that aren't supposed to be able to fly and little old ladies in rest homes all over who keep praying, keep on praying, as if...

He skips another stone and sits another twenty minutes that stretch along the day like the stones across the water and he thinks of Christ walking on water and a guy he remembers now as Crazy John from the Academy who shocked them all by getting drunk and wading through the pool, mumbling about how easy it is to walk on water after all, look at him, they could all do it, every last one of them could, but Clayton Bleu had only stood at the side of the pool, watching, afraid to try for fear it was true.

He skips another stone, feeling the heat on his neck, listening to the gulls cry like babies overhead.

The waves slop the sides of the reservoir, hitting the rocks with reliable rhythm, teasing the girls with cool, wet spray. Gray clouds build in the west, gathering like bubbles in boiling liquid, gaining height, coming closer. Still they lounge on bright red and purple and yellow and blue beach towels with pictures of sailboats and beaches woven into them. Birds whistle in passing, and someone's dog jumps from the water not too far away, its bark carrying across the water.

Crescent sucks in the air, snorts the breeze that has kicked up, the furry weeds along the grassy edge, even the hot tar of the asphalt, pungent and steamy. Down the hill that forms the embankment sits her mother's car. A real triumph for her to get permission to borrow it.

"Light Sky," she says to Hope. "Now that's a name."

Hope dabs at her legs again with the tanning lotion. A cheap brand, it smears into white, refusing to fade into her skin. She strokes, then rubs, transfers the excess to the other leg.

Crescent's left eye, the one closest to Hope, opens. She watches her friend rubbing the lotion along her calves, thighs, sees that she is being ignored. "You're hopeless, but I guess that can't be helped, in your family."

"I guess not."

Crescent sighs and closes her eyes, takes in the heat, wonders if eyeballs can burn up, if eyelids are enough to prevent it. She decides to try another tack. "Don't you think Denny's been acting weird lately?"

"What do you mean, weird?" Hope pauses, then smooths the lotion into her upper arms.

"Well," Crescent says, propping herself on her left elbow to face her friend more squarely. "The band stuff, for one thing."

"So?"

"So? I mean, he's entirely into it. In the extreme, don't you think?"

Hope holds out the lotion bottle to Crescent. "Do my back for me?" The sticky bottle changes hands. "A lot of people are interested in music, have bands. I don't see what's so weird about that."

"Well, yeah, but I mean, he's really into it. It's like his life. God, Hope, this bottle is a mess. Can't you get the lotion out without smearing it all over the outside?" She presses it into a towel to wipe it off.

"You try using lotion and getting it on your hands to get on your body and then keep it off the bottle." Her back goes rigid and Crescent knows she's bracing herself for the cold against her skin. "Careful, too. That stuff comes out like crazy and then you can't smear it in."

"I hear you," Crescent says, but she drops a mess down Hope's back and ends up cupping the excess into her hand and rubbing it into her own legs and arms. "But he's absorbed, Hope. Immersed."

"We're losing the sun," Hope says, looking up, her hair reaching down her back so Crescent has to drag it away from the sticky skin with her elbow.

"Why couldn't you put your hair up or something? It's getting into the lotion and everything."

"Why don't you put yours up? Same reason," Hope says.

Crescent tosses the lotion bottle down, drops Hope's hair so it mats into the smeared white mess on her back and shoulders. "I don't know why I try to talk to you about these things." She means Denny, means that she wanted Hope to tell her more, reassure her about him, about them.

The line of thunderstorm clouds is gaining on them and Crescent scans the banks of the reservoir. Around them picnickers are packing up, the dog has been summoned into the back of someone's pickup truck down the hill. Other sun worshippers fold towels and blankets, pull on jeans and long tee-shirts to cover up. A line of moms and dads and kiddies heads down the slope to parked cars.

Crescent sniffs the air again, inhales the scent of the incoming storm. "I guess we'd better head out," she says.

She tugs the bottom edge of her bikini briefs to uncrimp them from her, tugs at her top for the same reason. She slides her rubber beach sandals on and stoops to snap up her towel and bend the corner of page 147 in Stephen King's latest novel. Hope sits on her towel, not yet moving. The first thunder rolls into them, the breeze kicking cool air across them.

Crescent shivers, pulls the towel around her shoulders. "Come on, Hope, move your ass before the rain starts. This storms going to be a killer to drive in, I can tell." With her toe she nudges the end of Hope's towel. Hope says something, but Crescent can't make it out. She is staring at the side of the reservoir nearest them. A quick lightning flash startles them both. "Come on, Hope—"

"It's my dad," she says, then she points.

A fat raindrop hits Crescent on her forehead and she swipes it away. She looks where Hope points and spots the man, out of place in his white shirt and loosened tie and light gray suit pants. He's sitting on the grass along the edge, a few feet from the water that laps the embankment. He clutches his knees close to his chest and the breeze teases a few strands of his light brown hair away from his head. From here, Crescent thinks, he looks thinner than she remembers him, and maybe even more handsome, but maybe that is his solitude. Another fat drop splatters across her, then another. "So? We got to get going."

Hope stands, her eyes steady on her father. She gathers her things absently. "What's he doing out here?" she says, but it is like an out-loud thought, a question she doesn't expect an answer to.

Crescent turns to look again at the figure across the water, the drops coming quicker and harder now, but he isn't moving. She shrugs. "Maybe somebody died."

Hope turns to follow Crescent down the hill toward the car, then stops to look once more at her father who sits while the drops come closer and closer together, the thunder coming louder. Still he doesn't move, his forehead against his knees, his face hidden from her. "Yeah," she says. "That could be it." Then she plunges down the hill ahead of Crescent, racing her to the car, ready to go.

Contessa has just become aware that there is someone with her. The lavender around her, the scent of vanilla air freshener, the hum of the air conditioner, she knows these all mean she is home. She clutches her skirt. By the linen feel she knows it is the beige dress with a brown leather belt. She wonders if she's remembered to drape the black, brown and white "safari" scarf around her neck. She slides her fingers upward, touches the plain collar of the dress and sighs. So many things she forgets these days.

The woman across from her is talking on, a pause here and there but not looking for Contessa's response. Contessa tries to sort her out from the town, the past, the family—she is not, for sure, a relative. Whoever she is has stopped by to see how she is, with Jack away getting the rest he probably needs.

"Remember that?" the woman asks, and lifts her teacup

in dainty fingers with spiny veins running through them, light green and vivid purple, distinct from even across the room. She laughs a laugh shrunken by the room and Contessa. "Remember?"

"I'm sorry—" But sorry who? What is her name? "I'm so sorry, I just don't—"

"Of course you do, Connie. You and Teddy and me and Sammy would all go to the movies and Sammy'd say, 'In the back, the sound's better,' and Teddy'd say, 'And darker,' and Sammy'd look at him like, 'Of course you dummy, that's the point.' But only Sammy and I'd sit in the back or up in the balcony. You kids would sit in the front because Teddy thought the movie could swallow you up there, and Sammy'd steal a kiss from me and we'd laugh and pick you two out of the crowd but there you'd be, watching Doris Day or somebody, just as polite as you could be with each other." The woman laughs again, her pink lipstick not smudging but maybe it's already smudged off onto the lip of the teacup. "You've got to remember that, Connie. Gosh, even then we should have realized that Theodore just wasn't interested, you know?"

She was going to pretend to remember and nod her head but the question at the end confused her. "Sure," she says anyway, glancing around for maybe a cup of her own. Why is she serving hot tea on such a hot day? Hot drinks, hot day, no, no, but a glance out the window tells her it's dark, maybe even raining or just trying to, but why can't she remember this all starting? Even this visit with this woman? It seems like more and more she is here and then gone someplace, then back again and things have changed in the meantime and she just can't keep up.

At least now she knows it's someone from the old days. If she could only remember their names, remember who dated Sammy in those days, then maybe she could place this blonde with the short hair and thin wrists and calves that look like they don't have much muscle to support her when she walks, her waist thick but not fat. Of course, maybe she looks different now.

"How are things, Connie, really?"

She pronounces this last word as if it carries a lot of importance and Contessa thinks maybe if she doesn't answer right away she might have to go away again, to rest, like Jack. She'd miss her lavender room if that happened. "Fine," she says. "Really, fine." The woman is looking at her closely and Contessa wonders if she notices the missing scarf. Maybe the scarf is as important as the question. "The reverend paid a visit," she says.

"That's nice, Connie. Reverend Bleu, was it?"

She isn't sure of the name. He was wearing a collar like they do in the movies. "A very nice man," she says, and the woman nods. This seems to be the right thing to talk about, this visit the reverend made. Contessa again sees him here, in this room, and their hands together, but like so many things, it's fuzzy now, but she remembers a good feeling from him. "I was glad he visited," she says.

The woman smooths her hair near her left ear and adjusts an earring heavy with round fake pearls and rhinestones. "You know, Connie, I've never thought of you much as a religious woman, but I guess when the Lord tries you, it's good to turn back to Him. The reverend, I'm sure, will provide you with much comfort."

"Do you think so?"

"Of course, dear, of course he will."

"Good," she says. "Good." The woman hugs her and Contessa squeezes her eyes closed. "It is so hard to be alone," she says, but she cannot cry, no matter how much her eyes burn for it.

She is sitting on her porch, in the same chair, in a dress

that could be the same or maybe is, and for a moment he wonders if she ever moves. Wonders if the threat of storm pushed her back inside, even for the few minutes it took to build clouds that promised so much but sprinkled only a few delicate drops while it floated on through, leaving the town humid and thick and worse now than before the whispered, broken promise of a soaking rain.

Eddy brushes off a quick notion that Mamie is here for him, that she waits for him, that she falls into a sort of hibernation when he's gone, like that Gypsy mannequin that reads fortunes in arcades, sitting with her eyes closed until the coin drops in the slot and she comes to life, her stiff hands moving back and forth over the yellowed, dog-eared cards, her mouth and neck creaking from years of wisdom.

She sees him coming down the sidewalk and smiles and waves. He bounds up the steps, sits without invitation. She has a drink waiting for him.

They sit, quiet, for some time. Last night he needed her more but then there was the girl to contend with. Finally, because he knows Mamie won't begin until he says something, drops the coin in the slot, he says, raising his glass toward the house across the street, "To Jack," and she raises her glass with him and they drink.

It is a green-shuttered, two-floor house with little panes —fake snow still in the corners from Christmas. The tiny porch, not nearly as hospitable as Mamie's, is a concrete slab with two folding, webbed chairs on it. "Kids?" he asks.

"They had a little girl, years ago, twenty now, I guess, since she died. Spitfire, she was, like her mother." Mamie leans her head against the back of the chair and breathes in. "Smelling summer," she says, but he thinks that probably she is also breathing the past.

"But how are you, Eddy?"

He covers her hand with his. "Glad you're here. I haven't had a sweetheart in a long time."

Her head comes up from the chair, a hand waves away his words, but the other hand rests under his, still. "Do you take pride in making old women blush?"

"Making you blush, Mamie, isn't making an old woman blush."

The near-setting sun flashes against the windows of the houses across the street, hiding aluminum and white-painted wood beneath bright orange. Eddy watches Mamie watching Contessa's house. She is puckered, Mamie is, and folded and round and all things inviting to him, her body curved and bent over a lifetime of wisdom, but her mind and her words straight and true.

"You know," Mamie says, "she was here a couple of days ago, before he died, with a macaroni thing she'd made."

"Nice of her to think of you, in this heat."

Mamie swallows from her glass. It is a long swallow, and Eddy expects her to cough but she doesn't. "I didn't think so," she says. "I mean, I'm happy to be left alone—you know what I mean." She squeezes his hand and he nods. "I maybe could have been nicer to her."

"You didn't know she'd be going through this." They are not the words he wants but he has said them anyway and is glad it seems she hasn't heard him. Words have never come easy to him. He stopped talking once and he found people understood him better, but were more afraid of him. With Mamie he shouldn't have to try; she reads his hands and eyes.

"I hope she holds up," Mamie says. "When Deborah died, Contessa had a bad time. Hospitals, even. Oh, she's not crazy, just had a bad time. Who wouldn't? But I've been thinking about her all day."

It is getting closer to the sun setting. The birds clamor their last songs of the day. A squirrel in the tree near Mamie's porch hops branches, hugging dinner in his cheeks until he's high enough up to eat in peace.

"At the plant, before the accident, there was talk about it closing," Eddy says.

Mamie takes this in as if it's an interesting theory to contemplate. "That factory's been here nearly as long as the town," she says. "Only recently it's been a pressing plant, but there's always been something in it, something made or shaped somehow. I would guess if the pressing company goes the plant will still be here, maybe in another incarnation, but it will stay."

A young man passes by on the sidewalk, a guitar case bobbing up and down in his hand with every step. He looks in no direction but straight ahead, doesn't see them, and they don't speak to him.

"It's too bad, Mamie, but plants just aren't re-opening any more, not even in reincarnations," Eddy says.

She takes another long swallow of her drink, wipes a hard three fingers across her lips. Her eyes follow a group of kids, two on bikes and one on foot as they pass on the other side of the street. They are in bathing suits, damp towels draped around them.

"I can't imagine the town without the plant," she says.

And for some reason Eddy thinks of what he's heard of the burial ground north of town, thinks of the remains of the lives there. Something shut them down, put them away, buried them, and the world forgot about them for hundreds, maybe thousands of years.

"Maybe the problem with Atlantis was cheaper foreign labor, too," he says, and she grins and they drink to the fall of Atlantis.

Ben Stevens walks the length of the pale gray carpet in this office that is sparsely furnished but rich in what is absent: only a small shelf of law books sits heavily behind the lean desk with its high sheen of black lacquer. The books that aren't here are in another room, a law library assembled over the years to ultimately save the time and money it was taking to drive to and from the county library twenty minutes away, the forty minutes to the larger state library two counties away.

No papers clutter Mason Pope's desk—nothing clutters anything. His office suite is slick and clean and decorated like a big-city office or an office in a soap opera his ex-wife liked to watch before she started interior decoration full time. This is not the way Ben Stevens works, it is too much concerned with keeping up appearances, with not letting seams show. It makes Ben suspicious. Even this second phone call, like the first, Pope has taken in the next room behind its closed door. Perhaps it's for the confidentiality of the client, but perhaps it's something else.

The door to the other office opens and Ben backs from the photograph on the wall of Mason Pope in golf cap with club in hand standing next to an equally rested-looking Ohio governor.

"My apologies again for the interruption," Pope says, motioning Ben to a chair. This is the third time the two have seated themselves, begun the conversation. "One of the problems with meeting after regular office hours is that the girl's gone home, there's no one to screen the calls." He gestures helplessly. "Now what were you saying?"

"About the burial site," Ben says.

"Oh yes." Mason Pope is all angles in this room, his face long and thin, his wire-framed glasses rectangular around his eyes, his bony hands in a boxy clasp in front of him on the desk. It occurs to Ben, looking at him this way, very nearly studying him, he can almost see why the man has found success. It is in his shape: long and thin, an arrow shot straight at whatever he wanted, aimed and fired dead on into the heart to make the thing his own. The image becomes so clear to him he must blink to erase it.

"—the removal of them from the property," Pope is saying, and Ben realizes he's missed the main point, must ask him to repeat himself. "What I'm saying is," Pope tells him, "is that there's nothing we can do for them."

"What do you mean?"

He shrugs, leans back into the thick leather chair. "It's not their land. It's Freeman's land. From what I can understand from poor George it's sort of exciting to have the burial ground. But to release his property to somebody else, that's another story. You see, I can make legal decisions on George's behalf under power of attorney, but making these other sorts of decisions has to go back to George, and he's just not capable."

"That means everything shuts down."

"Not necessarily. I think I could defend pretty well the idea of the excavation and maybe even the auctioning of some of the artifacts, maybe all of them, because that would enhance his estate. That would be the type of decision a person would make, to make things better for himself. But to just say to these people, 'Come on in and take this back to your reservation' or whatever, that doesn't advance his estate, it doesn't make things any better for him. It would be harder to justify that to a higher court if I had to." He pulls himself from the chair, paces the room. "I've thought this through pretty thoroughly, Ben, and I just don't see where the Indians can make us do anything."

The carpet under Mason Pope's feet silences his steps so completely that Stevens doesn't hear but feels him stop behind him, feels the man move away again. "Can they get a state order or something? I hear this Yellow Wolf character is a lawyer himself and he seems pretty confident about getting what he wants."

Mason, behind the desk, near a window, waves the comment away. "He won't be able to prove ancestral relationship, under NAGPRA. I did a little checking."

"NAGPRA?"

"Native American Graves Protection and Repatriation Act. But Yellow Wolf is really all visibility, an attempt to intimidate." He looks out the window onto Main Street, a view Stevens knows shows him a few parked cars in front of what has been, over the years, a grocery, a bar, a record store, and is now an insurance agency. "I want to know what it is you want, Ben," he says.

"Me?"

"For the town, about this. What are your thoughts."

Ben pulls himself straighter in the chair, knits his fingers together in his lap. "Of course I've been thinking, too. Had a meeting the other day with the plant manager over here. They wouldn't give me any sort of assurance that the plant won't close. Now, with Jack Welch's accident and OSHA investigating, that might just be the straw that breaks that old camel. So we need something else."

"The burial site." Mason sits, folds his arms in front of him, listening.

"Right. The university folks are concerned flat out tourists could be trouble, hard to keep the place secure against looting. But Landers and me were wondering about a museum on the site. Build up around the dig, charge admission. They tell me grant money can pay for the building because it's so historical."

"A museum, eh?" He leans his head into the cupped palm of his left hand, raised to meet it, strokes his cheek with his fingers. "The Indians couldn't very well object to that, now could they?"

Ben shrugs. "It'll change the farm."

Mason chuckles. "The least of our worries. The question is, can we make it work? Financially, I mean."

"Couldn't tell you that, Mason. All I know is that we need something. It won't employ like the plant, but with the right advertising and promotion, maybe this could be more of a tourist center, folks could open other restaurants, motels, businesses that would cater to that crowd. Hell, we could even have a theme town or something. Little shops could sell moccasins, things like that."

Mason grins, drops his hands, leans forward. "You have been thinking about this."

"Because it's on your—Freeman's—property, you'd stand to gain from the site itself, directly. Plus any extras you might put around it. Then the town, the town benefits from the folks who'll come through who need to eat and sleep and buy things while they're here. Plus some workers who'll be employed at the site, guides, souvenir sellers, jobs like that."

Mason is nodding. "Could be done."

"When you consider we got a certain amount of tourist trade through here anyway, what with the lakes and the Erie Islands and even Cedar Point, we could tap right into that market."

He envisions as he talks, seeing along Route 20 new strips of Comfort and Holiday Inns, Red Lobster restaurants and department stores. A couple of summers ago Sandusky added more than a dozen new movie theaters just because of the summer tourist trade, so he pictures, along the route, a multi-screen movie complex.

"Let me check into this museum idea, Ben," Mason says, coming around his desk to shake hands. "I do believe you're on to something."

9

White gray haze lies smooth and silent across blazing wheat, eager for harvest, and supple green corn to either side, nearly knee high now, this first day of July. The day will be still and clear and hot, Eddy can feel it already—another in a long chain that binds the summer.

Once there were trees through here, hickory, oak, maple, thick enough to shade the ground from this same hot sun, underbrush cutting naked shins except along the few trails that ran from summer campsites to creek beds. They grew the Three Sisters—corn, growing straight up; beans, wrapped around the corn stalks; and squash, spreading big leaves to trap moisture in the soil—and hunted among the trees.

They were powerful, the trees, but then they were slashed at their bases, slaughtered for all intents, and hauled to the Atlantic coast where they were shipped across the ocean to England.

Everything, in all ways, began to change. Not even the ground is the same, the landscape slashed this way and that, the earth itself chucked full of chemicals and rot. If the ancestors came back, where would they turn? How would they know their way if not by stars or sun because the trees have been robbed of the power to guide them, to shelter them?

None But The Dead And Dying

Would they even believe they were in the same place, that these are the same hills they walked, the same sky they studied?

At the edge of the pit Eddy sits staring first at the sky, now at the ground around him, amazed at the number of bodies once buried here and the countless possessions left with them. It might have been the population of a clan, dropped by rivals or illness. More amazing is that they were denied gentle journeys the way most of the dead are laid to rest, faces up to the Sky World, their direction toward the rising sun. Not these. A few bodies were dropped haphazardly into the pit but another dozen or more were laid north-south, face down to Mother Earth. Now, uncovered, the backs of their heads to the open sky, they are vulnerable—attacked from behind, it seems. Or maybe just unwilling to let their jaws gape miserable smiles of greeting to those who might unearth them. Eddy listens, but the dirt in their mouths keeps them silent.

The sky gathers color and he knows the workers will be coming, eager to start again, but he has a little time, too. Out here, like it is further west where the land is even flatter, the sun emerges into the day slowly, creeping like a cat stalking prey, so patient.

Bands of pastel shimmer along the horizon, then stretch like arms around a yawn, waking up, getting bolder, brighter, while the sky opposite surrenders in deep blue.

Eddy fingers an unlit cigarette. When he snaps the match across the bottom of his boot he watches it flare, die a little, burn the paper down. He blows it out before using it to light his cigarette, tosses it behind him into the whispering corn.

It is past time to move on, he is thinking. Past time to take a quiet leave.

He stands, stretches. Down the driveway he sees movement in the gray morning, hears a chanting that he recognizes though doesn't understand. They are preparing the drum. Before long, the university excavators. Then who knows who else will come along.

He finds his footing down the far slope of the dig and steps quietly past the watchman who sleeps noisily like a buffoon in a comic strip, his rifle across his chest.

Along the back side of the property behind the house he makes a long jump over what looks like a water line digging. The house, this way, seems cut away from its own land by the scissoring of backhoe slices through it. The yard once was smooth, he can tell, but it is ruptured this way and that by jagged slashes of upturned earth thicker and darker than blood.

In a wide arc he traces the edge of the property, shunning the house, the drive, the Indians gathering in morning ceremony. He jumps the irrigation ditch that separates the front lawn from the road, and he breathes easier, the walk will feel good, good in his legs and head, though it will take more than an hour to get back.

He follows the narrow strip of asphalt, the county road void of markings, lines, speed limit or route signs. It is as private as someone's long drive and as promising. Red-violet and yellow wildflowers poke at him, tease him into tugging one free of the earth. He sniffs at it, discovering its empty beauty, empty scent. Despite that, the petals are bright and he thinks of gathering a bunch for Mamie, but he knows the petals will bend, faint from the growing heat and humidity, from his eager grasp.

Thoughts of Mamie often lead him to thoughts of Lone Hawk, a deep-lined, deep-wisdom woman from the reservation. She too sat on her porch, but her porch boards rested over the ground, her house flaked white paint, scorched and tired of hanging on, to show gray wood rotting all over. Lone Hawk gathered wildflowers, the scattered few, and ground them, sifted them, dropped berry juice into them, smeared them over his tired shoulders, his fingers and palms rubbed raw from his first paying work. She soothed the mixture into him, and with her words and chants and tales of the buffalo days and better times he fell into her cures and became strong. When she died last year he wanted to go back but knew he could not. Instead he pulled flowers like this one from along interstate roads three states away and laid them on sticks over dirt. He lit them and thought of her. She had been his mother and father, his only reason for going back.

The flower in his hand is wilting already, the pale green and yellow stem leaking clear liquid, vital fluids, over his fingers. He tosses the flower into the ditch that trails next to him, wipes his hands against his jeans.

The slick white door with the wreath is wide open, the screen door not pulled completely closed, as though someone has gone in in a hurry. The reverend slams his car door. He hasn't wanted this return, the chills that made him wrap covers around him tight as a secret last night, those chills telling him now to get back into the Chevette, back down the driveway, find another way to help. But this is what he must do, he must minister, must do the job he's been sent to do, must not let anyone see the part that should never have happened.

From the porch he hears voices, Contessa and a man, Contessa in that same flighty, distracted voice from yesterday. He is surprised that this early in the day she has visitors. He knocks and the voices become confused and he thinks for a second about what would have happened if they had been interrupted by the door, wonders what might be going on inside, but now in the screen door stands Theodore Thompson looking healthier than at his mother's funeral. Theodore is confused, though, concerned, grateful to see him. "Please, Reverend, come in," and to Contessa, "Look, Tessie, Reverend Bleu has come to say hello."

Contessa crawls from the sofa, glass in her hand teetering amber liquid. She glides to him and suddenly he's nervous. More people are here than he first thought—Theodore and Elizabeth, Contessa's sister, a woman from his congregation, are two he knows. There are two others, both women.

Contessa is reaching out to him with her free hand and he automatically backs from her, scoops her hand into his and she clutches it, tugs him close. "I'm so pleased you could come, Reverend," she says. "I know you've been concerned, but don't you worry because our prayer was answered. You remember that prayer, don't you?" She pulls him toward the sofa, hands him her drink. "Eat, drink, be merry and all that. Or is it drown your sorrows?"

"Tessie, perhaps the reverend would prefer not to drink," Elizabeth says, reaching out to take the glass from him, but Contessa reclaims it with a frown, a warning. "Would you like lemonade?" Elizabeth asks.

He nods, afraid to speak, to start the words tumbling to this woman who is their former choir director and current leader of children's Sunday School, this woman standing in the same room, the room he's sure will give them away, some smell coming through to her like a heart pounding through the floor, some image wrenching her attention away from lemonade to him. Contessa watches them, her eyes heavy with blurred mascara and a dreamy vagueness.

"Contessa..." he begins. The sister walks to the kitchen but the others are here and he must be careful of the words. What might set her off? What set her off before? What made him not stop her? He's sorry, suddenly, for the lemonade, his hands will shake and they will know.

"I was so pleased with your last visit," she says, and he

can't tell how much double meaning she intends. "I'm so happy you've returned. I'm so happy and so pleased that Teddy and Elizabeth are here. And do you know Frannie and JoAnne? Maybe Pete'll come and you'll be able to meet him. You'll like Pete. He's a farmer but he's still a nice person, you know. He's Elizabeth's husband. You probably know Elizabeth from church, but he doesn't go, so maybe you don't know him, but maybe you did meet him, at least once, at some church thing?"

"Maybe," he says, nodding to the other women. Elizabeth hands him a cold glass of iced lemonade, a wedge of real lemon floating in it.

Theodore switches Contessa's drink with a glass of lemonade and she smiles her thanks, waits for the reverend to sip his before she takes a drink. "Gosh, another hot one. I made a casserole to take to Mamie this morning—" she says. "Or maybe it was the day before...."

"I'm sure you should be thinking about yourself right now, Mrs. Welch," Reverend Bleu says, wanting to take her hand to reassure her, but afraid, so many things now meaning so many others. "We'll make sure Miss Van Allen is looked after."

Her expression is smiling and vacant. "Of course you will, you are so good about that, Reverend."

They sip in silence, wipe sweat from the glasses with their hands, wipe sweat from their brows with handkerchiefs. The reverend exchanges an uneasy glance with Theodore.

A sudden burst erupts from Elizabeth, a cry, and Contessa rocks her, her arms circling the rounded woman, but over her shoulder she rolls her eyes at the others in the room. "There, there," she says, patting Elizabeth on the back of the head as if she were a toddler suffering a learning-to-walk wound. "There, there. It's going to be okay."

She winks at the reverend and he wonders if Theodore sees this, he's looking right at her, and the reverend sets his glass on a leather coaster on the end table. He covers his hands, one with the other, over and over.

Elizabeth has gathered herself back together, is sitting up again on the sofa next to Contessa and she is looking at him. He realizes she has said something he's missed. He begs her pardon and she says, "I was wondering if you would lead us in prayer, Reverend."

He clears his throat, clears it as thoroughly as his head is of prayers. "Dearly beloved," he mutters, chokes back another cough. "Dear friends, dear God, in your presence...Our Father, who art in heaven, whose wisdom and infinite glory we seek...help us to understand and be enlightened to your mysterious ways, so that mercy may be shown upon your servant, Mrs. Contessa Welch, and her soul may be comforted in this time of grief—"

"Amen, amen," Contessa says. She's waving her hands at him as if waving a white flag. "Amen already."

"In the name of Your Son, Our Savior—"

"AMEN I said."

"Amen."

He hears the mumbled echoes from Theodore, Elizabeth and the others. Contessa applauds, stands to give her ovation. "Thank you, Reverend. I just know Jack is fine, thanks to you." She is upon him, pressing her hands into his, clutching them to her cheek. "You are a fine reverend, Reverend."

"Thank you," he says, untying his fingers from hers, glancing at Elizabeth. "I really should go now, and leave you with your sister and friends and let you know that if there's anything more that I might do, please call."

Elizabeth dabs at her eyes with a ratted tissue. She shakes her head. From her perch on the blue and white and lavender sofa, she says, "Please know that we appreciate your visit, Reverend," and he walks to her to take her hand. The sopped tissue clings to her palm, to his, and he can't wait to get back into the car.

He thinks of the reservoir, but remembers the sounds of the children laughing, the dogs barking, the boats puttering across the water, too many sounds when he just wants peace. There are enough sounds in his head.

He thinks of the burial site. It is early yet, maybe no one is there yet. He has heard that there are Indians with drums and chanting and he wonders if this could ease his mind, if these sounds can create peace, so he steers his car north.

Sandra knows, he thinks, the radio turned to classic music, the windows down and the air gushing in at him, blowing his hair around. She knew right away, the way I kissed her couldn't have been the same. And I couldn't pray with her and her quiet waiting for me, but I couldn't...

The sun climbs higher, its earlier collage of pale rainbow colors fading into daylight, everything turning blue in the sky. He thinks of smoking, after twelve years without. Maybe it would stop his hands, his heart, from shaking.

The worst is that he wants more of her, even today, when he should be repulsed by the very memory, but all he wants is to feel her close, her hand on him that way, again.

He has tried since yesterday to call up the scriptures, the parables that he needs, but all he can think of is, "Let he among you who is without sin..." and he casts it away like a fish too small and falls in after it.

He comes up on the burial site but sees that there is already a mob gathering, a cluster of people in the driveway and the Midwestern State car trying to drive around them, angry words shouted. This is not what he wants today. He drives past.

The roads through here, among the fields of rustling corn and the wheat that waits out its days before harvest, these roads narrow their way between ditches deep on each side, and he's glad no cars approach.

Up the road he sees a man walking, sees him thrust something away from him, his head not following its path. He seems to not hear the car until the reverend edges behind him and leans out the open window. "Say there, give you a lift?"

When the man turns he sees it is the Indian everyone has been whispering about, the one who came when the site was discovered, long before this new group. Some say he is the conjured spirit of one of the dead and will walk until the bones are put to rest again. He is lean and strong looking, and the face that turns to answer him seems never to have smiled or seen joy, but he does smile and the smile seems oddly to fit him, to soften his fierceness, to ease the power in his eyes.

He climbs into the car. "Thanks," he says, his knees rubbing the dashboard, maybe for luck. "Good walking until the sun got hot."

Reverend Bleu nods, not sure what he might add. "Heading back to town?"

"Probably should," the man says. He gestures at the reverend. "Clergy?"

His fingers automatically stroke his neck but today he's left his collar on the dresser. Sandra, he remembers, was puzzled but seemed relieved. She's wanted him to abandon it the way other ministers have. "It makes you look Catholic," she tells him. Today he said it was just too hot, and she accepted it, though the heat has never stopped him from wearing it before.

"How can you tell?" he asks.

The Indian, he notices, toys with an unlit cigarette between his index and second fingers, flicking imaginary ashes from it. He's turned his attention to the roadside, the cigarette dropping dry tobacco bits onto his lap. "I've seen you around town in this car, in your collar."

"You're observant," Reverend Bleu says.

The man grins. "Yeah, and I can hear all kinds of things when I put my ear to the ground."

The reverend looks at him, doesn't know whether to smile or grin or laugh or ignore it. "Me, too," he says.

The man's laugh startles him, and the hand thrust out to him pleases him. "Eddy Light Sky, sir," he says.

He takes Eddy's hand, shakes it. "Clayton Bleu."

"Reverend? Pastor? Father?" The fingers play, the cigarette begins to bend.

"Today I just want to be Clayton."

With a decline of his head, Eddy shows his understanding. Maybe, the reverend thinks, he's already got his ear to the ground, the way in Nebraska the kid Clay used to drop next to railroad tracks and embrace the steel rails, his ear to the grimy steel hoping and waiting for the vibrations travelling from miles away. "Drop you anyplace in particular in town, Eddy?"

"I don't want to take you out of your way, Clayton." He shifts his long legs in the cramped front seat and the reverend thinks he must be uncomfortable.

"No place is out of the way, really."

"The plant, Birdseye Street lot?"

"You got it."

Driving Eddy to work somehow relaxes him. His hands still twist around the steering wheel, holding it hard to hold them steady, but the drive, meeting Eddy, has given him something to do, something to do for someone, something safe that won't do more harm than good. He pulls into the lot, idles the car near the plant entrance.

"Thanks, Clayton. What do I owe you for the lift?"

The question is proof again the man isn't from around here. Clayton shakes his head. "Glad to do it."

"Sure?"

"Well...Got another cigarette?"

Eddy looks relieved, smiles, tosses him a near-gone pack and a book of matches from the Buckeye Inn. "Thanks again," he says.

The reverend watches the man's back as he heads for the plant. He sits, the heat crowding in around him in the idling car, and watches until the man is gone. He pulls a filtered cigarette from the soft pack, strokes it, reacquaints himself with the feel, the smell, the heat of the lit match close to his face, the taste. He breathes out a long stream of spent fire and takes the car out of park.

Landers has never had cause to drive down this street in town before, so he has to look carefully for the number. Street numbers are a little hard to see sometimes—most visitors know the houses, know who belongs in which one, and that's all that's important. When he asked in town where he might find Gasman George Freeman's house everybody knew the street but not the number. "Won't need it," they said. "You'll know it when you see it."

A crumbling wooden house that was probably once bright white with green or black shutters bordering the windows slumps in a lot of trampled dirt and evergreen trees. This must be it then, Landers thinks, heading up its cracked cement sidewalk. To his right, along the side of the house sits a rusting '62 Chrysler and Landers is surprised that it's in pretty good shape, considering its age, considering its lack of good care. Probably worth a little something, he thinks.

The porch, low to the ground like wooden sidewalks in western movies, creaks under the weight of Landers' step. Next to the front door with the torn screen sits an ancient ice box, rounded shoulders and front gaping without its door making it look like a toothless old man.

Landers raises his hand to knock, is startled that before he can Gasman appears on the other side of the screen, his face pressed toward him, eyes wide, chin trembling.

"Mr. Freeman," Landers says, "you maybe don't remember me, but I'm the man who works your farm out there off 101." The face doesn't change; there's no sign he understands, so Landers goes on, "Well, we got us a little fix out there, Mr. Freeman. You heard about it?"

"Huhn?" the man maybe says or maybe grunts, it's hard for Landers to tell.

"The farm?"

Gasman nods his head or maybe Landers just thinks so. Landers clears his throat, shifts his weight, wishes Gasman would come out onto the porch. The boards creak under his own feet. "You know about the burial ground out there?" he asks, watching the man's face, trying not to squint through the screen but it's so hard to see for sure. "Mr. Freeman, this could take just a minute. Could you just step out onto the porch here?" Landers backs away from the door, gesturing a sort of invitation. He turns away a little, trying not to seem too interested in what the man decides to do. "It's nice out here, weather good today," he says, "though we could use some rain."

He walks to the side of the porch where it drops without a railing to the ground. No shrubs surround the house, nothing nestling up next to it, nothing to soften it. He hears the screen door screech, the boards of the porch floor bending and creaking with the man's weight. He turns slowly, sees that Gasman George is in his worn clothes that might have been somebody's uniform. So, Landers thinks, he does understand, at least some things. "The farm can maybe make you rich, Mr. Freeman. Did anybody tell you that?"

The man is standing in the middle of the porch, the roof of it not too much above his head, the man not so much tall as the porch sloping, dragging under the weight of years of rain and snow and pounding hail. He looks at Landers, then out past him to the street where a couple of boys, maybe junior high age, ride by on their bikes, one of them dribbling a basketball alongside. They call to each other and one jerks his head toward Gasman. One waves and the other laughs.

"Did you hear me, Mr. Freeman?" Landers asks. "The farm, with the burial site, could be worth some real money now. But you got to be careful they do what you want, that Mr. Pope and Mr. Stevens don't start to make it their own little project."

Landers sees that Gasman isn't looking at him, and turns to see what has captured his attention. He sees the boys on bikes on down the street; when he looks back to Gasman the man's eyes are on him again. "Do you know what I'm saying, Mr. Freeman?"

Gasman nods his head, slowly, a definite nod, and Landers grins. Maybe the man can't talk, he thinks, but he hears, he understands. "Good," Landers says. "Now, Mr. Pope and Mr. Stevens and Mr. Olson, you probably don't know him, but he's one of the university people, they want to make a museum on your land out there. Make it so it's not so much a farm anymore but a tourist place where people can come to see this Indian stuff. But I'm telling you, they're the ones who'll make the money, and you'll be lucky to see much of it." Landers looks at the man's house behind him. "They sure haven't been taking much care of you as it is."

The man twists his body though his feet don't budge, not even a quiver from the boards beneath him when he twists to gaze at the house behind him, at the cracked window in the front room where his sister has pulled aside the curtain to watch. "My," Gasman says. "My."

"Yes," Landers says. "It's your house. Your sister and you take good care of it. And your farm used to belong to your folks, remember? And now I farm it but there's the Indian burial ground there and you got to decide what it is you want to do about that. I'm guessing they might talk to you about it, but you got to tell them, somehow, what it is you want. You got to let them know, Mr. Freeman, or they might do what you don't want. And it's yours. Yours. You need to decide."

"My," he says, and he raises his hand to motion to the house.

"Yes," Landers says, "yours. Your house. Now tell me, do you want the Indians to have the bones or do you want the university people to have the museum? Should Mr. Yellow Wolf—oh, shit, I didn't tell you about him, did I?" He swipes his Cleveland Indians hat off his head, wipes his forehead with his arm, slaps the hat back atop his head. "Mr. Yellow Wolf is an Indian who wants the bones from the burial to be turned over to his group so they can rebury the dead. Do you think he ought to be able to do that?"

From behind them, from the doorway, a squeal where the sister Eileen stands, her red hair going grey in long, ratty streaks down her shoulders. "Hey, mister!" she says. "Hey mister! Haircut and shave? That what you want? Go get me some crackers, will you? Ritz?"

"Eileen?"

She cackles, and in it Landers hears why the kids have always called her the FreeWitch. Except that her face is stunningly pretty, with a long, straight nose sprinkled with delicate freckles and eyes green as the summer grass, she could be a witch, her voice shattered by that laugh and her eyes busy here and there, her hands quick as houseflies against the door, then her head, then through the hole in the screen. "Georgie, lemme out, I been good, can't I just be on the porch? When's Momma coming home and will you PLEASE get out of that tree once and for all?"

And, with a quick step backwards into the dark of the house she is gone, vanished from the other side of the screen door, her cackle coming from somewhere inside. Gasman reaches for the doorknob.

"Wait, just one more second, Mr. Freeman," Landers says, holding out his hand to stop him, but his fingers on the man's sleeve frighten him, and Gasman shakes it off with a swallowed cry. A tug on the door and Gasman, too, is gone, back inside where, no doubt, it is safer and much, much easier to understand things.

Landers knocks on the door, calls out to them, but after several minutes it is quiet except for his voice and he knows it is no use. They have left him alone on this decrepit porch with everything that is on his mind.

Crescent licks dripping strawberry, sucks along the side of the sugar cone, lets the fruity cold lie on her tongue, lets it disintegrate there until she swallows. The concrete beneath her is hot, the asphalt patch of parking lot under her feet hotter still. She stretches her legs along it from her perch on the curb in front of Room 7 of the Buckeye Inn. The clock at the Credit Union on the corner next to the motel reassures her that she won't have to wait much longer. She's wandered out this way to get an ice cream, hang out. Just a convenient coincidence that Eddy Light Sky's room is so close.

Maybe Eddy will drop some wisdom on her, help her to understand Denny and Hope and school coming up. And what about that burial site stuff, she wonders.

She glances across the parking lot to the digital clock. Date, time, temperature. She munches the end of the cone, wishes she had a napkin for her fingers, a cold glass of water for her throat. The clock goes through its cycle again. A minute passes. Two.

It never occurs to her that he might come home with a woman on his arm or that he might not come at all. She can't imagine anything other than him walking up the road, his face falling into a long smile to see her.

Three-fifteen. His shift ended a quarter of an hour ago.

Any time now.

A gray Chevette pulls into the motel lot from the direction of the plant and Crescent peers into the front windshield to try to see the driver but the sun is in her face and she can't. She thinks that this looks an awful lot like the car Hope's dad drives and she wonders about that, Hope's dad the preacher at a motel on a weekday afternoon, but the passenger door opens and Eddy climbs out of the front seat as if unfolding himself from it, emerging from it like the twelfth clown from the tiny car in the circus show. He gives the driver a wave and heads toward her. When he sees Crescent sitting on the curb he almost stops. "Well, well," he says.

"Hi, guy," she says. She stands up, brushes off the behind of her white shorts.

"What are you doing out this way?" His long hair is damp, drops of sweat bead on his brow, soak into his shirt, his jeans.

"Came to say hi."

"Oh." He shifts his black Thermos from one hand to the other. "Well, I wasn't really expecting you—anybody—"

"If you're worried about your place being a wreck, don't. I mean, that's okay, I can even give you a hand, I'm good at cleaning stuff up." The heat is her excuse for the bikini top she wears with the shorts so short the beginning curve of her ass shows. She's told herself that if this doesn't do it, nothing will.

She moves close to him but he backs away. "You're not scared of me, are you?" She wants to laugh or giggle, anything to loosen him up, but nothing is happening.

"Cress, I'm just off shift. I'm not really ready to see anybody." He tucks the fingers of his right hand into his pocket for keys.

"I can straighten while you shower, if that's what you're worried about," she says.

She expects that grin, that flashy bright smile that doesn't entirely fit his face, but he's reserving it. "A maid comes in. Thanks for your offer, anyway. Maybe I'll see you later."

"At the bell tower?"

"I don't know, Cress. Maybe." His keys are in his hand, but he lingers in front of the door, crosses his arms across his chest.

"Look, Eddy, I just want to talk, you know? How come you're so cold with me all the time?" She's heard a tone in her mother's voice that seems to sometimes work on her dad. She tries this voice now, but he doesn't seem at all affected by it. "If it's that shower thing, you don't have to for me. I sort of like the smell of sweat."

"Cress...." He shakes his head, knots his fingers together at belt level. "Look, I just got a lot on my mind. It's been a hot, rough day, I need a shower and some sleep, and I appreciate your stopping, I do, but I'm just not going to be much company."

She swallows, feels her cheeks burn. "Then the bell tower, okay?" but she can't face the shake of the head she knows he'll give her, so she walks away from him, dropping her hips with her steps, hoping his eyes are following her, thinking of later.

10

he wink haunts the reverend. Her face, her hands, her wise yet simple-minded voice and eyes haunt him. He stirs in the night and he walks to the back step and lights cigarette after cigarette, wondering if she sleeps soundly, thinking she probably does, probably with the hint of a smile at her lips, lips pink yet from forgotten lipstick, on a face otherwise as stripped as the rest of her. He thinks of her this way, feels his fingers shake for wanting to touch her, for wanting to follow the patterns of gold the street lights scatter beneath trees lit from above, silhouetted like cut-out valentines and old-movie scenes of passion. He wipes his damp upper lip, brow, temples, neck, with his hands, then scrapes his hands across his terry robe, white but yellow-looking in the dim back porch light.

He has been asked by her sister Elizabeth to handle the ceremony. And the plant wants him to lead prayers in a memorial service for his co-workers. He has said, "Yes, of course," to both yet he stands here not knowing what he will say about this man she's been married to, slept with, created a child with.

He creeps back into the house, crawls into jeans and tee shirt and emerges again from the back, steps across the asphalt, unlined street, feeling against his feet the warmth still there. He'll walk, he'll think, maybe he'll pray, maybe he'll sort it all out.

A street away he knows where he's heading, knows he should turn back but knows he won't, can't. His path severs the streets, the houses split between him, the lawns cool and lush, even the dogs quiet in fenced yards. The town is dark and this is like a dream he often has, a dream where he is running, running, breathless and fast, through the town, between houses and across yards, cutting through to the shadows, afraid to be caught by something he never sees, never hears, something that maybe, just maybe, isn't even there.

He follows the splattered light, telling himself he has no need to run, not tonight, that he can walk, following streets and sidewalks, hurrying from one patch of street light to the next as if connecting them.

Mamie has fallen asleep on the porch again, but a steady slap of feet on pavement awakens her. She lifts her head in the direction of the footsteps, leans toward the sound of a man's mumbling, careful that the chair might creak.

From Mulberry Street comes the Reverend Bleu, staggering like a drunken man, chanting nearly, "Dear Lord in Heaven, lead me in the direction you wish me to follow, show me the way you wish me to go... Dear Lord in Heaven, lead me in the direction...." Circular, his voice comes round like the rhymes Mamie remembers neighborhood kids and school kids on the playground chanting: "Hell-o everybody, this is Harry Cemetery, if you're good you go to Heaven, if you're bad you go to hell-o everybody, this is Harry Cemetery..."

She blinks, dampens a tissue with the wasted scotch and melted ice, touches it to her eyes, cooling them. The reverend pauses now in front of Contessa Welch's house. His tee shirt is smudged as if he's used it to clean something, his jeans torn in two or three places, unravelling. His fly looks like it could be open. Mamie settles against her chair, dabs the tissue against her eyelids again. When he wavers toward Contessa's house, Mamie wonders whether she's glad she fell asleep, whether she's glad she awoke again, here.

Contessa Welch is pleased that the reverend has returned to her. She knows he has been paying unusually frequent visits and thinks it has something to do with Jack, but she isn't sure. Tonight he's left his preacher's clothes at home and somehow she's relieved about this. He never seems comfortable to her in them.

She opens the door wide but he slips in, closes it quickly. He is out of breath. "I'm sorry about the time, Mrs. Welch," he says. "I hope I didn't wake you."

She glances toward the clock—two something, it reads—and the dark windows explain for her the reason for his apology. She drops her hands against the front of her dress, wishing she were dressed for bed. Won't that be what he's expecting, at this hour? Won't he wonder why she's still up? "Oh, Reverend, any time is a good time for you to call," she says, and sees something in his look that she can't read.

"Are you having a difficult time? Adjusting, I mean?"

She thinks, He's talking about Jack's being gone. He's a minister, why can't I talk to him? Do I have to be so on guard with him? Is he just checking for the hospital people?

Her fingers knot and twist around each other. "Reverend—"

"Please call me Clayton, or Clay," he says. "Sometimes we just need friends."

"And you can be my friend?"

"Absolutely, Mrs. Welch, that's why—"

"Tess, please call me Tess, why does everyone keep calling me something else?" She drops onto the sofa, traces with her fingers the raised pattern of lavender lilies and blue irises and healthy green leaves.

"I'm sorry." He sits next to her, lets her take his hands. "How can I help you, Tess? This must be a very difficult time for you...."

"A lot of people say that to me," she says. His hands are soft and she wants to crawl into them like her fingers can, close those hands of his around her, feel safe and not alone.

"It's hard to know the right thing—"

"It's nice that you came," she says. So many things I could say, she thinks, but which ones are the right ones? Which ones if I say them will he send me away for?

"You must miss him."

She nods. "But he—" She wants to say something about him needing his rest, he's been working so long and so hard, but maybe the reverend—Clayton—Clay—won't understand.

She leans into him, presses her head against his chest, wants to press those lost words into him, pull sympathy and understanding or caring back out. She feels the blood rushing through him, thrumming, thrumming, steady, and he is so warm. His arm is gentle around her. He smells of cigarettes like Jack and something about him is familiar. She knows him. She thinks it is a secret that they share, but she can't remember what. "We're friends?"

When he whispers yes to her his breath is sweet against her cheek, his soft fingers easy through her hair, stroking her head, her neck, thrumming in her ear, her fingers reaching to feel that rhythm, that heat that builds next to her.

He doesn't tell, she thinks, somehow I know that. She says, "We have a secret, don't we, Clay? Tess and Clay, who are friends?"

His hands catch her fingers and she pulls them to her breasts, pulls them against the buttons running down the front of her, buttons and thin summer cloth stretched between that warmth and her nipples hard with cold, without Jack. "Can I tell you another secret?" She plants the words in his ear, the words the secret themselves and knows the answer before he gives it, feeling his hands cup her, then drag the dress open from neck to waist.

He glances quick around the room, dark because she never turned the lights on. "Someone might see," he says.

"Carry me," she whispers, arching toward him, making room for his hands beneath her, against her naked back, and she moans and he stumbles up the steps but never falls until the bed catches them and they cover each other with hands and legs and arms and hair and lips and tug away jeans and tee shirt and dress and cover each other again, then again, with not many words, their secret not needing them now.

She waited in the bell tower tonight, waited not for the music this time but for him. She couldn't sit, could only pace from window to window, peering out, peering between narrow slats in the openings that have them, telling him in her head to come. But he didn't. Theodore played, maybe longer than usual, she can't be sure, she barely listened.

Crescent wanders the streets now that the music is gone and the town is dead silent. The breeze lifts her hair from her shoulders, her neck, her forehead, and she helps it along with her fingers, pulling it away from her face, pulling it tight against her head, knotting it over itself. Homemade ponytail. She passes Theodore's house on the walk home, passes in time to still see the attic light on, dim, barely a light at all before it goes out completely.

She walks toward the house, thinking of Theodore climbing down from the attic, down to bed, alone. She circles the house, hoping for lights in windows, finally catching one behind faint, filmy white curtains. She thinks of hiding herself behind a clump of bushes bordering his yard or in the thicket at the back property line, but too afraid she will miss this moment of his privacy, she waits, arms dangling against legs, firm in her position.

She doesn't know what she hopes to see, thinks she might see.

He is a silhouette sometimes, sometimes not. He moves as if performing a ritual—fluffing pillows and turning down the topcover. He unbuttons his shirt but turns away and she glimpses only the back of a man who could be any age— maybe not firm, muscular, but not flimsy and fat. In a flash he has the light off, is, she imagines, in bed. Pajamas, though. She has seen enough.

No wonder he's alone all the time, she thinks. *Pajamas!*

Ben Stevens sits in the kitchen chair. It isn't the sort of kitchen chair he would have guessed would be in Landers Stone's house, seems instead the two-story, aluminum-sided farm house would have a chrome-rimmed, formica-topped table and matching chairs with heavy vinyl seats and backs, something in a faded red or school-bus yellow. Or maybe instead a strong wooden table and chairs matched only by their dark walnut stain. But this table is blond pine, almost a picnic table in its plain lines and sturdy frame. The chairs are Shaker, straw seats with delicately patterned floral cushions. Soft blue and off-white brighten the room. It is a shining room where everything seems perfect except for a faucet that drips and drips below the window where deep night throws the reflection of the room, of their faces, back at them.

There are four of them: Mason Pope, Michael Olson, Ben and, of course, Landers. The clock clicks silent seconds past two-thirty and Ben thinks maybe they should dim the lights, light a few candles, the mood seems right for shadows and whispering, plotting and planning.

"So we are in agreement that we should pursue erecting a museum to preserve the site on the property?" Mason Pope asks, looking first at Ben, who nods, then at Olson, who raises his brows, flicks his hand, saying "Of course." Pope looks across the table at Landers, who has been quiet most of this long, restless meeting. "Well?"

Rubbing his hands across his face, ruddy hands against skin toughened, like his land, by the sun, he says, "Not really up to me. Seems like you got it all planned out."

"You don't sound very convinced," Olson says. "Maybe you should share your concerns with us."

Landers looks at him. He stands, walks to the sink to pour down the drain the coffee that has gotten cold in his cup.

"Listen," Pope says, "if it's about work, don't worry about it. Much of the farm will remain untouched. We'll find a way to compensate you for any wages you might be losing for the loss of that portion of land on which you will no longer be farming."

"Spoken like a true lawyer," Landers says, not very loudly, his back to them, his reflection in the mirror the window makes staring back at them.

"Excuse me?" Pope says, moving his chair back from the table.

Landers waves away the remark, steps away from the sink to face them again. "What does it matter what I think? I just work here."

"Mr. Stone," Olson says, rising to stand next to him,

"we do care what you think. You'll be the one most directly affected by any changes. Your lifestyle could be upset. What you think can make the difference in how things are decided."

"Sounds like everything is decided."

"Well, like whether or not the house will still be convenient for you or whether it should be a gift shop, whether it would be better for you and Mrs. Stone to have a new house a little away from the site, from the people who would be working here, from the people who would be visiting."

Mason Pope rises from the table, pulls his jacket from the back of the chair. "Not that you have to decide such a thing tonight, Landers. But I think we will be needing to finish our plans so we can propose to the bank, to the university, what we're thinking of doing."

Ben sits in the ladder-back chair, his fingers stroking the sides of its seat where the straw winds around the frame, bends from topside to underneath. The straw is smooth to his touch if he rubs it in one direction. In the other, it bristles, itches his fingers. He fingers his mug, stares at the pattern on the porcelain.

The men around gather their jackets.

"I talked to George Freeman today," Landers says suddenly, and they all turn to look at him. His face tells them nothing except that he is glad to have their attention.

"You what?" Mason Pope presses his hands onto the top ladder of the chair he was sitting on, leans into it.

"I went by his house, asked him what he thinks about all this." Landers gestures around the room and at first it isn't clear whether he means the burial ground or the meetings they have been having here and there, this one and that one—now finally all together.

"And he couldn't tell you, could he?" Mason says, standing upright again, sighing. "He can't understand this, Stone, I'm telling you. Didn't you think I really spoke to him when

None But The Dead And Dying

I said I did?" His voice rises. "Do you really doubt that there is no way he can decide any of this?"

He walks to Landers, his face reddening, his hands in fists, clutching his suit jacket. "And what did you find out? Nothing, right? Because the man's an imbecile, he's retarded, what does he know?" He jabs a finger at Landers' chest, nearly shouting. "Stay away from Freeman, Landers. He is my client, he can't handle these things. Understand?"

He doesn't wait for a reply. The door bangs behind him and they hear his car start in the driveway.

Ben thinks about the Indians in their campers parked along the township road. What do they hear? What do they think?

Olson claps Landers on the shoulder, shakes his head because there is nothing any of them can say, except, "Thanks for the coffee." Olson heads for the door and, there, turns. He pushes his glasses up his nose, runs his hands through his red hair. "We really will try to design something that won't invade your lifestyle," he says as he walks through the door.

Landers rubs his palms against his eyes, breathes out long and heavy. Across the room Ben sees that Bessie has heard them, has come downstairs, her robe pulled around her, her graying hair bunched around her head, destroyed by tossing and turning and, if she's been lucky, by sleep. Landers crosses to her and holds her, folding her into him, and Ben knows that he has been forgotten, so he gathers his own coat quietly and makes sure the door closes gently behind him.

Eddy stands outside the motel door but even in a town this size, with not so many lights, even here it is hard to see the stars. Like the glint in someone's eye from across the room they wink at him and they are just as fickle, teasing him, waiting for him to flinch just once so they can vanish on him. He tries to hold their stare but can't. He wishes for a cigarette but he has given the pack away to the reverend. He wishes for sleep but he has maybe given that away too, to Crescent, the girl with the legs and the dreams that should stay in her sleep.

He strolls into the parking lot, away from the lights next to the doorways that welcome no one, but the stars get no brighter, no closer. From here there was no saxophone tonight, the stretching of the town out this way to the highway too far for it, and he misses it. He wonders if this could be why he hasn't been able to sleep.

Maybe it's not the girl and her invitations at all. Maybe it's not the visions that keep coming back of the man on the cement factory floor, of the blood someone had to mop up when everyone else had gone away. Maybe it's not the reverend with his odd way of not wanting to really be a reverend. Maybe it's not the wish for a cold, cold beer like the sign in the carry-out across the road keeps saying to him.

He walks to the cyclone fence around the pool that sits unfilled. No one, they've told him, ever uses it so why fill it? He climbs the fence, unstacks one of the plastic chairs and sets it near the edge of the deep end. Slumping into it, he stretches his legs out in front of him, crossing them at the ankles.

Maybe it's not the burial pit or the dozen or more bodies that must have been buried there, long ago, paid the proper respects and now brushed and posed and photographed like prized dogs for a judging or a Miss America in all her bathing-suit empty-smile glory.

Maybe it's not any of that. Maybe it's the silence, even the trucks along Route 20 stopping in for the night, the birds nestled in, the crickets and locusts and train whistles done until dawn. Maybe it's the silence, the sound without the horn, without the soul of the man who sings to the town his joy and fear and sadness. Just the silence.

11

hen Eddy Light Sky enters the sanctuary, he sees the eyes follow him, sees the hands cupped in front of mouths and knows what's being said behind them, knows that any appearance he makes outside the plant or the Bahama Lounge or motel parking lot creates this chatter about him, and how can he blame them? What is this Lakota doing in this Ohio town, in this Protestant church?

He finds a seat and, sitting, tugs at his collar. The new shirt is stiff at the collar and cuffs and the new boots are hot in the summer heat. The pew is flat and unpadded, the wood hard against his back. He wants sleep, and when he bows his head at the reverend's command, he hopes he'll stay awake.

"Dear Father," Reverend Bleu says, "we reach out our questioning souls to you on this day to ask after the fate of our friend, husband, coworker John 'Jack' Welch, that we may be led to understand your mysterious ways. We ask that you bless us with an understanding that may help us to understand our own lives better, that we may be more thankful than perhaps we have been for those we take for granted...."

Eddy glances up to see the preacher clutch a handkerchief to his face, wiping sweat or tears and Eddy knows he's wishing for a cigarette, knows he's wishing he were in the country or anyplace other than here, doing this service for a man they're saying knew the die was dropping, had time but didn't move, almost smiled they say, to see it slamming toward him. But why not move? Why not save yourself? That's the question now.

He recognizes the widow, Mrs. Welch, elegant in her black chiffon dress that looks more suited to dancing than a funeral for a husband. He recognizes her from the glance they traded at the Country Inn downtown that day, then from her porch across from Mamie Van Allen's. Her back is rigid, her head directed at the reverend.

But the reverend never looks at her, avoids her even when making mention of Jack Welch's husbandly loyalty and devotion. He gives her no look of sympathy, understanding, support, of whatever it is ministers are taught or learn on their own that they should convey to grieving spouses. The reverend is talking quickly, scrambling words sometimes, a twitch at the corner of his mouth.

Eddy wonders if preachers like Reverend Bleu drink. Wonders if he should suggest they go for one afterwards, or maybe tonight.

Eddy tugs at the collar of his shirt again, gives in to the starch in it and undoes the top two buttons, rolls up his sleeves to the middle of his forearm. He's the only man here not in a sport coat or suit. He notices this, but it doesn't affect him. He's in black. He didn't know Jack that well.

Crescent crosses her legs at the knees again, knowing this pulls her hem high up her thigh, wishes Eddy would look this way. If Eddy would look maybe it won't matter so much that Denny is sitting with Hope. They invited her to join them, but she shook her head and said something polite although she didn't feel at all polite, felt even worse when Eddy walked past, not noticing her, and she was too embarrassed to say hello to him. He's sitting alone, too, though, and for that she is glad—sees some reassurance in it.

Her parents are here somewhere, too, but she hasn't bothered to sort them out of the crowd, and crowd there is, the pews nestling people next to each other who haven't spoken in years. The humidity, the sticky air that hangs heavy in the church, will pull this afternoon's service out like a rubber band—stretch it and stretch it until the thing snaps and the service is over, everybody breathing again in fresh outdoor air.

Theodore Thompson comes in, late, and he looks for a place to sit, his brow furrowing deeper and deeper, so she waves him over, moves tighter to the man she thinks runs the barber shop at Main and Buckeye. Theodore wedges in next to her at the end of the pew. His suit is the same new one he wore for his mother's service. He is quiet next to her until they sing and when he offers up his tenor it is clear and wonderful and for a moment Crescent wishes he sang at night, too, and thinks maybe he does but no one can hear that part.

Something about him being next to her or Eddy across the room or Denny and Hope together up front remind her of school soon, of Ohio State and of not being here, and it occurs to her that even before drafty winter gusts force him to close the windows around the attic she will have stopped hearing him. As loud and long and clear as he plays, the sound will never carry all the way to Columbus.

She touches his hand, not caring that he doesn't know why, and when he looks at her, surprised and puzzled, she smiles sadly and gives his fingers a squeeze, nodding toward the closed coffin as if this has to do with Jack Welch, though it doesn't at all, and when a tear drops across her

None But The Dead And Dying

cheek he hands her his handkerchief.

The service ends before long and they walk together out of the church, she dabbing at her eyes a bit more before handing him back the handkerchief. "Oh," she says, reaching for it again, pointing to a smudge of black against the bleached white, "Oh, I'm sorry, Mr. Thompson. I must have smeared mascara into it." Scattered flakes. Indelible.

"Don't be silly, Cress. I can get another," he says.

They are at the curb, people pouring around them who discuss which car to drive to the cemetery. He folds the handkerchief neatly, presses it with his hands, flattens it back into his pocket. He looks at her and she knows what it is he is going to say. "I saw you."

She smiles. "The thing is whether you liked seeing me there or not," she answers, walking away because it doesn't matter what he might say.

She couldn't imagine sitting in the church today for the service, and so she has made this visit to pay her respects and now Mamie shifts in the soft sofa, wishes the iced tea weren't so far, so awkward to reach. Once she was so good at this visiting, sitting in front rooms with parents to discuss in earnest tones the progress or lack of it in their children. Now it is a rare thing to venture out, to expend the energy, the time it takes to sit and pretend concern or amusement or interest. But the death they're now calling suicide and the Reverend Bleu's visit here to see Contessa have brought her across the street, have seated her in this gaudy lavender living room, seated her just far enough from her cooling drink to make her suffer even more for it.

"My it's been a hot summer," Mamie says. It is a simple comment, the sort of remark everyone is making these days, but it stirs Contessa to examine the control for the central air conditioning.

"Perhaps I've overused it," Contessa says. "Perhaps they've cut my supply." She twists the knob on the wall.

"Maybe it just needs looked at. Do you have the Yellow Pages?" Mamie asks.

"Oh, yes, we must find someone who can come out and make the adjustment," Contessa says, carrying her skirt to make it flounce like a square-dancer's petticoated dress. She fumbles in a drawer near the telephone and with a "Voila!" brandishes the thin directory. "Let's see... What do you think it would be listed under, Mamie?"

"Try 'air conditioning—repair.'" Mamie struggles to the edge of the sofa, reaches across the gap to the coffee table, brings the glass to her lips. How can she worry over Contessa's struggle to make a call when she has so much trouble herself just picking up a glass? But she listens anyway, listens for the way she describes the problem, the way she gives the address, directions, sets a time. All seems okay. Mamie sighs. Maybe she has been overreacting.

Contessa drops as if exhausted into the chair near the sofa, collects her own glass and sips. "This heat must be awful for you, Mamie," she says.

"No more than for anyone else, I would guess." But she doesn't want to talk about the weather. She is studying Contessa's pose in the chair, her daintily crossed legs, the angling of the ankles, the tilt of her head, the pressing of her arms across her chest to create deeper cleavage. "I've noticed the reverend has come by to help see you through this, Contessa," she says.

"Yes, to help me through. Yes, of course he has. And my sister, too, don't forget. And Theodore. Lots of people have come to help me through. And here you are." She giggles the high school giggle Mamie had shushed in class many times.

But nobody else came at two in the morning, Mamie

thinks. "I'm glad, Contessa," she says. "I'm glad everyone has been so helpful."

Contessa sips her own drink. "Poor Jack," she says.

"Yes," Mamie says. "Poor Jack."

Bessie is telling him about the funeral, listing the names of the people who were there as if she memorized the guest book to tell him. Many of his old classmates showed up, it sounds like, and Landers wishes again he could have gone but it seems more and more he has to stay at the farm.

Today more press have arrived. Word of Daniel Yellow Wolf's appearance continues to spread and more camera crews are back, some of them with the same reporters and technicians who hollered hello to the crew in the pit and to Landers. It's been like a reunion here, a reunion Landers would rather miss.

Bessie finishes rinsing the dishes at the sink and Landers punches a few more numbers into his calculator at the desk. "Something weird about the reverend, though," she says, and Landers looks up.

"What, honey?"

She picks up a dishrag, starts drying a mixing bowl. She made up some potato salad in it for the funeral dinner though she didn't stay for it. "You seen the Reverend Bleu lately?" she asks. He shakes his head. "Well, something's not right there. He just stumbled all over that eulogy today and I felt so sorry for Connie about it but she didn't seem to notice, poor thing."

"Not right in what way?" he asks. He punches a few more numbers but they don't mean anything. He's given up trying to make sense, this afternoon, of the bills, the government forms he's supposed to finish filling out.

"I'm not sure I know."

"Maybe he just had an off day," Landers says. He piles the receipts and papers neatly atop each other, sets the calculator over everything.

Her rag still in her hand, she comes to him, hugs him where he sits, and he scoots his chair out from under the table. He slaps his hands on his thighs. "Come sit, Bess," he says, and she grins, it's been so long. Maybe they'll collapse the chair, but they don't, they just hold each other this way.

Through the screens in the door and windows they hear the drum start again, the chanting. When it was first quiet Landers went outside, maybe some trouble was starting, and that's when he saw the camera crews back, Yellow Wolf in the midst of them, telling them they should not photograph any time they wish but need to listen carefully for directions about appropriate times to film and snap and ask their many questions.

Landers pats Bessie on the back, kisses her cheek, and she gets up from him. One last hug and she leaves him to wipe more dishes while he wanders to the screen door.

The men at the drum sit just outside the circle, each one with a stick in hand outstretched, hitting, hitting, hitting for the rhythm they need. One man chants, the others join sometimes. These chants are beginning to sound different from each other to Landers. They are for different purposes, he is sure, but he cannot bring himself to ask about them.

Daniel Yellow Wolf chants with them, sits in the drum circle with them though he does not hit the drum. For the next chant he dances in a circle and the women fall in behind him, their feet shuffling in a way that makes Landers think of syncopated walking, and, watching them, makes him want to join in.

After the dance the drum is quiet for a few minutes and Yellow Wolf announces to the gathered media and local people who've come back that there will be a dance at dawn, a ceremonial dance and calling to the spirits. "We know there is unrest here," Yellow Wolf says, "because there has been a disturbance. Those who are trying to move on have been stopped, are being held back, and they want to be free to make their journey. If you return at sunrise," he says to the crowd, "please bring no cameras, no taping equipment of any sort. You must respect the sacredness of this."

Cameras click and snap and whirr while they automatically wind and rewind and Daniel Yellow Wolf steps to the edge of the circle to speak to the reporters waiting there.

He is cooler in handling this than any of the rest of them, Landers thinks, watching from the back door of the house.

"What's he going to do when he finds out about the museum?" Landers asks, but Bessie, least of all, knows the answer.

He is beginning to know that the farther out he must park along the road, the longer he must walk, the more people there are at the site and the more attention they are all getting. Mayor Ben Stevens, knowing these things, slams the door of his car and starts down the hot old tar of the road toward the house.

The sun falls all over the land. Ahead, the road nearly squeezes shut with the cars and trucks and trailers and vans and portable satellite dishes and people walking, some carrying coolers and he wonders if this means they have come to picnic. He nears these folks who might be migrant workers or might be Indians, calls out a hello but they make only the smallest waves before crawling into the camper backs of trucks. Ben curls up his shirt sleeves. It has to be over a hundred degrees in there, he thinks.

The driveway is choked off by a crowd of people in shorts and tee shirts and damp flesh, the sun licking at them, leaving them sticky and smothered and miserable. Only the television people are unaffected, their bright white smiles and crisp shirts and blouses and dry hair separating them from the rest of the crowd, even when they are not clutching microphones, staring into cameras.

Ben is glad he has worn a shirt meant to be open at the neck, glad he has thought to put on running shoes instead of dress shoes. He sweeps his hand across his head, tracking down a few loose hairs and pressing them into place over the thin spot. He waves to Landers Stone where he stands on his back porch, a few steps up, elevating him just enough to see and be seen over the heads of everyone else.

It is a quiet crowd, talking, waiting, hands on hips or cupped around eyes to see past the others. On tiptoe Ben looks, too, sees that a wide circle has been staked out and in the midst of it Indians sit near a silent drum, talking, eating sandwiches and drinking from cans of Pepsi and Coke. To one side he sees a particular man who is speaking to a reporter he recognizes from Toledo's TV-13 news.

He nudges his way through the throng and climbs the porch steps, shakes Landers hand. "Quite a turnout today, eh?"

Landers looks at him. "You make it sound like you planned it."

Ben shakes his head, chuckles. "Not me. But this has got to mean that they'll all have to eat and sleep someplace."

"A lot of them are staying here, camping out." Landers nods toward the migrant camp down the road a bit, heading up the rise. "Using water from the camp there. Seems like the migrants and them are making friends."

"You'll feel that in your water bill," Ben says. "You could tell them you need to charge them to make up for it."

Landers unfolds his arms, drops his hands into jeans pockets, sighs. "I could."

They watch the crowd shift as the drum beat starts, can see from here that some dancing is starting, slow, around the circle, men and women. "You must be getting pretty tired of this. I mean, they do this all day long, don't they?" Ben asks.

He shrugs. "Could be worse, I suspect."

"Worse? Why? Have you heard something I ought to know about?"

Landers studies him and Ben thinks there is a smirk in his eyes, on his lips. He shakes his head.

"Come on, Landers, you know we got to keep on top of this."

When Landers starts down the porch steps, heads toward the digging, Ben follows. The path is well-beaten, has been much-travelled. Across the yanked-up earth in the back yard Ben can see that the new water line, the digging that started all this, is being laid, and piping sits along the fresh ditch. It makes him wonder why nothing was found along there, why only here, in this spot.

Diamond Richards guards the way while behind him, new activity, the erection of a chain-link fence, silver white and blinding when it catches the sun the wrong way. A dozen or so men unwind the fencing, pull it taut from one fence post to the next. The fencing cuts further into the back yard of the house, further into the nearby corn, the dirt fresh at its base.

Inside the new stretch of fence they reach the edge of the pit where the workers stoop over their finds, this day looking no different to Ben than the earlier visits he has made. There are so many things to catalogue, to identify, sorting one rock from another because one is an ancient hammer, maybe, and another is just a rock.

Olson has seen them and scrambles toward them. "We think we've just about uncovered all we're going to," he says. He gestures around the perimeter of the site. "The site is confined, we're sure, to this area."

"Is that good?" Ben asks, squinting against the sun to

glance around the edge of the pit. On down the hill on the one side he sees the top of the silver fence wavering, uncoiling, circling the area.

"It means you can plan a building, something more permanent, because the site area has been defined," Olson says.

"Good, good." He looks at Landers. "You call Mason about this yet? He can talk to that architect he was thinking of."

"He knows about it," Landers says.

"Given the mood, that there are those who wish to see the excavation end, I think we should move quickly," Olson says.

In front of them Ben counts fourteen adult skeletons, arm, leg, rib, spine bones intact, a few of the skulls gaping laughter or screams or shouted words from another world. Most, though, lie face down, as if they were shoved head first into the pit, faces jammed into the ground for good measure. Around them, atop them, are those of little children, of babies. "What do you know about what killed them?" Ben asks and Olson blinks, then looks back into the pit.

"Well, that's what we need to find out," Olson says. "Of course what's been most unusual around here is the number of what I like to call breech burials—better than three-quarters of these burials are face down rather than face up. We've of course seen this before but not on this scale, so the practice has never been examined very closely. We still have more questions than answers, I'm afraid, like, were they buried by friends or enemies? Why in this position? Could have been a disease that was thought to bring evil, so they were interred this way to protect the living or something. Who knows?"

A disease, way back then, before smoking, asbestos, AIDS, Ben thinks. What sort of diseases were there?

"A colleague of mine at the university is starting the grants application process," Olson says, "and I've asked him to request that we make this a working lab so we could get some equipment here, do much of the analysis on site so we don't have to disturb very much. There's so much we can tell just by the arrangement that we would prefer not to move things around. Certainly we can record placement and we can be very exact about it, but already a few people have expressed some interest in coming down to see the site itself, so the longer we can retain its form, the better."

"Whatever you think is best," Ben says. He turns to Landers. "I'm going to send down a couple of our regular force to help out Diamond. How he gets his sleep is beyond me."

Olson removes his glasses, takes a handkerchief from his back pocket, breathes on the lenses and smears away the dust and sweat. "With these extra people coming around, it's a good idea to bring on more security."

A breeze kicks up dust around them. In the pit someone sneezes, and there is laughter. Landers calls out "Bless you," and Kathy calls back, "Thank you."

Ben glances at the crowd in the driveway. "You think the Indians are planning anything?"

Olson shakes his head. "They're the last ones to disturb anything. What they want is for things to be left alone. I'm telling you that the worry is in artifact traders."

"Arrowhead hunters?" Ben asks. As a kid he hunted them himself, walking long rows between broken corn stalks in the warm fall, eyes on the ground, watching for a glint of something that always, for him, turned out to be a sliver of plastic bag or a bottle cap.

"It's more than that, now," Olson says, starting to explain, while beside them Landers turns and walks away, toward the corn, away from the burial site through the space the fencing hasn't yet filled.

The dim bar, even at this late afternoon hour, takes a minute to get used to, and so the reverend blinks, rubs his eyes to smudge the darkness in, opens them to the thought that here he can think. A drink to clear his head. Or jumble it. Either one will do.

From the end of the bar Eddy Light Sky holds an amber glass up to him and Reverend Bleu follows it like a beacon, slides onto the neighboring bar stool. In front of them, against the dark wood wall, sit dozens of bottles and glasses. They're dark like the room, most of them, dark and private.

The men drink. The reverend bums a cigarette, sighs, swallows long and hard. "Baptize 'em, marry 'em, bury 'em," he says. He snubs the cigarette out, swallows a handful of peanuts. "Doesn't matter where you do the job, it's the same damn thing."

"What about the rest of it?" Eddy asks.

"It's all babysitting in between. Doesn't matter whether you're at their house or they're at the office or in some old people's home or at the hospital, it's all hand-holding. Babysitting. Or maybe like courting." He swallows again from the heavy glass mug, motioning for a refill. "Maybe too much like courting."

"Then why keep doing it?"

"Maybe because it's like courting," he says, and grins, but it is the very question he has been asking himself for days, maybe even for months now. And the question just keeps going around and around, gathering half-hearted answers the way Sandy collects towels and laundry for the wash: Because people need it. Maybe because I need it. Because Sandy wants me to. Because this is what I know. Because it's secure. Because it's easy. Maybe because there's nothing else.

"The question assumes options," he says, licking foam from his lip.

"You don't think there are any?"

None But The Dead And Dying

He shakes his head, raps his fingers against the bar. "No offense, Eddy, but the plant isn't for me."

"Who said it was? What about other things?"

"This is what I know. This is what I do."

Eddy fingers an unlit cigarette. "I think it's something else keeps you tied into it," he says.

"You going to smoke that thing or play with it?" the reverend asks, and Eddy hands it to him. He lights it, draws on it and feels the red hot burning inside him and it hurts but it is the right thing to feel. "Like what?"

"Like a title," Eddy says. "Identity. This is who you are. And it's easy. When you're a preacher all kinds of things are already decided for you. You don't barely have to make any tough choices, I bet."

"So?"

"Good way to never have to think about anything."

"Bullshit," Clayton says, but he knows that Eddy is right, that it is not thinking that he wants, not about Contessa or Sandy or Hope or what happened to Jack. "You don't know shit about being a preacher."

Eddy drops a twenty on the bar, gives the reverend a clap on the back before heading for the door. "Devil make you say that?"

At first, the reverend doesn't know whether to laugh and when he does, Eddy has already stepped back into the town.

12

he bulbous clouds hang heavy, withholding rain with a mean stare, a triumphant rumble far away and not getting any closer to this back porch. The reverend is wet already with sweat dripping from armpits and upper lip and behind knees, and when he wipes his hand across his face the sweat is light, easy to flip away, but nothing dries or stays dry in this humidity.

He is a little drunk and he has been trying to remember the last time he has had so much to drink. A small glass of champagne at New Year's, a bit of wine on a special occasion, but drunk? And he wants another cigarette but is afraid Sandy will see that he has violated this half of a vow they made after Hope was born, the little girl named for their hope they could keep it: he would quit smoking if she would take off fifteen pounds and keep it off. This has been the way they could cheat on each other—eating or smoking.

Even the little things, he thinks, are coming apart.

Her footsteps come across the laundry room linoleum, heading for the door he leans his back against. He straightens up, gives her room to come out if she wants but she stands over him behind the screen. "Honey, where's Hope?" she asks.

"Haven't seen her," he says, watching a squirrel dangle

upside down in the overgrown mulberry at the corner of the porch. The tiny front claws grab berries, stuff them into the mouth that's guarded by fangs the reverend imagines would pierce him like a cluster of needles. He shudders.

"She isn't still hanging around with that St. Clair girl, is she?"

The screen door snaps and twangs and Sandra is beside him, her fifteen pounds still gone, with maybe a few more lost as well. "That girl is no good for her, she hangs out with that boy Denny who is nothing but trouble." She sits with her bare feet on the next step, her blue-jeaned knees high in front of her and she leans her elbows on them, resting her head in her right hand. Her soft brown hair drops along her shoulder.

He watches the squirrel. He doesn't know Crescent that well, doesn't know Denny at all. "Maybe he's a nice boy," the reverend says.

She drops her arms, raises her head to him. "Clayton, what's going on with you?"

He expects her touch but doesn't feel it. The squirrel scampers down a limb that falls closer and closer to the ground, clambers toward the hard berries, but he's halfway down the length of the next branch before the reverend sees it as a way out.

"What are you thinking about back here?" She scans the back yard, the sky, the trees that beg, too, for rain, their leaves trying to wave the rain down, frantic for it. The air is moist but it isn't enough and everything seems to sigh in disgust and frustration.

He is thinking about the squirrel, that it is an animal but that it has more guts, will take the risks. He wants to put his arm around his wife, feel her shoulder in the palm of his hand, but he can't think how. Once he would have prayed with her about what was bothering him, but it seems like not enough now, that the only things that matter are the squirrel and the clouds, the clouds storing up their rain but not letting it loose like a kid at a water fountain holding the cold, wet liquid in his mouth, his cheeks fat, not swallowing. Maybe somebody should smack the clouds like somebody pinches the kid's cheeks to make the water squirt. Maybe that's all it needs.

He knows he should answer her about what he's thinking or about Hope but he hasn't had any answers for so long, just questions, and he's empty.

"Clayton," she says, but all he can tell her is, "Not yet. Not yet."

The pipe in his hands is cold, has not been used in a long time. Eddy's fingers cover its smooth surface, the long thin shaft with the dangling leather straps and beads. Lone Hawk saw to its making for him and it has always carried a bit of her. So far he is from his people, his homeland, where the smoking of the pipe is sacred and shared and something he never thought he would miss. The elders knew, though. He remembers Granger Running Deer at Rosebud and Little Turtle Climbing at Pine Ridge and the looks on their faces when he said goodbye. He remembers their words to him, words about finding places that no longer exist, finding places that never were. Eddy had smiled, sure of all the answers, and said, "Maybe a place yet to be."

Through four pairs of shoes and three trips through all seasons he walked, looking and looking and listening for the right sounds and feeling for the right spot on Mother Earth's belly. Now he holds the pipe and it is still cold.

He's wished for someone to talk to, but it seems everyone he meets would rather talk than listen, too.

Going on or staying, he thinks, are almost the same thing. All this time going, going, never getting, and staying is not enough, either. He thinks of the people at the burial site, the people who are his people though he doesn't know them, the people alive around the drum, the people who know the ways of those who have now been awakened, after so many years asleep.

He places the pipe to his lips but its bowl is empty and he cannot smoke it anyway.

No one, he thinks, will disturb Jack Welch.

The rain is coming, they can all feel it. It has taken so long but now it races for them, coming at them fast and angry and they must hurry to pull the tarp overhead. Olson shouts orders to his crew and they circle the site, stepping carefully around to pull the tarp across but the breeze grows into wind and they struggle with the weight of it, the bulk of it, trying to hold it, to catch the flying ropes that must anchor it to the fencing around.

"I don't think this will be enough," Olson shouts to Landers. "It'll be too high. We're going to have to drop the tarp over top, weight it somehow," and he is looking, already, for things of weight that won't crush what is underneath, but there is nothing, it will all take on water.

"Anchor it low, angling it down off the east side for runoff, then fortify the sides." Yellow Wolf signals to a few men who watch him pull a corner of the tarp against a fence post and begin tying it, yanking it strong into a knot that holds it safe. They scramble to anchor the sides a few feet above the rim of pit, reaching nimble fingers through the fencing to tie its ends. "There might be some damage to the inside edges," he says to Olson, "but it should help."

One of the drummers who is fuller through the middle when he stands, watches the sky shift and blow overhead. "Coming from the northwest," he says, and they scramble to fortify that side, propping bedrolls and blankets, hanging some of them from the fence to close those sides in and when they are done they stare at a tent low to the ground, a circus big top for tiny people.

The rain comes fast, fat drops splattering heads and shoulders, and in the scramble for cars and trucks and vans Landers pulls Olson and Yellow Wolf toward the house. The wind grabs hold of the tarp, yanking it, trying to lift it off, but it holds, shuddering but intact.

Inside the kitchen they laugh uneasily and whip rain from their clothing, flapping arms and hands and shaking their heads. "Came up sudden," Olson says, but Yellow Wolf and Landers smile to each other.

They stand near doors and windows, watching the storm come in, watching the tarp waver in the wind. "The one side slants some," Yellow Wolf says, "and that should send the water running off it, should send it down the ridge and keep it out of the pit entirely."

Olson walks to him, extends his hand. "Thank you," he says. "I can't tell you how I appreciate it."

Yellow Wolf ignores the offered handshake. "We didn't do it for you," he says, but there is no meanness in it, it is only a blunt admission, and Olson nods his head, understanding.

"Coffee?" Bessie says, holding up a pot to show that it is already brewed and the men nod and settle around the kitchen table.

This, Landers thinks, is more like it. He introduces the two men and they eye each other, and behind them Bessie cracks open a Pillsbury tube of cinnamon rolls, arranges them in a round cake dish.

The rain rattles against the window, a hard rain. He sees in his mind a corner of his tomato fields where the rain drains poorly, listens for the rain to back off, a sign it might not flood the low areas, that it will be just enough to bring the crops back, not take them under again, another way.

And so they speak of the rain and of the crops and finally, the room washed in the scent of cinnamon, Landers says, "I think, Mr. Olson, you ought to tell Mr. Yellow Wolf just what you've got in mind for that burial site."

Olson is surprised to be put on the spot this way, Landers can see it in the way he swallows his coffee, the look on his face. "I really don't think now's the time," he says.

Yellow Wolf looks from Landers to Olson. Today he wears a black band around his forehead, his hair loose on his shoulders and wet from the rain. Landers says, "Now's the best time. Just us. Next to George Freeman, we're the ones who count. So, you want to tell him about the museum or should I?"

Olson nearly drops his mug and Landers, for a second, feels sorry for the man. Behind all those freckles and that pair of glasses and the university title, he's just a kid. A kid playing in the dirt.

"Museum?" Yellow Wolf says. "This must be what your late night rendezvous was all about." He leans back in his chair but accepts a refill in his mug from Bessie and smiles his thanks when she loosens a roll from the cake pan and slides it onto a plate in front of him.

Olson looks at Landers but Landers nods to Yellow Wolf. He is an honest man, speaks his mind, says what he wants. He has missed that lately. "I tried to talk to George Freeman about that," Landers says, "but Mason Pope isn't so far from wrong when he says old George can't quite understand."

"What do you mean?" Olson asks.

"Well, I think he understands pretty well, but he has trouble getting across what it is he thinks." Landers turns again to Yellow Wolf. "George has had a problem nearly all his life with talking to people. Most folks think he's real retarded, can't make sense of things that are much complicated, but when I spoke to him yesterday he seemed to maybe understand. But he just can't talk."

Yellow Wolf finishes the last forkful of the warm roll. "Thank you, Mrs. Stone," he says. "That's quite a nice thing on a night like this." She says he's welcome, that he should feel a little more at home, she hopes, and he nods. To Landers he says, "So Mr. Pope can't really know for sure what it is that Mr. Freeman wants."

"Well, certainly he has Mr. Freeman's best interests at heart," Olson says.

"Money isn't everything to everybody," Yellow Wolf says. He rises from the table. "I thank you Mrs. Stone, again, for the wonderful baking and coffee. And you, Mr. Stone, for your hospitality and understanding." To Olson he says, "Though you think otherwise, a museum is not what you want to do here."

"We would be preserving the site," Olson says. "It's the best way to keep from disturbing things, to keep the site and still be able to appreciate it."

Landers knows this is the wrong thing to say. Yellow Wolf steps closer to Olson, sits again in the chair beside him at the table. "It is the best way for you to keep what you want. It is the best way for Mr. Pope to make money and for Mr. Stevens to bring in more revenue to the community. It is not the best thing for those who were put to rest only to be disturbed again. They have not asked anything of you, Mr. Olson, so why do you think you can keep taking and taking from them? What right do you have to disturb the peaceful resting place of the dead?"

Olson stares at him, blinks, and Yellow Wolf nods one last time to the Stones before stepping out into the rain.

When the rain slams into the earth, hitting the ground hard, Contessa Welch is standing on the asphalt edge of

None But The Dead And Dying

Arch Street, at the dead end where street ends and cornfields begin. The rain shivers down on her but she stands rigid, not feeling it, seeing again the refrigerator—so simple it had been, to flick that handle, break that seal, open that door that held tight her Deborah. From one side a seal so sure and tight no amount of pushing or screaming or begging or cries for Mommy could loosen it. So hard to die, so hard to find, curled up in the corner, shriveled, it seemed, from fear and despair and giving up, the refrigerator not cold enough to keep her but so hot and tight and no way out and why oh why oh why oh Mommy Mommy please come and get me Mommy why oh oh why did I ever want to play this stupid game and why did I think this would be the best place to the very best place why don't they find me why won't the door push open when it pushed closed so easy?

And the law not helping because some people not paying any attention, it's back on the property nobody's supposed to go back there I had no idea some little kid might come onto my property and get into it anyway how can you blame me the man said, and my little girl had to die because he thought the law wasn't for him, my little girl dead, me Contessa Butler Welch who never ever hurt anybody—

"Mrs. Welch? Mrs. Welch?"

She turns into the sound, expecting to see flashing ambulance lights before they take Deborah away where she won't see her again no matter how many times she asks but it is a plain car, a dented car with rust and a young man in it—is that Deborah with him? No, of course not, it's the reverend's daughter and some boy. Clayton—Clay's daughter. "Yes, children?" she says, feeling rain on her, her feet so cold and wet but it hasn't been raining, has it? Today so hot and sunny and dry but maybe that was yesterday.

They are motioning her into the car but maybe they want to take her to the hospital again, the hospital not like the one Jack was in, a hospital with bars and men who touched her rough but she smiled at them anyway and they laughed at her smile.

"Mrs. Welch," the daughter says, "you'll catch a bad cold if you stay out here." The girl's hair is getting wet where she is leaning out the car window, matting against her forehead. Her arm waving Contessa toward the car has rain on it, beaded rain like clear soap bubbles or tiny champagne bubbles.

The girl shouldn't be getting wet, so Contessa gets into the back seat. "Thank you," she says.

"The rain came up pretty sudden," the girl says. "I mean, sunny all day and then—whoosh!" She laughs a stunning laugh and the boy driving laughs and Contessa laughs, too.

The boy says, pulling the car into her driveway, "This is it, right?"

And Contessa says it is, and thanks them. She thinks for a moment that the girl might invite her to her father's church, but she only waves as the car pulls out of the driveway.

Like the day, the night music is sad, whining from the attic windows, moaning into the streets. The rain comes again, trying to shush the horn but the horn blows past the sheer drop of it, careens alongside it, dangles over the edge of it, hangs there before giving up the fight, giving in to the thunder and lightning.

From the street Crescent sees the light high up go out, traces his path through the house by watching the lights go out one by one. She slides her bare feet along slippery grass and watches the bedside light go on, glides again to the front, to the door, tries it and by luck or chance or plan it is open and she's inside, in the dark, her chest pounding, her clothes dripping in quiet pats onto the thinning carpet. She remembers the stairs, mounts them, pausing at creaks, and at the top she follows the sliver of light from an open door.

In the hallway, smooth to the skin she drops her shorts, tank top, slips sideways to stand nervously in the open doorway, her breasts high, nipples rigid, her silken panties shimmering.

His book, paper covers curled in the damp air, in the damp clutch of his fingers, falls flat against the sheets. She steps closer. To him, she knows, she is a dream, a faded memory, vivid again, and frightening in its power to startle him, he who has become so accustomed to the rhythms of his life, the even patterns of now and then and the clear lines between them. These shadows, in this room, blur those patterns.

She strolls toward him on feet steadier than she feels, and crawls from the end of the bed over him, placing with the care of a cat her hands and knees in the crevices between his calves, thighs, arms. The edge of the bed is high off the floor, high like a stage, its blankets and curtains and its headboard the proscenium, Crescent the heroine, crawling forward, her body moving easily despite her shaking hands, the churning inside her that could be fear or excitement or both. She presses into him, the blankets thin between them, her breasts strong against his pajama shirt. She rests her head into the hollow of his shoulder. She sighs, listening, hearing his heart beating but she cannot feel his breathing. "Shh," she says, touching her fingers along the row of flat white buttons, picking at them, tugging them, opening him to her.

"Crescent—"

The attempt is feeble, unneeded, unheeded. His arm drops across her back, his fingers scratchy but kind along her spine, tracing her lines like a painter, pausing low, hesitant to venture further.

"Shh," she says again, and it becomes for them a breathy,

soothing chant, a reassurance. She peels his nightclothes, kisses his graying chest hair, letting the trail of it lead her lips downward, licking the saltiness from him, lathering him, feasting. Her hand guides his lower, lower. "Touch me anywhere," she whispers, showing his touch the openings, the curves, the sleek skin and wet insides.

When she wants him inside he fumbles, nervous hands in the way, not knowing the way, and she guides him, believing but not comprehending his innocence, and this carries her further, strengthens her, and she crawls atop him, sits high and sets the rhythm, swallows his eyes with hers, leans to feel him deep, leans to thrust her breasts, her flat stomach toward his gaze, his amazed eyes, his squinted gasps and release, feeling her own thighs gripping in a relief she has no control over.

He clings to her beyond it, grunting and clawing, and she holds him, kisses his eyelids and temples and neck and lips until he is still, his hardness still within her, his breath heavy, his hands firm about her. She smiles, and rests with him, dozes next to him, then rolls under him, letting him take her, this time.

"And the fireworks," she whispers to him, "aren't for another two nights."

When the July night glows into dawn she unfolds herself from him, retreats in slow motion, watching his dreaming eyes flicker, and tiptoes into the hallway to pull her shorts and tank shirt back on. Down the stairs and onto the walk, then toward home, she can't help thinking how wrong they all have been.

13

ddy sees the man fall from the newly-painted kelly green bike: sees the bike coming smooth down the brick street, close along the orange-yellow curbs that warn not to park there, sees the bike collapse under the man with the twitching head, sees the fall like a cruel joke, a chair made to collapse under an innocent victim. Even from here Eddy sees the surprise in the man's face as he tumbles forward, his arms and legs scattering across the narrow strip of lawn between the sidewalk and the street. Eddy clips into a jog, is at the man's side to help him up but gets the same look of surprise and panic from him. "Hey," Eddy calls, "you okay?"

The man scrambles to his feet, quick but unsteady, and grabs the bicycle. His feet feel for the pedals, his hands clutch the handlebars, but Eddy sees that the back tire is flat, sees it was probably the cause of the fall. But the man, anxious to escape and gaping at Eddy in a toothless, frightened, open-mouthed way, sits on the saddle, his feet trying to pedal then trying to walk the bike, but his weight is too much so he sits on the tattered black vinyl seat trying and trying to go nowhere, his feet slapping the puddles along the curb where the street dips toward sewer grates.

He reminds Eddy of a frightened colt, corralled for breaking, eyes burning, hooves clawing the air, driving back all who come close. "Shh there, friend," Eddy says. "It's okay." He reaches out to the man—not to touch him, not to frighten him further, but to show his hands are bare, an ancient gesture. He carries no weapons, bears no mystery, intends no harm. He points to the curb. "Why don't you come over and sit a minute, catch your breath?"

The man stands, the bike between his greasy pantlegs, the factory-issued green shirt torn and his thin, baby-fine hair sticking up and out. His John Deere hat lies crown-up in the damp grass. He points to the hat. "My."

"Yessir," Eddy says. A breeze ruffles between them like a rude guest at a crowded party and the hat starts to roll. Eddy stoops to pick it up but a child's wail erupts from the man and Eddy freezes without touching it, backs away.

"Mine, *mine*," the man says, and Eddy nods, beginning to understand.

The man drops the bike and it crashes against the curb again. In three long strides the man has collected the cap, set it on his head, its bill askew, its green dark in spots from the wet grass. The man doesn't smile. No look of triumph crosses his face. "Mine," he whispers, and Eddy nods again.

Back to the bike the man walks, tugging the cap firm around his head. Raising it to inspect it, he holds it by the seat, running his fingers across deep gashes in both fenders, slashes of curb paint, black and white primer and missing green. "Ahh," the man says. "Ahh...nahh...." His twitch is a shake now, rapid and fierce and angry and a quick hand to an eye erases a threatening tear. "Ahh...ahh nahhh...."

Helpless, unsure, Eddy stands near. "It's paint, friend. It can be painted again. Your bike can be repainted."

Thick, rough with dirt and work, the man's fingers trace the scrapes as if they were scars of the flesh, as if the bike had died there on the street and these were its wounds and the man now must mourn it. His attention is caught by the flattened tire and he wails again. "Ahh *nahhh!*"

"It'll be okay," Eddy says. He takes a step closer. "It maybe isn't so bad. The rim doesn't even look bent." Even if the rim is bent, he's thinking it might not be too hard to fix.

But the man lets go of the seat and the bike clatters again to the street where a car drives slowly around them, the mother and children in it peering through open windows. The spokes of the bike spin some, and Eddy marvels at the quiet of it. A smooth bike, despite creaking fenders and bright paint.

A few doors have opened along the street and among the onlookers Eddy sees Mamie on her porch a few houses up the street. The man seems unaware of them, is staring at his bike as if daring it to defy him one more time in one more unimaginable way. "Nahh...." he says, his shaking gone now but the twitch back. He walks away from Eddy, from the once bright green, new-looking bike. His step is long and quick and he's soon out of sight around the corner at the end of the block.

They sit on swings in Community Park and gaze at the maze of covered bridges at the bottom of the hill that jump the creek that feeds from Waterworks Pond, bridges with names like The Minuteman Bridge. Another picnic table from the covered, cement-floored shelter near the woods floats in the bend of the creek between two bridges.

"We used to do that," Crescent says to Theodore. "Throw the tables into the creek."

"Goodness," he says, making her grin. "You and Hope?"

She laughs. "Me and Denny." She pumps her legs to swing, swing higher, farther out over the hill. "Come on," she calls to him on a swoop past, "Pump it up, come flying, don't just sit there!"

He struggles to make the swing move but he doesn't get much momentum going, has to hold his feet above the puddles from last night's storm that have made the sand beneath mud.

Crescent soars past him, floating, letting loose her hands, balancing, frightening him, his face giving her a mixture of surprise and amazement and horror. She has been wondering about Denny and Hope, but not so much today, not since last night, not since tempting Theodore away from his lawn mower and leading him by the hand down here as if he were a younger child she were babysitting for the day.

I have the saxophonist, she thinks. I have the midnight musician. Hope can have Denny and Eddy can leave because I still have something nobody else has ever had.

She slows her rhythm, lets her legs go limp, catches the mud with her bare feet like putting brakes on, splashing them.

"Hey!" Theodore scolds but she laughs and he laughs. "You're all muddy," he says.

He never knows what to say, she thinks, and that just makes it even more fun. "I know," she says, stopping the swing, sitting next to him for a minute. She jumps up. "Time to rinse off."

"What?"

But she is running, her arms out next to her, flying on the ground this time, skipping and slipping and managing not to fall down the hill, squealing like a little kid and laughing and feeling her heart pound away at her like there's somebody even farther inside who wants out. At the bottom of the hill she turns to see that he is gingerly stepping sideways, cautiously coming after her. "Hurry!" she says, and it's enough for him to skip a bit.

He's still out of breath when he catches her and she reminds herself he's old. Maybe even older than her parents. "What are you up to now?" he says.

None But The Dead And Dying

She jogs to the edge of the creek, slipping down to sit on its bank. It is maybe two feet deep and runs about seven feet across. The banks are weedy and stony, but they are enough for sitting, for fishing. She plunges her bare feet and legs into the water, swishing them to loosen the mud. "Rinse cycle!"

He laughs and his face wrinkles in places she can see it's not used to. "I don't know about you, Cress," he says, shaking his head, but he crouches to sit next to her.

"I know about you," she says, knowing her words will surprise him, and they do.

"What do you know?"

"I know that you haven't been happy much," she says.

He pulls his legs up, clasps his skinny knees with his arms, his hands holding his elbows. He stares across the murky water. "Tomorrow night I guess this is where people will be," he says.

"Fireworks, yep," she says. "You're changing the subject. I know about your mother, how she was sick all those years. That must have been very hard. Some people decide on nursing homes, but you didn't."

He shrugs. "Didn't seem like there was any sense to that," he says, and she isn't sure if he means to the nursing home or the illness that cost so much life.

"You had to miss out on a lot," she says. "Is that why you came back from college like they said you did? Because your mother was maybe already sick?"

She's heard the stories, the clinging mother who was always just a little too close to her son, who couldn't bear their distance; the timid son who let the saxophone speak for him because the words never came out right, who couldn't find the way to make it speak for him someplace else.

He unfolds his legs and she thinks for a minute he will stand and leave her, but she sees that he has been watching the ducks sail on the water toward the other bank along the pond where a young mother and two little kids crumple bread from a bag and toss it into the water.

"You'll be leaving this summer, won't you?" he asks.

"*The* Ohio State University," she says, wondering, is he asking because he will miss me?

"Looking forward to it?"

She paddles her feet under the water, watches the foam churn on the surface. "It's a way out of here. I can't wait."

"Here isn't so bad," he says. "Here you have friends and people know you, can help you if you need it."

"There's the plant and the bars and the churches. Though maybe the burial ground will make things more interesting for awhile. But they'll probably figure out a way to fuck that up, too—excuse me!" She presses a damp hand to her mouth. "Sorry. Excuse my language."

He does look surprised, but doesn't, she can see, know what to say. She goes on, "I just can't understand why somebody with the chance to get out, to be other places, do other things, would ever want to come back here."

She dries her hand on her tee shirt. Leaning back on his hands, his body and feet outstretched in front of him, Theodore moves his head in a sort of "Well..." response. She pulls her feet from the water and crawls closer to him, wraps her arm around his waist. "You can tell me this," she says.

He studies her a minute and she thinks that he is not old again, that he flashes back and forth as though there is a little time machine right inside of him that pulls him in and out of the years, yanks him from fifty to twenty to thirty to fifty to fourteen.

Across the pond the children squeal and the woman there picks the smallest one up. Maybe a duck has snapped at it, come too close to a finger while grabbing bread. When the woman gathers her children to walk away along the bank, the ducks follow, dozens of them now, squawking and honking and fluttering their wings.

"The maestro, he looked sort of like Einstein, was everything I thought a music teacher at a university should be," Theodore says, and he is there again, eighteen, speaking to her from the campus practice room his time machine has taken him to. "Funny I can't remember his name, after all that," he says. "He had these thick eyebrows that went up and down all the time but mostly seemed to frown at me. He was never happy, never. No matter how I practiced, no matter what I did. 'Hush, hush, don't scream it out so,' he'd say. But the saxophone is a band instrument, really, and that's what I wanted, not some orchestral instruction, but I didn't know that."

"And so you didn't know to change teachers?" she asks.

"It was more than that," he says. He puts his arm around her, draws her close. He tells her was as if the maestro conjured the composers during his lessons, making him feel they were all looking over his shoulder, watching him, taking notice of his missed breaths and notes and dropped keys, and all Theodore ever wanted was one kind bit of encouragement until one day he dropped into the chair for the lesson, exhausted and lips sore from late practices and the maestro for the first time looked at him in a fatherly way— the smile so like his dead father's had been, the voice soft, as if the words coming would be hard for him to accept. He asked if Theodore was having a hard time adjusting to college life and he was, the boys in the dorm playing tricks on him, removing his mattress to the lobby of the girl's dorm across the quadrangle not even the worst of it.

"I kept telling myself I had my music," Theodore says, "that no matter what they did or said, I had something. I would work hard, I would show them all. And when I had my recital in the spring my girl would be there, she'd sit near the front by the stage, pretty and womanly, and then nobody would wonder anymore, nobody would tease me. But there never was a recital, of course."

"What happened?"

He releases her, draws into himself again and she nuzzles next to him but they are apart though next to each other, their legs and shoulders and arms touching. He sighs, wipes his face with the heels of this hands, looks out over the pond, quiet again with the ducks back in the water and the shore clear, the water in between flashing sunny shards of lightning into their eyes. "Not anything as exciting or mysterious as people think, I'm sure."

"Well, what?"

He shrugs, looks at her. "He just decided I wasn't passionate enough, that I was stronger technically, that I had what he called promise as a scholar, that I would be a superlative teacher, but not a performer. And, of course, I have never had a desire to teach. All I've ever wanted is to play. And there I was, the man not looking at me, not even looking at me when all I wanted at that moment was for him to at least pretend that I mattered, pretend that what I wanted was at least possible. But he didn't."

"And so you stopped playing for people," Crescent says, taking his hand, feeling him press her fingers against his palm.

"Yes," he says. "Because I stopped thinking I was any good."

Crescent pulls bunches of grass from beside her, flings it into the creek. She feels for rocks, stones, throws everything she can for a minute, yelling sounds that don't mean anything. "Ahhh! I can't believe it," she says, calmer. "What an asshole. What an utter, raving, idiot, fucking asshole."

He grins at her.

"Repeat after me," she says. "What an asshole. What an utter, raving, idiot, fucking asshole."

And he repeats it, saying the words as if for the first time.

None But The Dead And Dying

The reverend is here again, sitting in that chair that seems too tiny for him, that chair that is straight in the back, with thin arms and legs and nearly flat padding, crewel work her mother did. Doesn't match the room but sits here anyway because her mother did the handiwork and that's enough to make it a part. This is where he sits, his blue eyes on her and a sort of smile across his lips. Contessa's sure he is expecting something from her but she can't think of what. So much, Contessa thinks, has been happening since Jack died, so much she has lost track of, so many days she can't remember, and she must get them back.

This morning she decided she was really going to pay attention, not lose track, remember things so she can be okay because lately something hasn't seemed right and it's time to take control. So she had breakfast and showered and dressed and watched Sally Jesse, and when she thought of Jack she reminded herself that he is not coming home from the plant today, that he never went, was never going again, that he was gone, gone, gone. Another part of her kept wanting to think he was just away, like in Toledo, and would be coming home maybe not today but someday, but she knew that wasn't right. It was like a battle inside herself, one part thinking some things, the other part telling her no, Jack is dead, Jack won't be back ever.

And this battle inside her seemed over until this man, the reverend, came to her door, a look on his face like he knows her better than he should and it makes her wonder about those days she can't remember, but she doesn't want to ask him.

So he sits in her chair with her mother's crewel work and is asking her something about how she is doing, the question everyone seems to ask. Sometimes she thinks it isn't so much losing Jack as it is dealing with all the people, answering all the questions, being friendly to those who never before bothered to even say hello in the grocery store. Maybe this is what has kept her so confused, all this attention when all she wants is to be left alone.

"Fine," she says, "I'm doing fine, Reverend."

"Clay. Remember?" He leans forward in that spindly chair, forcing his weight onto the front legs. He's not a big man but strong and she worries for the chair, the tiny legs like those of a horse, too small-looking to hold so much.

"Clay?" He has said this, his first name, as though they've agreed she call him that. She wants to tell him to back off, back away, get out of her chair. "Clay. Of course. Well, don't you worry about me, Clay. I'm fine. I'll be fine." Shift the focus, she tells herself, take the conversation down another path. "Mamie Van Allen was here the other day. So thoughtful, it was, for her to come here in the heat. We didn't have much to say, so little in common you know, but it was nice of her to visit. Made me wish I'd spent more time visiting around myself. And Elizabeth, that's my sister—"

"Yes, I know."

"—Elizabeth has come quite often and it's all been quite helpful." She knows she's babbling but there is something in the way he is looking at her, something he thinks she knows, something he's expecting and she can't figure out what it is. She has given him something to drink, offered him food. She has let him sit in this chair. What has she forgotten? "Well, Clayton, it was so nice of you to come," she says, and his look is nearly a leer but maybe it's her imagination. Maybe he knows something about the other night, maybe his daughter told him, because that's one thing she does remember, the rain and the mud and the ride in the car home. "I'm really all right," she says, standing, extending her hand to him, hoping now he will say goodbye.

His hand is gentle in hers, friendly, something different

about this touching, though, than when he took her hand after Cecelia Thompson's funeral. His thumb massages her knuckles, caressing her, and he leans to kiss it, to rest his lips against the tips of her fingers, one by one. He turns her hand over in his, rubs his across it as if clearing a path. His eyes shine. He holds her hand to his face, kisses her palm, licks it, and a throbbing starts in her, starts in hidden away places and in places men stare at when she walks down the street.

She snatches her hand away from those minister hands, preacher eyes, the need he's touched real but hers alone. "Oh, God," she says, turning from him, but he comes to enclose her with his arms and she pushes him away, trying to remember, thinking, there was Jack dying and then the people, the reverend, Elizabeth, maybe even Theodore, but there is something else, some last thing, but she can't see it anymore.

"Go away," she says, wondering if he can hear her. "Please go away."

It is that easy. He is at the door, not really smiling, confused maybe, but still that gentleness haunts him, and he says, "Call, Tess, if you need me."

She closes the door. "I don't need you. I don't need anybody," she says, but of course he can't hear and wouldn't understand that so far nobody has done her any bit of good.

Clayton sits in the sanctuary, wishing it was winter, wishing snow was falling on the cross, that night was coming, that last winter was coming instead so he could take back things. He scrapes his face with his hands, feeling, in a habit formed in his nervous teens, for the tiny hints of larger pimples to come, for the scars he feared would linger, never letting him forget, like any scar from any war.

He runs his hands through his hair, down the back of his neck bent forward, thinking that's where everything started. Fourteen years old, the outbreak that wouldn't leave him, would leave him only dateless and teased and the punchline to school-wide jokes, early moustaches and beards never enough and Christian schools the one place he thought things would be different but weren't. Then, in the seminary, Sandra. Slight and blonde and dimpled and smiling. Beatific, he thought. She'll be the perfect minister's wife, everyone said. But still....

Women like Contessa never looked into him, never found him attractive, never wanted him. And no amount of praying healed him from that. Her desire, the look in her eyes, the firm, confirming legs around his back all gave to him something he had never had, but there has been a bill running up for it he wonders if he can pay.

A sound startles him and he looks at the cross through the window in front of him but sees only the sun on it, the sky deep blue and perfect behind it.

"Mr. Reverend?"

Twisting in the pew, he sees Mundee Manway hobbling toward him down the aisle, her straw bag losing strands as she walks. She's in white today, a white vee-neck Hanes undershirt like a blouse and a white cardigan sweater stretched over it, its vivid red flowers of yarn with the yellow centers matching the flowers on her purse. These must have been quite a find for her the day she got them. The long white pleated skirt is oversized and she wears white high-topped sneakers.

Oh God, he thinks, she's here to be married again.

"I guess I'm early, huh? I guess I'm early and I guess it's I'm excited that I'm early, huh?" She grins, grimy and innocent, and the reverend nods. He looks at his watch, wondering how much of the evening he will have to sit, watching the door with her, listening to her mumble and ramble, waiting for witnesses who will never come.

He wants to shake her hand but sees the clutters of stains from years of smoking and lack of proper washing, the deep wrinkles hoarding dirt the way a prospector protects gold. She clutches the huge straw bag, rubbing dirt into its handle. She props herself next to him on the pew.

"They aren't coming, Miss Manway," he says.

She looks at him, her eyebrows twisted, unsure. "What? Did they forget?"

He shakes his head, feels pure and clean and in control next to her. "It's not the day."

She looks around. Frantic all at once, she pulls open her purse and starts rummaging through it, shuffling around papers and clinking objects out of his sight like a magician rummaging a crowded hat for the rabbit. "I'm sure this is it," she says, more to herself than to the reverend. "If I could just find the invitation. I went to such trouble, you know, printing them. Maybe it's just my being excited about it, maybe that's why I've got the wrong day. In here somewhere, I know it is."

The filthy fingers work quickly, drawing out old tubes of lipstick, compacts, crumpled papers and clear-barrelled ink pens, a Dum-Dum sucker like the ones the tellers give children at the bank, candy wrappers and loose sticks of chewing gum, combs, a toy truck and a change purse of tired red leather. In a pile she drops these until they lose their balance and scatter over the pew and onto the floor. The reverend reaches to pick them up, feeling them slide in his fingers, stick to his hands from things spilled on them.

"Oh, I'm sorry, Mr. Reverend," she mumbles, "sorry," her face dropping into red embarrassment. "It's the paper I'm looking for, you know. The paper about the date, about whether today's the day or I'm too excited to get it right, and if I'm early or they're late. But you're here, Mr. Reverend. Maybe that's a sign I'm excited but still I'm right about today, huh?"

"There isn't a wedding, Miss Manway."

"But then, when?"

He reaches for his handkerchief, blots his fingers into its folds. When he looks into her eyes he wishes he was born more intuitive, or maybe a mind-reader, born one of those people who who can read other people through their eyes. "The eyes are the windows to the soul," didn't someone famous say that? Or is it "mirrors of the soul"? It doesn't matter because no matter what, he doesn't know what to say to Mundee Manway.

"When?" she asks again, and he stands, offering his hand to help her up.

"Not even you know, Miss Manway, do you? Really? And who would you marry?" he says.

Her eyes wrinkle at the corners, studying him. She blinks. Her attention goes again to the pile of things on the pew and she busies her fingers in collecting them, jamming them back into the purse, her hands moving like a piece of earth-moving equipment that scoops and drops, scoops and drops. "I guess I not only got the wrong day, I got the wrong goddamned church, so excited about it. Sorry about your time, Mr. Reverend, sorry."

A few steps from the door leading out of the sanctuary she turns, her eyes not leaving the carpeted runners stretching down the sloped aisle. "You're invited anyway," she says.

"Thank you, Miss Manway," he says, but she is gone.

He wipes the pew with his handkerchief, flicking errant crumbs from her things onto the floor. Behind him, in the hallway, he hears Ben Stevens greeting Mundee. "Beautiful outfit today, Miss Manway," he says. "What's that you say? A wedding! How wonderful for you. Congratulations."

And so Reverend Bleu knows what is coming and prepares himself. The mayor is Lutheran and has to be here for reasons other than spiritual, though this is getting easier and easier for the reverend to manage. They shake hands, the mayor in his clip-on tie and Dockers and the reverend in his jeans and short-sleeved shirt.

"Nice and cool in here," the mayor says, though they both know he has just stepped from his air-conditioned car into the day for only a moment before crossing the driveway into the church. He sits on the pew where Mundee has just been.

"What can I do for you, Ben?" The reverend knows there should be more verbal square-dancing first, some promenades and do-si-dos, but the little left in him after his visit to Contessa has been stolen away by Mundee Manway, swiped and tucked into the far reaches of her huge, broken bag.

This throws the mayor off and he squirms a little, sighing, finding a way to start. "Landers Stone's been getting quite the company out at his farm, you know," he says.

"The burial site," Clayton says, "I went out there one day. Looks like a madhouse."

"The way I see it is that these folks bring in some business to town," the mayor says. He unclips his tie, holds it in his hand. It is a garish flash of fuschia and ochre that he folds and tucks into a back pocket. "You know we're probably going to lose the plant," he says to the reverend. "That could just take this town apart."

The reverend nods. Nearly everyone works in the pressing plant or has a small business kept alive by the income generated by the people who work there.

"But we also got a strong farm community, and you'd know that by your church members, good, Christian people." He hesitates, pressing the fingers of one hand into the others, his hands forming a pyramid, a tent, a church steeple.

"What are you getting at, Ben?"

Stevens looks the reverend in the eye. "I'm asking all the ministers to talk to their congregations this Sunday about the burial site, about how we need to support the effort it takes to uncover the truth about our history, something like that. How you do it is up to you, but we need the support of the community."

"You want this tomorrow? July Fourth Sunday?"

"I know it's real sudden and that you probably got your sermon planned and all, but Landers is nearly beside himself out there with all the protesters starting to come in and Mr. Olson, the archaeologist, says there could be looting of the grave. We surely don't want any of that to happen."

The reverend slaps his hands against his thighs, stands up. He paces, looking at the cross that looms at them from behind the glass. He hasn't planned anything yet for tomorrow, nothing except his usual rah-rah-good ole USA talk. But what is there to say about the burial site? Whose business is it of his to stir people up? "What is it, exactly, you want us to try and accomplish?" he asks.

Sitting in the pew, his tie gone and the neck of his shirt open, Mayor Stevens looks more the factory worker on his day off and, seeing this, the reverend remembers how Ben Stevens earned his living before politics, thinks of how some things have changed, kept on going, moving—if not forward then at least somewhere. Moving at all seems triumphant.

Ben Stevens lounges in the padded pew, winding his arm across the back of it, crossing his legs. "We need to reclaim what's ours from the outsiders," he says. He leans forward, uncrossing his legs. "We're talking about a museum, right there on the site. Olson says this find is worth studying for a long time. That, with the tourists, can really help the town out."

The mayor is beaming, he is in a selling mode, all positives and no negatives that can't be flipped around to somebody's advantage. The reverend says, "A museum will benefit Mason Pope most of all and the rest of the town very little. That's the bottom line. And if he's got you convinced otherwise, you're—" He stops himself, unwilling to call the man a fool, to insult him, because he likes Ben Stevens. "Otherwise you're not thinking clearly."

The mayor stands, reaches back to shove the tie into the pocket where it threatens to spill out. He studies the carpet a minute, then, to the reverend, says, "If the plant goes, what else is there?"

"I'll see what I can do," Reverend Bleu says. It's not a promise and Ben will know that, but it does offer him an escape, an escape he already knows he will probably use.

Mamie has moved her favorite wicker chair onto the back porch so she can watch Eddy at the head of her driveway in front of her garage. He has muscled up the door after years of its holding in her car and lawn mower, things she doesn't use any more, things others offer up to her when the need for them arises. "This your car, Mamie?" he asks, walking into the dark part of the garage she can't see from the kitchen doorway. She heard him whistle and was pleased he was impressed, though she had no idea why an old car would impress anybody.

He went into the garage in search of tools and managed to find a few, a box of essentials her handyman kept there, a man gone over seven years, the tools still around, unused, because she calls someone else now, someone who, like the boy who mows her yard, brings his own equipment and tools.

Eddy wields a screwdriver, loosening the wheel from Gasman George's bike where it sits in the driveway. He strokes the rim, feeling for tears and gashes in the rubber.

He wipes the screwdriver with a clean rag she found for him, and lays it next to him on the cracked cement. He wipes rust and dust and maybe even old grease from a pair of pliers, measures where he needs to work the tools, searches the box for something else.

She's poured him lemonade and every once in awhile he remembers it, picks up the glass, sips it, and in doing so, remembers Mamie and toasts her. They smile and he works again.

So she sits and drinks her scotch, smiling and toasting, wondering about this man who is maybe thirty, his body strong and taut and deep with mystery. She wonders where it is he sleeps at night and whether he stays alone. She wonders where he's come from and why he's chosen this place to stop. Shifting in the chair, she crosses her feet at the ankles, pressing her toes into the cement of the porch, pressing energy into them, getting the blood to circulate just a little more. She wonders if he will take in the fireworks show tomorrow at Community Park, if he knows about it, wonders what he thinks about it. She wonders, too, about his earnestness with Gasman George's bike. He saw the fall, he told her, helped the man as best he could and was amazed when George walked away, abandoning the bike he had so fiercely possessed.

"When you take the bike back to him, he might not seem to appreciate it," Mamie says, "but he will."

Eddy looks up at her, his face behind the spokes of the wheel he spins, checking for kinks and twisted metal. He smiles. "I know."

"Do you mind if I talk, or does it interrupt your train of thought?" she asks, sipping, wondering if he will tell her the truth or if he will be kind.

"I like it when you talk, Mamie. You know that." He sets the wheel down, pries the tire from the frame.

"You have maybe heard about the burial site north of

town?"

He takes the front tire off the bike, bounces it on the driveway next to him. "What about it?"

"It's Gasman's farm."

Eddy catches the bicycle tire in his hands, lays it down, looks at her, looks at the bike as if it might clarify what she has just said.

Mamie goes on, "Landers Stone leases it to farm it. Mason Pope, an attorney in town oversees things, has power of attorney over George's business interests. But it's George who owns the land. He inherited it from his father some years ago when he died."

He slaps at a mosquito, turns to watch a car pass on the street too fast and too loud. "Why do you tell me this?" he asks, his eyes on her again.

"Just thought you might want to know that."

He stands, unfolding himself from the cement, comes to stand next to her. On the porch, in her chair, him standing next to her on the ground, they are very nearly eye to eye and she thinks, there is something about him. "I'm sure you could tell he's a little different," she says. "You're very good to help him this way, Eddy."

He looks at the bike, propping his foot on the edge of the porch and leaning his arms across his bent knee. Suddenly he grins at her, straightens up, kisses her on the cheek. "I'm only doing it to impress you," he says, and turns back to the driveway. "Tell me, Mamie. Did you buy that Bonneville in there new?"

"Brand spanking new. It was 1969 and it was loaded." She chuckles. "I guess it still must be unless some sort of gremlin snuck in and stripped the thing while it's been sitting there."

"Those gremlins can be nasty," Eddy says, toasting her. He holds up a can of kelly green paint. "Thought I'd stick to what he knows," he says, and she nods. "But what do you think? Should I add stripes? Give George a bike back that's loaded?"

"Yellow. Something bright."

The afternoon stretches this way, the sun crossing the eaves over her head, shining into her face, dropping its rays over Eddy who's been in the shade until now as well. Late but still hot, he sweats at his task and he reaches to pull off his tee shirt. He looks first at Mamie. She shrugs, shifts her feet.

His lean arms and chest are crisp with strength and muscle and she feels herself sigh. He bends over the bike, stroking the paint into it, and she watches the shapes of his shoulders change, muscles tightening and loosening, sees his hands turning, fingers working.

She rises from the chair, wrings the door open, its spring coiling and creaking, catching his attention. She waves, pulls her eyes from him. It's hot, she tells herself. It's time to go in.

14

ands of setting colors—raging pink and violet, soft amber and blue-green—stripe the western sky, a bonnet covering the crowd around the drum, around a fire built near the circle which even Landers has become accustomed to stepping around. They have transformed his dirt and gravel driveway with the hollow thunk of the drum and the shrill calls in words he cannot understand, though he listens and listens, cannot stop listening, the drum and singing persistent and earnest.

Daniel Yellow Wolf has spoken, off and on all since the creation of the fire this morning, of the spirit and power of the flame, of the light, of the fire. "We light this with the coming of the new day when the power to create is strong, when all things are coming alive again, out of the dark, out of the death of the night," he said this morning. "We will nurture the flame and tend its power until our ancestors are set free to follow their journey again."

The campfire crackles and snaps its own rhythm, but much seems the same to Landers. Circles of dancing, though tonight the traditional ceremonial clothing is everywhere. Even tiny children, barely walking, hop in the dances, bells banging around ankles and wrists, leather fringe bouncing and swaying with each step, their own regalia magnificent miniatures of what the adults wear, with fine beading and embroidery, with feathers and jangles and ribbons of all colors streaming.

Not many other than the reporters have stayed this late for more of the ceremony, most leaving early, tired from trying to listen past what sounds like simple syllables to hear the rich stories of ancient peoples as Yellow Wolf had told them. There are more migrants tonight, many of Landers' families gathered around the circle, joined by dozens—maybe a couple of hundred—from other farms. They watch with interest, some joining in the dance when invited, learning step by step next to willing teachers. The men lead, the women follow, elaborately stitched and decorated fringed shawls draped over their arms. Every now and then a dancer breaks free, unfurling her shawl, fanning it out, dipping and turning further into the dance.

From the back of the crowd Rico emerges, walking alone toward Landers from where he, too, has been standing apart, chatting with a few of the other men.

"Mr. Stone," Rico says, and Landers nods his greeting.

"Interesting, I'd say," Landers remarks, nodding his head again, this time toward the group of dancers and singers and drummers. When Rico glances at the Indians as though just noticing them, Landers realizes something much more than a ceremony has been going on here all day, and this is what Rico will tell him, he knows.

Above them the sky steps with the dancers and drummers into deeper night, the colors collapsing into each other while stars begin to appear like shy glances from behind stage curtains, one at a time, here and there. Landers looks for a moon but doesn't see one. The voices behind the circle end a song and begin another, a quicker beat to this one, the vocals tricky for the soloist who follows a winding, hilly path of notes and words thick as brush.

"Mr. Landers," Rico says again, and Landers motions

for Rico to sit on the back step but he shakes his head no so they stand nearly eye to eye, though Rico, despite being in his late-twenties, is the shorter of the two, unable to match Landers' hearty six-foot-three. Rico has been with the Stone farm every summer since Landers can remember—probably since birth. His father's death two years ago made Rico the most senior laborer. No one else has been with the farm so long. Like it is on so many farms, the generations of workers stretch alongside the generations of farm owners, but those who tend the land, who minister to its nourishment, are often those who pass on their commitment to the land from father to son without legal deed, their responsibility stronger than paper.

"My father," Rico begins, and Landers nods, "my father, he said we should always work hard and do our jobs and we'll keep coming back."

"I hope you think your father was right," Landers says. "He was a good man, your father."

"Yes," Rico says. He pauses, watching the campfire dancing, listening to the beat of the drum build louder and faster, the chanters following its lead. "Mr. Landers, we know you got to do what they tell you. We know that. But we just cannot let the desecration go on. We just cannot keep on working like it's not happening—"

"Rico—"

"My father, he used to say that we keep working and we go nowhere. We get a little bit but we need a lot. He used to say that sometimes it's not worth it, no matter what." He stops, looks toward the men he was with earlier. They are watching him, watching Landers.

"What're you telling me, Rico?" Landers asks.

"We cannot keep working, you know, while the desecration goes on. If they will just let the graves be buried, we will work. If they will keep on disturbing the resting places, we will not work. We need our jobs, Mr. Stone, but this is what we will do. Not just us here, Mr. Stone, but everywhere around, you know. Other farms, too. I don't want to lose my job, but my father, he used to say sometimes some things are more important."

Landers runs his hands through his hair. Near his neck he has been sweating and his hair is damp. He sighs. "And they said the only inconvenience would be a few strangers around," he says.

"Señor?"

"Nothing, Rico." He drops his hand on the man's shoulder. "Listen, you all have the fourth off anyway. Take Monday off, too, and we'll see from there, okay? You can understand why I can't be having you just take off with the pickles and tomatoes coming ready next month."

"Pay for Monday?"

"Pay for Monday."

"And the grave digging?"

"I understand how you feel about it, Rico. Hopefully I can get something arranged about that by Tuesday. Just don't pack up for someplace else until I can see about this, okay?"

The sun has long vanished over the horizon, abandoning behind it a pale version of its own glow that struggles its own path to its own setting. The darkness brings with it a cool edge that everyone seems to breathe in at once.

"I don't know about the other farms," Rico says.

"That's their business," Landers says, though he knows it isn't true, it is up to him, up to Mason Pope, to Michael Olson, but up to him most of all and he has no idea what he can do. And tomorrow when the phone rings it will be neighbors with complaints and suggestions and ultimatums, friendships around here safe unless somebody threatens a farm, and this is exactly what promises to happen. "I can't negotiate for them, Rico, you know that. All I can tell you is I'll let the folks who're in charge of all that know—" he gestures to the burial site, where Diamond and a local cop smoke cigarettes, vigilant in the night—"and see what we can do to get this stopped," he says.

Get this stopped, he realizes, is exactly what somebody needs to do.

Rico nods and they shake hands. "I will be here early Tuesday," Rico says, meaning he won't go directly to the fields, no one will, not until they talk again.

"I understand," Landers says.

Rico heads back across the driveway to the men waiting for him and in the dim light, beyond the edge of the flickering campfire, Landers sees the men smile and clap each other on the shoulder.

It's all got to stop, he thinks, but it is a runaway stage coach in a western movie, the horses gone wild and the innocent schoolmarm in the coach screaming for help. And the cavalry, Landers decides, is the last thing she needs.

She's glad Mamie is not on her porch tonight. She's considered the screened-in porch at the back but for some reason wants the street, to see it, feel the cars along the brick surface making noise like tongues along ear corn or a monotone xylophone or a virgin aunt sounding disapproval in her voice. So she sits here, on this fold-out chair with the plastic straps that cut into the backs of her thighs, thinking maybe she should have worn a skirt instead of this robe. She wonders if the neighbors can see her well, in this light, because she must be so careful.

She tries to remember about the preacher, the way he touched her, kissed her, and today, Elizabeth on the phone saying, "Yes, silly, you know he's married. Goodness, Connie, if you're looking already, don't head for the reverend. Nobody much is crazy about Sandy, but she's a preacher's wife, after all. Besides, it's too soon for you, dear."

Contessa strains this way for the lost time, for the meaning of those looks, that kiss, the caress of her fingers and she thinks for a moment maybe she imagined it all but there is, too, that look on his face when she told him to get out, that stricken, sad, hurt, puzzled, lost look. It's that same look she's seen, she decides, in her own mirror.

The dark, faded strains of saxophone whine in the distance. She closes her eyes here on her front porch, leans back in the chair, and sees Theodore at seventeen, on that shaky wooden stage in the middle of the gym, cut-out cardboard hearts painted bleeding, near-to-dying red, cut-out stars sprinkled with silver glitter catching lights, shimmering, making her want to believe it is a Parisian café and Theodore a wandering minstrel, an expatriot American jazzman captured by the romance of France. He dedicates songs to her, plays a few he even wrote for her, telling anyone who hears that she is his, his inspiration. She sways alone near the bandstand, vowing to remember every note, every song title but she hasn't had to—he plays them at night through the streets like this.

She hugs her robe to her though the breeze is warm. She imagines he cried when Deborah died, maybe at the funeral, and she sees it in her mind though she wasn't there.

Tonight the sounds dance, running from him, kicking up heels. This music smiles and laughs and teases, tripping in its grinning excitement. She hasn't heard it this light in a long time, maybe in years, maybe since he played those high school dances.

Where are the mournful sounds for me, Contessa wonders. Where is the slow, desperate breathing and fear and coming home again, broken?

So she sits, waiting through each song, tolerating the mood she doesn't feel, waiting for the crying she can't do for herself.

None But The Dead And Dying

She listens not from the bell tower but from a plastic chair on Theodore's own front porch, her feet pushed against the railing, her arms folded across her chest, smiling with the music.

If you're happy now, Crescent thinks, wait till you're done. Wait until you crawl into bed for the night in those stupid print pajamas. Yeah, if you think you can make music now....

Eddy finds him sitting in the dark sanctuary, staring through the tall window, the backdrop of the altar, staring into the nothing where the cross stands but can't be seen anymore. He looks as though he hasn't moved for a long time.

When Eddy moves closer up the aisle, he sees that the Reverend Clayton Bleu is clutching a chipped, gold-painted lipstick cartridge, running it through and between his fingers, turning it this way and that as if memorizing it by touch. Eddy takes a seat next to him, unwilling to say anything that might interrupt something private, something crucial, but his sitting causes the reverend to stir, to look at him.

"Oh, Eddy, sorry. I forgot. I got tied up."

Eddy shrugs. He waited awhile at the Lounge after working on the bike, then decided to come looking. "You okay?"

"Peachy. You?"

"I want to show you something." He hasn't planned this, isn't even sure it will work, but needs to try it. Needs to try something. "Got your car handy?"

They drive to Main Street and Eddy directs him. "I know where we're going," Clayton says. "Cops out there. We could get shot or something."

"Just me. They wouldn't shoot a preacher. Not a local one, anyway. Now drive." Eddy kicks back as much as he can in the cramped Chevette, pulls a cigarette from his pocket and passes it to Clay, who swings the car onto 101 from Main Street. They cross Route 20.

"What's that guy pointing to, anyway," Eddy asks. At the top of the hill in McPherson Cemetery a statue of General James Birdseye McPherson points west.

"Fremont," Clayton says, chuckling. He lights the cigarette from the car lighter. "Who knows?"

"He needs a big, giant yo-yo. He looks pretty bored."

"He was the youngest general killed in the Civil War, I think," Clayton says. "Youngest general killed in one of the wars, anyway."

Eddy grins, blows cigarette smoke into the night through the open window. "Couldn't have been a very good general, then, eh?"

They turn off 101 onto a skinny township road. "Park on down the road," Eddy says. "We'll creep in the back way."

"I should have met you at the bar," Clayton says, putting the car in park and climbing out. "I could sure use a drink."

It's dark, nearly too dark to see and they move slowly. "Watch for the ditch here, come on, jump," Eddy whispers, leaping the crevice where water tickles the ground.

"How the hell do you know where you're going?" Clayton asks, and Eddy shushes him, takes his arm to show his position.

He points to the house though he guesses Clayton can't quite see his gesture. He figures they'll track around the property using the house, the burial site on a diagonal from here, through the house, best he remembers, so they use the house to orient themselves. "Watch for the water line," he says. "We'll have to cross it—I'm sure it's not covered yet."

"Why does it have to be so fucking dark?" Clayton says, but he is laughing, trying to stay quiet, holding the back belt loop of Eddy's jeans to stay in step.

"Shh!"

They circle around, watching for signs that they might be awakening people in the truck campers or in the house. Eddy's eyes are adjusting and he spots bushes and clothesline posts to avoid. What he doesn't expect is a tent along this back edge of the property, and then another, leading Clayton too quickly, too noisily, the twigs and grass loud under their feet. Before them, from the nearest tent, there's a man Eddy can't see too well. He gestures for Clayton to get down behind him. "Oh," the man in front of them says. "I guess I don't know you."

"Eddy Light Sky."

"You just get here?"

"Just now."

"Well," the man says, "we can use all the help we can get."

"I'll try not to disturb you any more," Eddy says, hoping the man's curiosity has waned.

"Don't go up around the site," the man says. "They've beefed up police and who knows with this small town but what they don't shoot first, let God sort us out."

"Right. Thanks."

The man gives Eddy a nod, goes back into his tent. "Ready?" he whispers, giving the motion to Clayton that he can relax, stand up, get ready to move on, but he is gone.

Eddy scrambles back to the car, where the reverend sits on the hood, watching him. "Where the hell did you go?" Eddy asks him, but the reverend laughs, takes a puff on a cigarette, offering one to Eddy. The orange from the reverend's cigarette is the only bit of color around, the house dark now since they first drove up, the whole world cut out in silhouettes of black, white, gray.

"What's the point, anyway?" Clayton asks.

Eddy leans against the car door. "You don't pay much attention, do you?"

"What're you talking about?"

"Listen, Clay. Just listen."

"Is this some Indian worship-the-world-around-you thing or something?" The orange waves in the dark, an angry eye, staring Eddy down.

"Look up."

"Stars. Space. Is this a quiz?"

"No," Eddy says. The orange eye, he sees, is about to go out.

Clayton flicks the cigarette onto the road and Eddy steps around the front of the car to stomp it out. "Listen to the night," the reverend says. "Look at the stars, gaze upon nature. Contemplate our beginnings and death. Is that what this is about? Shit, Eddy. Do you think I don't do all that already? Do you think I'm this stupid? This out of touch?"

"All I know is that you're in trouble somehow. No preacher suddenly takes up drinking in bars with some stranger. And for some reason I don't think it was devotion that had you welded to that pew tonight when I walked in."

"Everybody's got problems. Look at this place. Everybody here feels like they've got something to win or lose, some claim to stake. Preachers aren't any different. What's the crime if I decide to have a drink or a cigarette and, by the way, who the hell are you to drag me out here and start in on me about it, anyway?"

He jumps from the car hood, heads for the driver's side and Eddy climbs back in the car. If he waits for an invitation, he might end up walking back to his room tonight.

The reverend edges into a three-point turn that takes a few more points on the little road before heading them back toward town. Stars hang overhead in a moonless sky. In the car, in this dim green dashboard light, Clayton Bleu looks too young to be carrying the worries of a congregation with him. He looks like he might never be old enough to bear it, or wise enough to know better, and this makes Eddy sorry for him. Miles of low green corn, soy beans, all of it looking the same in the quick darkness, clip past them.

"You know Gasman George?" Eddy asks as they near the outskirts of town.

"I know who he is. Why?"

"Know his story?"

"Not much. Retarded, maybe because of his mother's suicide or his sister who's nuts. Why?"

Eddy turns his face into the rush of cool air from the open window. They pull up to the stoplight by the cemetery and he looks out the back window at the statue of the general pointing. He's pointing the wrong way, Eddy thinks. He's pointing me home.

"What do you suppose makes him different from you and me?" Eddy asks.

The reverend makes a right onto Route 20, steering for Eddy's motel. "I don't know. Why are you so interested in Gasman?"

"Just curious. I'm fixing his bike." Eddy inhales the night, tastes the exhaust fumes from the late-night trucks and misses already the smell of weeds and fertilizer from the farms.

Mamie lights a candle beside her bed. It is a thick bed with fresh sheets in this house she had redecorated fifteen or so years ago. Very contemporary, she had a sale to flush out all of the old. She was a senior citizen that year and she decided she would not have a little old lady's house, crammed with ancient dark wood and doilies. From Cleveland came a woman in flouncy scarves of primary colors who planned and rearranged and called in carpenters who cut skylights through her roof and moved walls.

She had a yard sale for her old furniture and things,

walked among people who thought she was dead because after all, isn't that usually the situation for a sale like that? And she heard amazing things: "Well you know she was an old maid, no man ever good enough, so full of herself is what I understand," things like that. And so she gave up more than her furniture and her past.

But she has a bed that is not very tall off the ground, a sleek Danish design in bleached wood like nearly everything in her house, bright and open, no hiding places for secrets, but she doesn't care because there is no one to keep things from. She can say her secrets aloud because no one will hear, no one will give them away.

And tonight she says a secret out loud, a secret about Eddy. She thinks about him and the way he looked today down by the garage with the bike, Eddy hot and drinking the lemonade she made, Eddy bare-chested and strong and smiling at her.

He will go away again, maybe soon, and she will miss him, but there is no other way that it can be. Two have died and Eddy will be the third, though he won't be dead, only gone, but it will be the same thing for her.

She leans, slowly, balancing herself, to blow out the candle and it shudders her first try but goes out for sure the second time.

The reverend watches Eddy close the motel door behind him, watches the light vanish from the sidewalk, watches for a flutter of ochre curtain, a sign of his life inside the room, the television going on, but sees nothing. He waits for the light to go out, another kind of sign, but it burns golden against the curtain, constant, betraying no movement inside. It's as if Eddy has walked into the room and ceased to exist.

He watches for a long time, watches into sleep, wakes on the fringe of a dream of Eddy soaring around him, winged in deep red and blue and purple plumage, scooping past him, the corn dried on the stalks, broken and withered, blown with the wind his enormous wings create, crackling around the reverend like fire. He blinks, sees that the light is now out in the window. He starts the car.

The lights in the Bahama Lounge are out, too, as he passes it, and he wonders how close to sun-up he is.

Maple Street, straight from the Lounge, would take him home. Instead he turns toward Buckeye. The street pavement rolls under the car in a whisper of conspiracy, the car taking him past dark houses and pulled shades. The saxophone, he knows, has been silent for hours, and he circles past that house, too, a dim light in the back the only one in the neighborhood.

He tells himself it's Mamie Van Allen. She falls asleep on her porch they say, and he should check. Should check on his way home, now that he's heading down Buckeye in the direction of home again.

Just Mamie, he thinks. Then home.

Her long porch is silent, a wicker rocker on one end of it tips in the breeze, doing its job for nobody. Her house, too, is dark.

He looks anyway across the street, can't help it, doesn't want to, but cannot keep his eyes away, and there she sits. Steady and statuesque in light leaking from behind her living room drapes, light that fingers thinly across her lap. He stops the car on the street, parking against the yellow-painted curb. He wonders if she sees him, wonders if she's getting up, tossing the moonlight off her, escaping into her house, clicking the lock behind her.

But she sits, her eyes on him but not really seeing him, he can tell. He climbs the steps. "Tess?"

She pulls the robe close to her, as if suddenly aware of the night, the cool air, his eyes. "Reverend."

Something has changed, I have to know what, he thinks. He doesn't ask to be invited, doesn't wait, just sits next to her on the matching plastic-ribbed lawn chair. "How are you tonight?" he asks, imagining that they can both believe it isn't this late, that the sun won't be up soon.

She inclines her head as if to say she's okay.

"What is it, Tess? You can tell me, we're friends, remember?"

"Are we?"

The question catches him, catches him in the throat and he coughs, trying to clear it, but it stands here between them like a soldier on guard duty waiting for proper dismissal or maybe a secret password. "What do you mean, Tess? Of course we're friends. Don't you remember? You've been through so much, I know...."

She smiles a smirking, cynical smile that is out of place on her, a smile strong in its own right, a smile that seems in control of her, and it frightens him. In this light, her face softened by a night without a moon, he still sees what he has not seen before, that she is old, that she is years older than he is. Why has he not seen this until now?

"Jack's dead," she says. "My Deborah first, then Jack. Or maybe I should say I lost Theodore first, to that damn horn, to that school." Her eyes travel the rooftops in the direction of Theodore Thompson's house. "Not that it matters. Not that any of it matters."

"You've had a hard time, Tess. A hard time." He fumbles his words, words now like juggling balls that keep falling around him, his hands too slow to keep them in the air all at the same time.

"And you've made it harder, haven't you?"

Oh, God, what does she mean? What the hell does she mean?

Shifting again, her robe loosens, drops lower between

her breasts and he wants to look, looking would remind him, bring her back at least in his head, because there was something that he wanted from her, something. He hasn't realized she is so much older, could look at him this way. She is daring him to speak the truth, to accept whatever she throws at him, whatever punishment she delivers.

"I'm not sure, I—"

"Yes," she says, voice and eyes and limbs and mind steady, smooth as steel and as icy hard. "Yes, you do know what I mean. What happened to us? What did you do to me?"

The cough again, the dryness in his throat, her question, and he has no answer for her. "Tess, you were very confused—"

"Of course I was confused—my husband was just dead. But you? What about you?"

"Tess, I don't know what to say, how to say—I don't know if I can explain—"

She stands, shakes her robe around her as if shaking herself loose of him, shaking him out of her like dust and dirt from a rug. She looks at him again and he fears she might even spit on him but she leaves him instead, the door closing quietly behind her and he thinks that this is even worse. Overhead the sky begins to lighten in the east, birds in the maples and along the street begin their morning songs and he knows he should leave before he is seen but it is so hard to get up from the chair when there's no place he wants to go.

15

The man at the back of the rental truck is wiry, but has a belly bloated from all the beer he's thrown down in motel rooms to calm his nerves after shooting off fireworks in little towns like this one. Eddy saw him park the Ryder—a quiet "Warning: Explosives" sign taped to the side panel—in front of the room next to his. The big-bellied man, alone, already looked weary, and when he asked Eddy for directions to the Waterworks Pond at Community Park, Eddy offered to ride along, to show him.

Now they stand in the heat, the fireworks man Bo taking the papier mâché bulbs out of a cardboard box, arranging them by size along the back edge of the truck in their brown paper, their dark blue, bright green wrappers like the ugly presents they are. It has taken Bo over an hour to decide how he'll set the show up, where to set the one-by-four racks, walking the ridge over the pond up near the baseball diamonds, looking out over the pond and its winding creek, deciding where the fallout would most likely be, given that the wind doesn't shift too much.

"Wind keeps up," he said to Eddy, "but you know how that goes," and they nodded, and he put Eddy to work hammering the mortars, aiming them straight up, so Eddy pounds

None But The Dead And Dying

nails in to frame the rows of tubing, his sharp hammering swallowed into thick, humid air that threatens to suck in everyone.

"First a rack of threes," Bo says, mostly to himself, "then probably a rack of fours'll be how I start."

Eddy counts: ten mortars to a rack of threes, six to a rack of fours. He wonders if he'll be able to count tonight when they fire, if he'll be able to see the difference. "What are these other sizes?" He points to dozens of other mortars, other sizes he's been fitting together.

"This show, fives, sixes and an eight. Sizes go way up but they get pretty damn expensive, hundreds of bucks apiece, you know. Detroit, Philly size. But this'll be a good show, here." He glances around the park, scratching his hot bare belly. His shirt is across the open door of the truck. Eddy wonders if the keys are in it, if it's sitting for a quick getaway. If the fireworks show goes wrong, if the rockets explode too low, singe the earth, do they run Bo out of town, side-panel sign and all?

Around the park a few picnic tables are in use, some toddlers in swings being pushed but the place is otherwise quiet. Eddy has heard that there will be baseball soon, followed by weird games of skill like balloon and egg-tossing that attract hundreds, pairing up mothers and sons, fathers and daughters, a family day. He wonders about Bo's family, their daddy and husband or boyfriend away every year, on Independence Day, on his birthday, he told Eddy. "A Fourth of July baby," he said. "Came in with a bang but in this business, got to hope you go out with a whimper." He laughed but Eddy could only eye the balls of fireworks as if they could go off by someone just thinking about it.

Bo says, "The eight I'll sink the metal mortar for. Good pop on that one." He grins a straight white smile that surprises Eddy. No missing teeth, no missing fingers. Must be good at this, Eddy thinks.

They dig in the heat, dig within the sixty-by-sixty or so square foot area Bo's chosen away from the trees that shade the picnic tables, away from the stands where the crowds will gather. They dig under a sun scorching them and they hammer, finally, a frame for the finale—a flag-shaped ground display.

"The Stars and Stripes Special," Bo says. "Two and a half inches, these." He holds a strand up like gourds with stems all knotted together into a single line with red paper at the tip. "Safety cap," Bo explains. "Goes in two seconds. The rest—" he snaps his fingers—"like that."

Eddy nods, and Bo says, "Gonna be a good show. We got a variety of rockets, your aerial cannon salutes and Oriental chrysanthemums, some multi-breaks." He motions across the blue sky as if it were black and he were already seeing the bursting chrysanthemums.

Eddy scuffs the ground with his shoe. The rain the other night loosened things up but it's been dry since. He supposes it's safe enough.

A tattoo on his arm, a winged lady in a flowing dress, dances in streams of sweat. Bo moves so smooth it would be easy, Eddy thinks, to forget these things are made to blow up.

"Are you going to need help with the show?" Eddy asks. It is so hot their sweat might soon boil, bubbling on their skin, sizzling the hairs that crawl down Bo's neck to his back, creep across his shoulders.

"Don't I wish you could," Bo says, "but it's got to be legal."

Eddy points to the fireworks lined up in the back of the truck. "You load those now?"

Bo checks his watch, shakes his head. "Another hour, maybe two. Show's at ten, right? So I'll probably start around six-thirty." He counts, pointing with his fingers, the bulbs of papier mâché, then the mortars, nodding. To Eddy he says, "But thanks, thanks plenty for your help, buddy. Enjoy the show."

"Sure," Eddy says, but he feels awkward with this, something unfinished here, thinks maybe he's waiting for a handshake, but Bo is busy, alone this time, and Eddy turns to head down the hill. It's not really his party tonight after all, and besides, there are things he must finish up.

He collects the bike from Mamie's garage. Its green is the color of artificial carpet, with thin yellow stripes around the fenders, even to the trim edges except near the back of the seat where Eddy slipped, the line wavering a bit. He holds the bike away from him, inspecting it, and decides again that Gasman George might not notice it. He walks it further down the street because riding it just wouldn't be right.

The address won't be hard to find, Mamie has told him, and he can see why as he nears the number. The wooden house with worn-away paint, a slope-shouldered refrigerator hunched on the front porch tell Eddy that whoever's supposed to be looking after George and his sister have failed. He reaches his hand out, but before he can knock, Gasman George is at the door, face near the screen, his eyes wide with curiosity or fear and maybe recognition, though Eddy can't be sure.

Eddy gestures to the bike. "I fixed it for you, George. Fixed it and brought it back to you. Here." He holds it at arm's length as if posing it for the man's inspection. George looks from Eddy's face to the bicycle and back again, then studies the bike, his hands pressing the screen door open when he leans closer to look.

"Mine," George says. "My bike."

"Right, George. Your bike, all fixed and with a new tire and new paint. Here." Eddy carefully nudges the kickstand with his toe, laying the weight of the bike against it to prop it up. He back-steps from it, and the porch moans under his feet. It looks new, Eddy decides, or very nearly new. It is the brightest, shiniest thing on the property and Eddy knows how George feels around it.

As if approaching an untamed animal or rabid dog, George slips from the house, closing the screen door gently behind him. He reaches to touch the bike, reaches his hand far out in front of himself, lets it guide him to the bike as if he were blind, groping. He strokes it, fender to fender, the polished handlebars, scrubbed seat. He crouches to squeeze the tires. "Ahh...ahh!" He nods, smiles a crooked, brown-toothed smile at it.

"Do you like the stripes I made you, George?" Eddy points to the yellow that binds the bike like a painted ribbon. "Do you like the stripe?"

George points to it, looks at Eddy, who nods. The man traces his rough fingers, fingers like brown leather gloves, thick and cracked, traces them along the line of the yellow, nodding, nodding until he traces the glitch, the slipped line. His finger and Eddy's breath stop. He looks at Eddy, points to the wavering pinstripe.

"Sorry about that George," Eddy says. "I goofed." It is all Eddy can think of to say, his mind full of scolding for talking to a grown man as if he were a child. Who knows what goes on behind those eyes? Who knows what he thinks of any of the rest of us?

"Goofed," George repeats. He stands. "You goofed. My bike, your goof."

Eddy nods, admitting his fault. "My goof, your green bike."

"Green bike." And he laughs, his mouth opening into a joke only he understands, laughs with shoulders shaking, tears in his eyes. He reaches out his hand to Eddy and Eddy takes it, shakes it, and laughs with him. In the front window appears a woman's face with angry eyes, red and silver hair stretching in all directions, turquoise cardigan sweater despite the heat. When she sees him looking at her a smile creeps onto her face like a question, a coy smile from an old Lillian Gish movie. And she disappears.

"Well, George, I'm glad to get your bike back to you in one piece. I guess I better go now."

George looks again at the bike and shakes his head.

"See you, George. Ride carefully, okay?" Eddy starts down the sidewalk. There is something else, something resting quietly on the back porch of his mind like a sleeping dog, something he should say, something he feels responsible for, something he shouldn't walk away from.

George waves. The fear seems gone from him, his hand steady and sure, his smile broad, creasing his eyes at the corners. "Thanks," he says, his voice like his sister's voice. "Thanks."

"Sure, George. Anytime." Eddy can return the wave but not the smile. Down the street he walks, trying not to look back because for all the steps he makes he knows he hasn't yet walked away.

The Reverend Bleu opens another package of Ball Park franks and rolls them onto the grill, the charcoal grease spitting back at him. He rubs his left hand over his right arm to wipe the sting away. He twists the hot dogs with the long-tined fork and wears an apron that reads, "For this I went to college?" but he's thinking it should read, "Hotter Than Hell." He is exhausted. Only the barbeque splattering grease at him keeps him awake.

All of the regular members have come to devour bread-wrapped hot dogs—less expensive than buns, the hot dogs lying diagonally across a choice of white or wheat bread—potato chips, Sandy's famous potato salad and baked beans, broasted and deep-fried chicken and every manner of cookies, cakes and pies. The families are well-practiced in picnic feasts which, food-wise, are so similar to funeral dinners and wedding receptions. They line buffet tables, passing serving spoons across or down the line, nodding and murmuring about the amount of food, guessing ingredients, taste, cooks.

The tables line the far end of the church property on the other side of the parking lot, a spot of grassy ground about half the size of a football field that church parents bought so raucous Cub Scouts could run off energy out here in "Capture the Flag" and so the Camp Fire Girls could camp out safely on summer nights. But the Cub Scouts never took to the games and the Camp Fire Girls wanted real woods, so the grounds have been abandoned by all but the men who rotate turns mowing the grass.

Six years ago, when the Reverend Bleu arrived, he bought badminton and croquet sets, baseballs, bats and mitts, but the younger members of the church couldn't be enticed into using the back lot that was always, it seemed, too hot or wet. He began thinking of selling the patch of land to one of the homeowners whose property borders the lot, all of them with more money for building pools or decks or maybe even a tennis court, but in the third year when he mentioned this to Sandy she would have none of it, suggesting they have picnics, holiday fairs, church bazaars "like the Catholics have" and carnivals. He relented. The Fourth of July picnics have been the only events out here since that conversation and many of the picnics have been cancelled because of rain or excessive heat. The reverend wonders why she's so sure they can win this year against the sun and heavy air, wonders at her faith despite it all.

He forks a gleaming hot dog onto Frankie Messer's plate, the fourth one for the boy who walks away without a thank you, his pale, bubbly skin pressed between his thighs, forcing him to walk with his legs spread a little, his roly-poly

None But The Dead And Dying

arms out a bit from his shoulders, holding his plate out in front of him as if he is offering a sacrifice to pagan gods.

Metal folding chairs have been carried from the church but the kids, Reverend Bleu sees, have commandeered them. He's thankful many of the older members have thought to bring lawn chairs with them, sitting in tiny patches of shade that shrink and move and tease, pulling them out of their chairs to shift them, circling, crowding closer.

The idea started a few years ago that they would gather and picnic, waiting for the sky to darken, for the fireworks to begin, the trees far enough across the lawn that the sky opens up to show every bomb that might burst in the air. Each year the picnic starts earlier and is more elaborate, the church doing more and more, the families attending doing less and less. The reverend, when he thinks of it, imagines that in another few years it will be a breakfast and he will be flipping all the eggs, toasting all the bread, frying all the bacon, serving his own congregation and maybe a few visiting from Fremont, Bellevue, Castalia, maybe even Sandusky and Tiffin.

He forks out another hot dog. He is thinking that if Sandy wants to have the picnic again next year she can play short-order grill attendant because this year is his last. He slits open another package of franks, frowns when he sees two more packages awaiting him in the cooler. He relines the grill with the meat, hot splatters of grease from the coals snapping at him. He nearly swears but bites his tongue. He needs a drink, the cool inside of the Bahama Lounge.

"How're we doing?" Sandy asks, her rounds complete, her plate full, standing across the grill from him.

He wants to say, "I don't see you sweating back here, what's with the 'we'?" but of course he doesn't, just tells her there are only two more packages left. He squints through rolling sweat and sun to the gathered parishioners. Mundee Manway isn't among them, and he wonders about that—she's a regular for free food, studying the weekly paper for funeral and wedding announcements, watching for locations, and no one turns her away when she shows up. They have always eaten their fill by the time Mundee has walked to the church, so her grimy fingers in the chip dip or reaching a dirty sleeve across a casserole are tolerable to them by then. She once told the reverend that the Baptists on Duane Street have the best services but his church has the best food, and he takes an odd pride in this. He's heard she sometimes bowls with the Lutheran League team because they always eat free afterwards—the six-lane bowling alley owned and run by one of the church trustees happy to accommodate the folks he worships with.

Maybe it's the heat or maybe it's their nature, but they are quiet, these people from his own congregation, nibbling from white paper plates balanced expertly on their laps, some of them sprawled on the ground but all of them placid, settled. Even those who've finished sit idle next to grounded Frisbees and baseballs. The badminton net sags in the sun, and the reverend thinks this could be a photograph, a still shot, still as the breeze.

"Do you think I should heat them up?" he asks Sandy, pointing to the cooler, to the two packages. "Or do you think everybody's about done anyway? I don't want to see them go to waste." But maybe they already have, he thinks. Maybe they should have donated the whole shebang to a homeless shelter or place for battered women or maybe to the Indians holding their vigil outside of town, the hot dogs and bread and potato salad and roasted chicken and plenty of knives and forks and spoons and paper plates for all of them.

"Go ahead and cook them up," Sandy says. "We can't have too much." She holds out a plate to him, heaped with salads and sweets. "Here," she says. "I fixed a plate for you. I know you're not much for sweets, but wait'll you taste Marcie Brannon's cake—three layers of different chocolates. She's real proud of it, Clayton." He is staring at her neck and is suddenly aware that he is. The gentle sweep of that neck down to her shoulders, down to her spine where her top vertebrae jut out, this neck is burning right in front of him, burning under the sun, and he knows that tonight there will be lines tracing the memory of her sundress, the sleeveless top and scooped neck and he sees the smoothness of her skin browning to the shade of her hair and he thinks, we're really not very old. We really haven't come that far yet, together.

She stands, holding out the plate to him. "Clayton? Are you listening?" The hand on the hip.

"I'm sorry, honey. It's just that—" He stops. She's never liked him to be intimate in public. Not becoming to their positions in the church, she's said, reminding him that this is a job they have together. She has always been better at this than he is.

He begins to pack up the potato salad, the crisp lettuce, tugging transparent wrap taut over the edges of the bowls, twisting closed the tops of chip and bread bags.

"Clayton?" Sandy says, nudging him. He looks up to see that Frankie Messer's back for a fifth hot dog.

"Sorry," the reverend says, forking the half-dozen weiners from the grill onto a plate, wrapping it. "This picnic is moving down the road." He walks the length of the table, spooning the final slices of strawberry short cake into the tin with the last pieces of cherry pie, stacking cookies and brownies and wrapping, wrapping, wrapping, careful not to crush anything.

Sandy follows, watching him wrap and stack, re-capping the two-liter bottles of Pepsi and Dr. Pepper and 7-Up, tucking them into the coolers where ice water sloshes around them. "What *are* you doing, Clayton? We're not nearly finished here. Frankie wants another hot dog."

"Frankie's mommie can do that for him," the Reverend Bleu says, snapping the lid of the cooler closed.

"Will you stop?" Her whisper is harsh and he looks again at her face, the pale brown eyes that seem to bleach every summer with the sun, that long slope of neck. "People are watching," she says.

He kisses her on that neck, in that scooped out hollow at her shoulder and she snaps back from him, flicking her hand at him as though his lips were a swarm of mosquitoes out to infect her with malaria, out for blood.

But he smiles and gathers up the food, making three trips to the Chevette to load it all in before, with a wave, he heads out of the parking lot, out of town.

The sun is starting its gradual drop to the horizon like a slow-motion roller coaster train on its descent from the highest hill, and it will go faster and faster the closer it gets to the bottom. It burns bright orange into reflecting windows and it changes the colors of things, but Crescent knows there is no hurry to get to the park, it will take hours for the sky to wash black after the sun itself is gone because it leaves so many trailers in its wake, reminders of the day bright overhead.

She tries to think of what could be the problem with Hope the way she rambles on about the church picnic today and her father's weird departure from it, but she knows there is something else, something underneath it like a too-tight bra under a tank top, squeezing everything else out around it.

They cross White Street again, not far from Crescent's house, when it occurs to her that it must have to do with Denny, since she's been so preoccupied herself with Theodore. "So give it a rest," she says, finally. "You didn't come looking for me to tell me about the idiot church picnic."

"Well...."

Crescent stops, folds her arms across her chest. She taps her foot. People are barbecuing all over town, driveways brimming with cars they have to walk into the street or way up into yards to go around. Her family has never celebrated much, Christmas, birthdays, her parents' anniversary worthy of a few gifts, maybe a cake, but no more. They don't vacation, they don't have friends or relatives in from out of town for a few days, ever. She will do it differently when she is on her own, she's decided. She carries plans in her head for the first party she will throw at OSU when she gets there in the fall. She will meet people who will become old friends who will visit her years and years from now on Independence Day when they can gather on her deck to barbecue and drink beer.

She taps her foot. "It's about Denny, right? Look, it's not like I'm too stupid to know you two are seeing each other. And it's okay with me, Hope, by the way, if that's your problem. Because I have somebody else now anyway."

Hope looks at her, eyebrows together, looking for the truth or the lie or the friendship. She sees something, sees enough to start the walk again, taking them past another stretch of cars along Main Street in front of the homes of funeral directors and the judge and the newspaper editor and plant foremen and school teachers. "I really like him a lot, Crescent," she says to the sidewalk.

Crescent runs to long-jump a stretch of hot black asphalt driveway. "Denny's a great guy," Crescent says, but it is too easy and she knows it. There should be something else, shouldn't there? When there was so much, for so long, and so many dreams between them, but now they're all changed, the dreams and them, everything different, rushing this way into the sunset and the fireworks and the end of the summer and going too far away in too many ways. "He's a great guy," Crescent says. "And, after all, you'll be here and I'll be gone."

Hope looks at her as if this makes no sense to her, but Crescent doesn't care, because it makes complete sense to her, and that's all that matters any more. "Let's go see if Mr. Thompson wants to go to the park with us," Crescent says, and she feels a little more right saying it, but not much.

It is as though he is waiting for them and Crescent can see that he is surprised she is not alone but what can she do? So she directs him: "No, no, don't bother with the chair, just a blanket. You got a blanket? An old one? That's it. That's all we need."

They walk Mulberry across South Street, Theodore following the girls in his Bermuda shorts, polo shirt and Off! Insect spray. Weaving through the crowd already forming around Waterworks Pond with their lawn chairs and blankets, their coolers and little kids with sparklers screaming circles around them, the girls and Theodore reach the opposite ridge of the pond from where the fireworks will be launched. In the fading light they can see a white panel truck and something that looks like the empty frame of a small billboard sign. They start up this hill facing the set-up, the creek cutting deep between the hills where a policeman patrols to keep kids from this area where the ashy fall-out will come.

"Here," Crescent says, talking over her left shoulder to Theodore. "This is a great place. If you get the right angle on the hill you can lay back and it's like they come right down on you." She slips the blanket from under Theodore's arm and hands a corner to Hope. They spread the olive green army blanket over the grass, smoothing out edges that kids running past ruffle.

Crescent and Hope drop easily onto it while Theodore bends more slowly to sit cross-legged, the cedar smell of the chest the blanket has been stored in drifting into the air.

None But The Dead And Dying

"Great, huh?" Crescent says to Theodore. She nudges her sandals off with her toes, then points to the sky, nearly straight overhead. "That's where they'll go off."

He cranes his neck to follow her finger. Stars are faint in the darkening stretch over their heads. Across the park, across the creek, a man makes announcements of winners in the water balloon toss from the baseball diamonds. "Now we're looking for girls aged eight to thirteen with their dads. Come on, dads, team up with your girls for some balloon tossing! We got a few, good, good, but we're going to need more. Looks like our champ dad from the fourteen to seventeen age group is back out there. Hiya Don! All those girls of yours in their teens this summer, eh? Come on and give Don some competition here! Father-daughter balloon toss, eight to thirteen! Tee shirts to the winning team!"

She has been watching the crowd but it is still sudden when Hope gets up, waving into the crowd further up the hill. "I'll see you guys," she says. Taking long strides up the hill, she leaves them alone.

Crescent twists to see that Denny stands apart from his friends, his arms outstretched, ready to take Hope in. Crescent turns away, sees the curiosity in Theodore's face. "Her boyfriend," Crescent says, trying very hard not to say more.

"I think the last time I was here," Theodore says, "they had coin tosses. And one year, I guess I was about your age, Jack Welch crammed fifteen hot dogs into his mouth in thirteen minutes to win a fast-eating contest."

"I'll bet that record still stands," Crescent says, and Theodore laughs, but she can only stare at the sky and wish it would get darker faster, that the man on the microphone would just shut up, shut up, shut up, and then there is finally the announcement they've been waiting for, something about the factory money making the celebration possible, with help from community project funds. The flash of lights around the now-empty baseball diamonds slam off, the park dark and ready, then a THWUMP and a burst of colored light—red, then white, then blue exploding over their heads. They lay back and it is like the colors are falling, chips of purple and silver and shimmering gold sky showering down, down, but never quite far enough, and Crescent oohs and ahs and claps and hopes that just one sliver of bright light might drop against her cheek.

At the edge of Mamie's porch, Eddy balanced on the railing and Mamie in her chair close to him, they watch the fireworks blossom between maple trees, over the roofs of houses. He has been telling her how they're fired, how the first fuse takes just two seconds, the charge fuse less than that to send it up, the timer fuse adjusted so it will go off at the right height, and she has listened and nodded and sipped her drink.

She thinks that after all these years of watching, this is the year she sees so much more.

When he asks, before they are done, if he can borrow her car, she says yes, though she will miss him beside her, the sky bright but empty without him. She tells him where to find the key and she hears him open the garage door, hears the car try not to start, trying to keep him near her, but after a few tries, it gives in to him and she understands that, and allows herself to wave back when he pulls from her driveway onto the street. Overhead a huge burst of red, white and blue thunders and showers on the town.

16

At first they were reluctant to take the food, watching him while he unloaded the car, taking out platters of desserts and chicken and casseroles that suddenly seemed the wrong things, too much or too sweet, but the Reverend Clayton Bleu didn't know what else to do but to bring them out of the car, set them down, let them decide about it all. If only he hadn't babbled on and on: "We were having a picnic out at the church and there was so much left over, well, actually, these aren't leftovers, exactly, I mean, most of it, well, some of it, hasn't even been touched, not that we would bring you only what we couldn't finish, I guess that sounds pretty cold, though some of the food is, the food that's meant to be, cold, I mean, you know?"

They silenced him, eventually, with their own silence, with the gentle hands of the women who carried the trays and packages and pie tins away from him as if transferring his burden to themselves, their smiles shy. And the looks on the faces of the men told him he was making a fool of himself, the smiles they gave each other, tried weakly to hide from him, but Daniel Yellow Wolf shook his hand, said they appreciated it, the situation was lasting longer than they had anticipated, and walked Clayton away from the group around the drum.

Out here, away from the town, a breeze stirred around them, combing the long grassy weeds into wavy masses in the ditches along the road. At the corner of Landers Stone's driveway and the road rested a huge rock and the two men perched themselves on it. Daniel Yellow Wolf has talked awhile but Clayton finds it hard to listen, watching the clouds overhead. He has lost track of time, but it is probably early evening, maybe seven o'clock, though the sun beats as though it is noon yet.

From here he can see miles across the fields to faraway farms and barns and thin strips of roads. Above, clouds gather and part like groups at cocktail parties, breaking up and re-forming, invisible attractions, powerful enough only to hold them a little while, pulling them this way, then that. They hang low, flat on the bottom, rising into the sky. Looking at them from here is like looking at a skyscraper from the side, seeing it climb, solid on the inside, the world of the clouds.

When he was a boy in Nebraska he watched clouds this way. He tells Daniel Yellow Wolf this, tells him he thought that if the clouds would just part a little more he would see God, or maybe Jesus, and then he would know. He would sit on the back wooden steps, the clouds longer and taller and heavier even than these, crawling over the widest horizon. He waited and watched the forms shift, the clouds giving up on him, moving on but never shifting far enough for him to see, other clouds crowding in to keep their secret hidden.

Blue sky days held no such secrets from him. God was accessible enough in goldenrod and grasshoppers and creek water splashing over rocks. Cloudy, stormy days were when He closeted Himself away, drew the blinds, hung out His Keep Out, Do Not Disturb sign.

Next to Daniel Yellow Wolf he watches for those secrets

None But The Dead And Dying

again, but they are no more his to learn than ever. Yellow Wolf claps him on the shoulder, stands. In the gathering dusk, so many things draped by the night, he is hard to see, even from a few feet away. "Thanks," he says, "for thinking of us with the food. We do appreciate it."

"Sure," Clayton says, and watches him walk back toward the group who have long finished their meal and cleaned their campsite. Clayton, thinking it is probably time to head back, begins to walk toward his car, picking his way through the fading light.

In the distance, a flicker, maybe heat lightning, so he stops to watch for it again and sees that it is the fireworks display going off in town, faint, the colors nearly gone this far away, but he rests again on the rock, the sky low down near the town sparkling glitter raining down behind the Catholic church spire. Another half an hour passes and he knows it has to be moving up toward eleven, knows that Sandy will be upset again, another late homecoming and tonight he cares more than he has about her anger, her jealousy. It is another thing that careens away from him, as though at the core of him is a firecracker of his own going off, spewing hot sparks in hundreds of directions, burning anybody too close.

He turns toward the road, sorting through the darkness for his car, sees the headlights of another car headed for them, steadily, until it nears and slows and stops along the side of the road. The headlights go out—it is as if the car vanishes entirely until the interior light flashes on and Clayton can see that there are two people, one getting out of the driver's side of the car, another sitting on the passenger side. The car is bigger than most people are buying these days, and it looks familiar to him but he cannot place it.

The light flashes out and Clayton walks in the direction of it, trying to watch his footing and the car at the same time. The interior light flashes again, the passenger door being held open for someone who doesn't seem to be getting out. Clayton picks up his pace, trips but doesn't fall in the long grass.

As he nears, he sees that it is Eddy Light Sky at the car, that Daniel Yellow Wolf has gone to greet him. He sees that the car is the old one Mamie Van Allen used to drive, and he wonders why on earth Mamie would want to be driven out here at this time of the night, tonight.

"Eddy," he says, coming close to the car, nodding in greeting, and he starts to say hello to Mamie, but there is a quick motion from Eddy and Clayton stops. In the passenger seat, his frightened, quivering face studying them all, sits Gasman George.

Contessa sits on her back porch, screened in from the booming firecrackers, watching the flashes of light from them shimmer against the grass and the house behind hers. It is as though somewhere high up a huge color television is on, sound distorted, throwing flickering images around but there is nowhere for them to go, so they fall all over the place, splatters of red or blue or gold, of purple and white and silver.

She dreamed last night that it was Jack's funeral again, but Deborah was with him, a sort of double coffin, and she was crying. The reverend was giving the eulogy, but what he was saying wasn't about Jack or little Deborah, but about Contessa, about how she used to date Theodore but hadn't trusted him in college, hadn't trusted he would come back, how she was caught this way by Jack Welch, by his eyes, his strong arms, by an urgency that brought them Deborah. The reverend talked about how she watched Eddy in the diner that day, how she'd wanted him, dreamt of him, how she even wanted the reverend himself, no wonder her husband and daughter had been taken. She sat alone, listening, and when she tried to leave, men from the town, men she didn't know, held the doors closed, sealing her in.

The congregation lifted Jack out of his coffin, held him up for her to see. "He did this because of you," they said, and when they picked up Deborah she was like a doll, long lashes closed, arms stiff at her sides, her ivory satin dress heavy with lace and promise, but they dropped her in their clumsy handling of her, not able to see how fragile she was, and she crashed, her eyes coming open. Contessa screamed and tried to run to her, to help her, but they held her and she struggled but couldn't get free. She cried and heard Deborah cry and she woke up, hot and sweating, her face and pillow and sheets damp.

She tried to remember, then, which pants he wore, remembered she didn't have them anymore, but that she still had his wallet, someplace, and tried to remember where it was. She searched the desk, the dresser, and, finally, tucked into a box in a drawer in a downstairs closet marked "Jack's things," she found it.

Once textured leather, it was worn smooth to her touch, shiny in spots, the inside lining torn, threads sticking from it, and she thought of how she meant to buy him one at Christmas, a new one, expensive, with Isotoner driving gloves to match and then she realized how silly, Jack would never have worn them, would have thought them too sissy, like so many other gifts she bought him he never wore, never used, never wanted.

Her fingers sorted through the slit plastic pockets, her picture—bathing suit, showing her figure—slipped in there, but she couldn't imagine where he took it, when they last went to the beach. Then, other things in the wallet: his driver's license with that slicked hair (did he really wear it like that?—a let's-get-it-over-with look on his face—did he give that look to her? in bed? alone?), his credit cards, an insurance card, his union card and journeyman card, AAA Plus card, and she stopped for a minute to think what she was hoping to find. Then, another card, names and phone numbers, lodge friends, people she knows.

"Come on," she said, "tell me. Tell me, Jack, tell me why." She flipped through the cards again, squeezing her fingers into tiny, flat pockets, empty except for one torn slip of paper. She drew it out, peered at it, leaned near the light to read folded ink that had bled with age, a phone number. "Oh, God, Jack," she said. "Oh, God," and then realized the number was hers, her parents' house, all those years ago, the slip she'd passed to him that day in the soda fountain.

She sits through the final flickering of the fireworks reflections across her lawn and house, sits until she hears the cars travel the street, the sudden slap and bang of illegal firecrackers, a now and then sizzle and boom of an illegal rocket. She sits and fingers the slip of paper, smooth like the wallet was against her fingertips.

The slamming of a car door comes clearly through the open doors and windows to Landers Stone and he rises to flick off the kitchen light. Only from darkness, he has learned, can he see clearly into darkness. The angle from the screen door shows that the circle where the Indians have been spending their days is filling again. Hours after removing the drum, after the media and nosy neighbors have gotten into cars and vans and pickups and have driven away, a group assembles again. It is hard to make out figures, details, the moon in its last quarter offering only the barest of light, but Landers thinks there might be two cars along the road.

From the back window over the kitchen sink he can make

out the burial site, though Diamond doesn't seem to be around. "Damn," Landers says, reaching to snap on the lights around the site. Sprawled along the front ridge of the pit is Diamond Richards and he scrambles up, caught in the light, and he aims his gun, shouting.

Out the back door, Landers leaps from the short porch. "Put that down, dammit Diamond," he yells, and Diamond obeys, taking his usual legs-spread-at-shoulder-length stance.

Down the driveway sit two cars and Landers heads toward them, passing Indians emerging from tents and truck campers, holding flashlights. High beside them, in the house, an upstairs bedroom light goes on, then out again, and Landers knows Bessie is settling near the window, in the dark, to watch them below her.

Daniel Yellow Wolf is heading toward him up the driveway with three men, one of them the Reverend Clayton Bleu. Landers sees that Gasman George Freeman is with them and he is right away relieved. "It's about time," he says, and holds his hand out to shake theirs. The third man is someone they call Eddy, who has brought George.

"Why don't you show George what all the excitement's been about?" the man Eddy asks, and Landers shrugs. Nothing can make this any more complicated than it already is.

George walks beside him, a loping, careful walk that still manages to find tangles of weeds and ruts to stumble over. "Sorry," George says when he trips a little, when someone steadies him. The path tonight to the edge of the pit is stretched long in shadows from the moon and floodlights. Diamond Richards steps aside for them and they stop, their breath heavy though not from their walk. The pit is bright and clear, the high-wattage lamps casting daylight over the site. Hatchets with stone heads and jagged bowls shimmer, the skeletal remains of fourteen or so bodies, their rib cages, eye sockets or backs of skulls dusted clean and smooth. Not the glossy white of plastic school science models, these—in their dull brown and off-white they seem to want only to fade into the earth, to keep on taking on the colors of the rich soil.

George stands looking into the pit for a long time, studying each figure, the objects around them. He stands a long time, his body still except for eyes that search and search for answers to silent questions.

Behind them a drummer begins a steady rhythm, the sound of their hearts beating loud around them, outside them, and a chanter calls out to them in hushed monotones. On either side of George stand Daniel Yellow Wolf and the man Eddy.

"Call Mason," someone says. Landers looks behind them to see that the Reverend Bleu is nearby. "Call them all. Ben, Mason, that archaeologist Olson," the reverend says, and Landers nods, heading back to the house at a walk, then a jog, then a run.

They are not yet in bed, the fireworks not that long over, and he reaches them all—the mayor already on his way, alerted by local police who thought Mamie's car was stolen when they spotted Eddy driving it out of town and radioed the chief, who knew Stevens ought to be alerted. They've been watching the odd Indian since his right foot crossed into the town limits last month, and figure that now the stranger is making some move. Mason Pope, not yet home from the Waterworks Pond park celebration, is left a message by his wife who tells Landers she's sure he'll be right there, so he creeps up the stairs without turning on the light to tell Bessie she just might want to get dressed and come down.

From the window he watches as they move the circle, winding it further back on the property, closer to the burial site. Dozens of Indians, men, women, children—he has lost track, he realizes, of how many have come here to pray in their way. "It's about time," he says, and Bessie frowns at him, she is so used to his complaints about how slow she is to dress, but tonight this isn't what he means because she is beautiful in the strange yellow glow of the room. He holds her and kisses her and she smiles so he knows she understands.

Holding hands, Landers and Bessie leave their house, stepping along in the hop-sliding way that is dancing, joining the Indian dancers in their trail from the driveway to the burial site. The Stones have heard the songs enough days now that they hear the difference in this one, and though they do not know the words, cannot know for sure, they sense its promise, its hope, its wish for peace, the drum, the singing, the dancing that is gentle over the earth, the toe-touching a whisper against the womb beneath their feet.

They pass the Reverend Bleu who stands to the side of the driveway, his hands clasped in prayer but his eyes on them, his lips moving to his own chant, his own wish.

The drum or maybe the screech of car brakes summons the migrant workers, too, who scramble from tight quarters in tiny shacks or overcrowded trailers, snatching on clothes to head for the burial site. Something is happening that has not been planned and that makes it important.

It seems like forever, it seems like no time at all before the mayor and the archaeologist arrive. "Got your message just after you left it, Bud," Ben says to Landers. "What's going on?"

"Look," Landers says.

In the center of a newly formed circle at the front base of the ridge, a pipe is offered to the six directions and sweetgrass burns. A man who understands things not seen leads the ceremony, a man they don't know, a man with a great deep voice and eyes that are nearly blind.

When it is time, they ask George to speak to them. "Tell us what it is you wish," Daniel Yellow Wolf says, and George nods. He stands at the edge of the circle, his back to the front ridge of the pit.

He hesitates before walking to the edge of the pit, before turning to look again into it, his back to the crowd, his head bowed.

It is the look on his face when he turns back to them that they will talk about around the town for years to come, the shine in his eyes that might be a healing or tears.

Ben Stevens sees it clearly, that look, the face so familiar in its frightened scowl that is now so calm, a face confused but now clear. Later, when he sorts this night through, he will decide it was his own fear that compelled him to do what he did, the fear that things changing are sometimes more terrifying than things staying the same, and it is this look on Gasman George's face that convinces him of this truth. To come to know someone one way and then see them change right smack dab in front of you, he will tell people later, that's something downright scary.

Later they will discuss, over coffee at the Country Inn, whether it was the power building in Gasman that stirred people, and Ben will only be able to ponder that, sipping the thin coffee to keep from having to answer.

Because of this power in Gasman George, at this minute, on the rise at the edge of the dig, Ben knows that if George speaks, his words will possess a final authority. Around him, the Indians settle into quiet, many in the front crouching or sitting on the ground. The drum is silent and the night spreads open many promises overhead.

Next to Landers, Ben tries to catch his breath, he has been rushing since getting the phone message that someone has brought Gasman out here, but nothing wants him to catch up, and so he pants, taking deep breaths, summoning the words, the courage. Mason Pope might not get here until it is too late; it is up to him.

He steps forward, excusing himself through the crowd, stepping carefully around others who stand, crossing carefully over those who sit. He makes a show of moving forward, and this causes the disruption he needs. "Excuse me, excuse me, thank you, so nice to see you," he says, stalling, moving, smiling, trying to keep smiling, until he is right in front of Gasman, holding out his hand to greet him, but Gasman looks at him, some confusion returning to his face, and for a minute Ben is confused: is this really what he wants, after all?

"I just want to say," Ben begins, nodding to Gasman, turning his offered handshake into a small wave, "that as mayor, we're tickled pink that you've allowed such generous exploration of your property here so that we all"—he gestures around the crowd, careful to include the Indians—"can learn more about each other. I think this might just be the time to let you know that our plans continue for the improvement of the property and the preservation"—he is delicate with the word, emphasizing it, caressing it—"of a bit of a valuable heritage. Without your cooperation, Mr. Freeman, such a project could never continue, and so you benefit us tremendously by your generosity...." There is more he needs to say but they know he is interrupting, babbling, and they begin to stand in the front, and he suddenly isn't sure what they might do.

He feels a hand on his sleeve and he turns. Daniel Yellow Wolf reaches to shake his hand. "Thank you, Mr. Mayor," he says, "for sharing your view on this. Tonight we wish to hear what Mr. Freeman has to say."

And they turn again and look to Gasman. In his few words, Yellow Wolf has pulled the crowd back together, back in again. It can't be this simple, Ben thinks.

Through the crowd emerges another, out of place in a light golf shirt and slacks, Mason Pope, snaking his way through the gathering, his smile slight, his steps graceful and confident. "May I just have a word?" he asks, but he doesn't wait for an answer, saying, "While we appreciate your perspective on this, Mr. Yellow Wolf, this is our situation, and will be handled as we see fit for the benefit of the community and for the benefit of Mr. Freeman. We have been quite liberal about allowing you to remain on the premises but you ought to be reminded that this is private property and that you are trespassing. My understanding is that you are here without the approval of Mr. Freeman, but are uninvited guests, as it were."

Daniel Yellow Wolf stands erect and silent, his arms crossed against his chest, waiting for his fellow member of the bar to finish. Mason Pope continues, "This has gone just about far enough and I must ask that you vacate the premises immediately. I have asked our police chief to stand by in case official complaint must be made or in case we need to have you removed."

"Well said, Counselor," Yellow Wolf says. "We agree to leave after we hear what Mr. Freeman wants."

"You've already been informed of the plans for this site," Mason Pope says.

The crowd shifts, finding more comfortable footing, easier sitting, but they are quiet, listening, the world around them silent except for this discussion in front of them. Ben Stevens stands among them, hoping vainly for the words he needs to come to him, but he can only stand to the side like a spare part, helpless. Across the way he sees Clayton Bleu and he wonders why he is here, of all people, and thinks that this makes two of them. Gasman George is maybe three.

To one side, near Landers, stands Olson, and behind him, arriving just now at a run, are his assistants and volunteers, chattering, whispering, gesturing—hushed by the crowd. Olson, too, motions for their silence. It is out of his hands. Whatever it is that he wants no longer matters.

None But The Dead And Dying

"No," Gasman George says. He has been watching with the rest of them, listening, showing no reaction, but now the word comes out, then erupts again, this time more emphatically: "No!"

"No, what, George?" a man next to him says. This man is an Indian Ben doesn't know but from the way Gasman looks at him they seem to be friends. "Tell everybody what it is you're thinking about all this."

"George, you don't have to say anything," Mason says. He steps closer to George, his hand out as if to stop the words. "I can handle this for you."

"Maybe you've already handled too much for him," Yellow Wolf says, and the crowd, for the first time, hoots a bit, claps a bit, and the man next to George, the other Indian, grins.

"I know what's in the best interest of my client," Mason says, and Yellow Wolf shrugs his shoulders.

"Maybe you know what's in the best interest financially, for both of you," Yellow Wolf says. "But maybe it's not what Mr. Freeman wants. He can tell us. Besides, if you're so sure what he wants is what you want, what are you worried about?"

Mason Pope has no answer for this, at least not one they can hear, for the crowd has taken up the chant of George's name, "Freeman, Freeman," so Pope's mouth moves, but no one is listening. There is only one person they want to hear.

Ben takes a deep breath, moves to stand near Bessie and Landers Stone again where the couple hold their arms around each other in a show of affection he isn't used to seeing in them. Around the semicircle in front of the burial pit other couples move closer, young men and young women whispering as the chant fades.

The man next to Gasman says something to him, and though Ben can't hear it he can see from the gesture that it is an encouragement to speak. Daniel Yellow Wolf motions for the crowd to quiet.

It is that time of the night when even the birds sleep, their heads tucked under wings, some of them with one foot up, an odd balance on branches lean and supple in any breeze. It is that time of the night when cicadas purr from hiding places, when cats in heat cry like babies in fields or under porches, when train whistles wail louder than at any other time. It is that time of the night, if you are alone, that you feel most intensely alone, and when you are with someone you love, you feel most deeply in love.

It is that time of the night when people aren't expected to gather, yet here they are, on this farm that has become nearly home to many of them. It is that time of the night when magical things are most likely to happen, a time when fantasy becomes real, when someone like Gasman George can finally find the words.

He looks at them and they sit in silence, waiting, watching that look in his eye change them all. "This is mine," he says at last, pointing. "But not mine. Not yours." He points around the circle. "Nobody's." He turns to look again into the pit, his back to them.

A few hours ago, when Eddy borrowed Mamie's car, drove to pick up George, he didn't know what to expect, but all he had to do was tell him: "George, they're making decisions without you. Want to go and straighten them out?" And he had nodded his head, that shaking, sparse-haired head, and he smiled. At last someone had invited him, asked him to his own property, let him know they were willing to take the time to drive him there, show him, help him to understand, and then listen. He changed his clothes right away, sat silent in the car but fiddled with the radio buttons, finding a rap music station from Toledo that Eddy laughed to hear.

"What would you like done with the burial site, George?" Eddy asks him now, looking with him into the pit. "Tell the people what you want."

"Leave it be," he says. "Cover'm up and leave'm be."

Mason Pope starts up the rise to him. "George, listen to me—"

"No," George says, stopping him with his word, the shake of his head. "Mr. Pope, no." He looks at the man a moment, then lopes around the outside of the circle of the pit to the outside of the crowd where he kicks his way down the slanting side onto the path to the driveway. Eddy follows. "Home," George says, and Eddy nods his head.

They try to reach them, speak to them, say thanks or scold them, the mayor trotting after them, but Eddy guides George through it all, telling him, "It was about time they let you say what you think."

"About damn time," George says, and Eddy looks at him but the night is dark and he cannot see the man's face, but George laughs, and this makes Eddy chuckle. He opens the car door for George. Somewhere behind them he hears Daniel Yellow Wolf asking that the lights be turned off. Not too far from the car Eddy sees a medicine man in subdued regalia, performing a ritual at the edge of the corn field. Tonight will be a reburial; tomorrow tarp anchors, light poles, and a metal fence around loose dirt will be the only reminders that anything at all unusual has happened here.

17

he reverend gets out of his car where he has slept the night. It is only in this early dawning that he sees the Christian cemetery across the street. All this time, the burial site across the road, and now he notices it. He tells himself it's been the confusion of the extra vehicles, the strangers that have been crowding around, that has made it invisible to him.

Wrought iron gates read "Block Church," in an arch overhead, but the church is gone, only the markers of its long-dead congregation left. In Latin, words beneath the church's name that take a few moments for the reverend to translate, it has been so long since he has needed it.

> *Through me is the way into the woeful city,*
> *Through me is the way into eternal woe,*
> *Through me is the way among the Lost People.*

Standing in the slant of the rising sun, he is struck first by the poetry of the words and only after rereading does he wonder at their meaning. What sort of a congregation saw death this way?

A thick bell the color of the wet cement sits at a crooked angle on the ground. It is warm already to the reverend's touch but it doesn't move, no swing to its body, no clapper dangling within it. The people are gone, lost, and they have taken with them their sounds, the music of their church.

Warblers swoop from the solitary tree, perch on a marker at the far end of the graveyard. Except for their songs the countryside is all quiet this morning, the township road empty save for his own Chevette.

They have moved so quickly, he thinks, they were all here and now they are gone.

He wonders about Eddy—has he left with them?

Wind cuts through the tree, shifting the corn, green and strong and not yet topped out, leaves flat and slashing each other like wild applause, maybe at the reverend's recollection that the quote is from Dante.

He leans against the bell, pulls off socks and shoes, walks the clipped grass, sharp against the bottoms of his feet. The church has left but the people aren't lost.

Josiah Bugell, 1847-1894. Emma Bugell, 1845-1907.

Infant 1862: "Our Lamb." Rebecca Bugell, 1865-1870.

Luther Vanderhauf, 1887-1958. Sarah Vanderhauf, 1890-1962.

His feet are heavy with needed sleep, but he walks and reads and ignores the sun on his head, the open door of his car behind him, the corn ripening around him. The latest death date is eight years ago. And someone comes and weeds and cuts grass and he imagines someone like Theodore Thompson.

When he climbs back into his car, he's lost time again, but thinks only about the women, so many women, who've outlived husbands and children.

Hope, his daughter, where is she?

He turns the engine over in the Chevette and drives away from the sound of last night's drums. Loud and strong they were like a heartbeat he can still feel. He drives toward town, fast down lanes already cracking, asphalt stretching to breathe under the hot summer sun. He tries and tries but cannot think of where to look for her first.

Ben Stevens rests the phone receiver back in the cradle, presses his hand to his head, wipes his brow. Every day now, the rest of this July and all the way into September he will sweat, all day, like a cleansing that is never done, that stops only when he steps in the shower but starts again faster than his towel can keep up.

It is the heat but more than that it is this news from Frank Jessup at the plant. They are closing. Headquarters decided, Frank has told him, that this location is unnecessary.

"Dammit, I knew this was coming," he says to Mariann. She never seems to feel the sweltering humidity, sitting today at the kitchen table in a light cotton dress, her hair soft around her smooth face. Have I kept her this safe from worries? he wonders, needing to touch her cheek to feel the softness of it, to feel the secret of it.

"You did your best, Ben. They'll understand that you did," she says, and he knows that she is right, that in November when they elect new council members his term as mayor will be safe, but today it doesn't seem as though it should be.

"They're closing. And now, without the Stone farm...." He shrugs, slumps into a chair next to her. He takes her hand. "I don't know what else to do."

He feels the pressure of her fingers against his, a squeezing signal they use among others to show they are in on something together. He squeezes hers back. She says, "The town will survive. It always has. Something will carry it. Something will keep it going."

She is smiling, her lips pressed into it, and he leans to kiss her, put his arm around the back of her chair, around her.

None But The Dead And Dying

He draws her near, closes his eyes, resting, already, so early in the day.

A dream, just at its edge but gone before she can hold it, a dream she clenches her eyes tight to see again. And her hand, holding something, sweating, is the way she awakens this morning, stiff in her chair on the porch, her bottle empty on the table beside her but she isn't looking at that; she is looking at her hand, at the other hand holding hers so tightly. Eddy. Eddy who came back sometime in the night to touch her through her sleep.

He is looking at her, smiling. "You're beautiful in the morning, did you know that?" he asks, and she feels herself blush.

"No one has ever been around to see it."

"No one? Not ever? What a shame for the men of this earth."

"Don't tease an old woman, Eddy."

"I meant it." He stands, still holding her hand. She feels the long ache in her arm and wrist and he rubs it gently for her.

"You're going," Mamie says, and he nods. "Will you come back again?"

"I'll try, sweetheart. In the meantime, I'll miss you passionately." He leans to hug her, she feels his strength, his youth, his hands caressing her back, his lips grazing her ears. She wants to tell him she will miss him even more, wants to kiss his cheek, but is afraid of tears and pleas and losing dignity. Instead she lets loose of him and turns away so she won't have to see him head down the steps, walk away down the sidewalk.

A clear night it was last night, after the fireworks, after the music of the saxophone, and she watched for shooting stars, mysterious cloud shapes over the moon, waiting, waiting, but only stars she couldn't name glinted overhead.

When she is sure that Eddy is gone, she peels herself slowly from her chair, limb by limb, and gets unsteadily to her feet. Across the street Contessa is on her porch, shaking a small Oriental rug, and she pauses to wave. Only days have passed but she seems recovered. With each one, Mamie thinks, the rhythm of death, of survivng it, becomes a little more familiar. Cecelia Thompson. Jack Welch....

With effort and another sliver of pain through her arm, Mamie waves back. She turns to head into her house where her own rugs need beating and where she needs to decide about them, about everything that has been hers, all these years.

They sit on Theodore's front porch, holding hands, him sipping his morning coffee, complimenting her on her ability to get the combination of water and coffee just right. She nods, smiling, sipping her own cup because it is a college thing to do, remembering last night, in his attic.

She sat with him there, perched on a chair, its stuffing picked clean, sat and listened and watched him breathe fire through the horn before smothering that same fire only to fan it again, run with it until it caught them both, swallowing them so fully they forgot to drop and roll and put the music out.

Last night he improvised, he told her, dividing the sounds of others into his own, playing for her, for his memory of the couples who used to dance while his music echoed in the gym. She closed her eyes and pictured the dresses, the tacky decorations, the cheeks pressed together, heard the swish of skirts and baggy pants.

"Thank you for letting me listen to you play last night,"

she says, holding her mug up as if to toast him, and he turns, smiles. It is early enough that the birds sing to raise the sun through the trees. A dog barks a few streets over.

"It was nice to have an audience for once," he says, and she thinks about saying something, it would be so easy, maybe he's ready to know that they have been there all along, listening, applauding him with quiet nods and whispers at open windows and front porches and even the Catholic church bell tower.

"I'm going to miss it," she says, watching him. She has fantasized this conversation, has imagined that he will try to talk her out of going away to school, telling her she can't go, he needs her too much to let her leave, saying all the things to her he wished, years ago, Contessa Butler had said to him. So far he has said none of these things.

Coming up the street is Eddy Light Sky, his gentle, easy stride carrying him toward them. She wonders again about him, this lone traveller, no real job, no real home, yet he seems to be in total control. When I feel lost, she thinks, I will think of Eddy. When I think I don't fit in, I'll remember that nobody does.

They wave. "Mornin'," Eddy says, passing by.

She knows she will never see him again. She holds Theodore's hand more tightly.

"You know, Cress," Theodore says, "you're doing the best thing to go to school, to get out of here."

She sets her mug down on the little plastic table. "It doesn't always work, you know that."

He nods. "It will be different for you, though. Somehow we both know that."

"It will be different in a lot of ways, for me," she says. They are both saying this is over, that maybe she will spend a few more July and August nights in his attic before she retreats to the bell tower, to share in the secret, to pretend that if she isn't with him she can't hear the music of the saxophone. For now they will enjoy each other, will enjoy their own secret, while it lasts.

She watches Eddy turn the corner to head for Maple Street. She holds Theodore's hand across the little white plastic table.

"What?" Theodore says, and Crescent looks at him. "You looked like you were about to say something," he says.

"I did?"

He nods. "You even moved your mouth a little, like the words were right there."

"Huh," she says. "How about that." The words are right there, she feels the power of them forming in her head and throat. All she would have to say is, "We hear you, Theodore," that's all. Just like that day at the church, after Jack's funeral, those three simple words he uttered to her: "I saw you."

"What were you going to say?" he asks, and she smiles. She feels the words inside her, knows that more than anything right now she wants to say them, that they want to be said, that nothing is more important.

The dog is still barking in its penned yard someplace. A boy on a bike flips the morning *Sandusky Register* onto the porch, his blue torn tee shirt flapping.

No one in this town is more able to change things than she is at this moment, sitting here, sipping coffee, holding Theodore Thompson's hand. In another month she will move on, and in another month or so after that windows will start to close against chilly autumn winds and even jackets won't be enough to keep people on their porches to hear the midnight music. But it is just midsummer, with so many nights to come before that, so many nights of music in the dark.

"What is it, Cress?" he says, clenching her hand more tightly, urgently.

"Nothing," she says. "Nothing."

None But The Dead And Dying

Bessie drops the curtain to the front window as Landers steps into the living room. "What now?" he asks, sure that the media must finally be gone, he is so ready for it, so ready to go on.

"The reverend was out there all morning, walking in that cemetery across the street, but I guess he's gone now," she says, shaking her head. "I don't believe I've known a more confused minister in all my years going to church," she says. She folds, from a pile next to her on the sofa, sheets and pillowcases and towels, snapping them taut, pulling them in to her, pressing them smooth with her hands. "All the goings-on last night, I forgot to get these off the line. Good thing it didn't—"

Rain. She stops herself to protect him from that word. They both know rain is something they need to worry for these days instead of against—that shower the other night was not enough nearly. "That's okay, hon," he says. "I guess I'd rather be worrying about that than what-all's been going on."

But another television van has pulled up outside and Landers sighs, can see them clearly through the sheers. "Why don't they all just talk to each other so all I got to do is tell them once?"

"Maybe we could put a sign up out front: Everybody's gone home and now it's your turn," Bessie says and Landers chuckles about it.

Even the university people are gone, left last night after they were all asked to give the medicine man privacy to work. They have not been back to see their almost two weeks of work covered again, obliterated by loose dirt.

Landers pulls on his baseball cap, removes it again to look at the Chief Wahoo emblem on it.

One more van full of cameras shooting the patch of ground where yesterday a pit lay open the remains of strangers' lives, one more explanation of what happened that won't come close to describing who Gasman George is, the strange strength in him last night, and it will, at last, be over.

"What about a marker?" this reporter asks. He is back from TV13 News in Toledo, and Landers has come to like him. They are on camera and so he only says there won't be one.

They decided, early in the morning while workers shovelled dirt gently over the site, the Indian medicine man performing sacred rites so the spirits could continue their interrupted journey, they decided a marker can only make it easy for someone to come do their own digging. Better to pass the word the old way, from land-worker to land-worker, the legend of the Indian burial ground on the rise behind the house, on land that shouldn't be tended but left grassy for soft bare feet on summer days.

None of this does he tell the reporter, leaving him to puzzle this one through, to ask the audience through the camera, "Have we really heard the end to this story?" Landers knows that they have, but they aren't asking him this one.

Finally, when the reporter leaves, Landers heads for the pickup truck to meet Rico, to ask him if he can arrange a crew for overtime. If he's got men and equipment George Freeman will let him paint that house. People can think what they want.

The truck bumps along the side of the road to the path that separates the corn from the wheat, and Landers, at last, breathes easy.